PURE DEAD BRILLIANT

Debi Gliori

A DELL YEARLING BOOK

For Rosemary Sandberg,

and about time too.

Published by
Dell Yearling
an imprint of
Random House Children's Books
a division of Random House, Inc.
New York

Visit us on the Web! www.randomhouse.com/kids

Educators and librarians, for a variety of teaching tools, visit us at
www.randomhouse.com/teachers

ISBN: 0-440-42006-7

Reprinted by arrangement with Alfred A. Knopf Books for Young Readers

Printed in the United States of America

August 2005

10 9 8 7 6 5 4 3 2 1

OPM

A Note to the Reader

There are few things more confusing for tourists than the Scottish population's halfhearted adoption of the 24-hour clock. Hapless tourists are asked to adhere to bus, train, and airplane timetables that lurch giddily between normal time (the train will depart at 5:30 P.M.) and 24-hour time (the train will depart at 17:30). The author apologizes on behalf of all mass-transportation companies, and advises her readers to seriously consider using an Alarming Clock for all their future travel needs.

Contents

Dramatis Personae

THE FAMILY
TITUS STREGA-BORGIA—about-to-be-thirteen-year-old hero
PANDORA STREGA-BORGIA—ten-year-old heroine
DAMP STREGA-BORGIA—their two-year-old sister
SIGNOR LUCIANO AND SIGNORA BACI STREGA-BORGIA—parents of the above
STREGA-NONNA—great-great-great-great-great-great-grandmother
(cryogenically preserved) of Titus, Pandora, and Damp
DON LUCIFER DI S'EMBOWELLI BORGIA—half brother of Luciano Strega-Borgia
NOSTRILAMUS, MALEFICA OF CALEDON—long-dead ancestor of the Borgia clan

THE GOOD HELP THAT WAS HARD TO FIND
MRS. FLORA MCLACHLAN—nanny to Titus, Pandora, and Damp
LATCH—butler at StregaSchloss
MARIE BAIN—possibly the worst cook in the Western Hemisphere

THE BEASTS
ALPHA—centaur and librarian
TARANTELLA—spider with attitude
SAB, FFUP, and KNOT—mythical Schloss dungeon beasts
NESTOR—Ffup's infant son
TOCK—crocodile inhabitant of Schloss moat
MULTITUDINA, THE ILLITERAT—rat, mother to multitudes, and Pandora's pet
TERMINUS—daughter of the above
THE SLEEPER—Scottish unreconstructed-male mythical beast

THE HOUSEGUESTS
ARIADNE VENTETE—student witch and balloonist
HECATE BRINSTONE—student witch
BLACK DOUGLAS—student witch and yoga tutor
FIAMMA D'INFER—student witch and impostor
ASSORTED PROTO-SORCERERS—an additional eight students from the
Institute of Applied Witchcraft

THE IMMORTALS
ASTOROTH—Second Minister of the Hadean Executive, with special
responsibility for pacts and soul harvests
THE BOSS—Astoroth's online manager, First Minister of the Hadean Executive

Strega-Borgia
StregaSchloss
Argyll & Bute
Scotland

Dear Dr. Agony Aunt,

My first egg hatched last Hogmanay (a boy!!!!!*****!!!)
but despite my best efforts, I cannot wean him off
dragon's milk and on to gasoline.

Please advise. Also, any tips on how to get him to sleep
at night?

Yours exhaustedly,

F. S-B (Argyll)

DR. AGONY AUNT
THE CENTER FOR LEGENDARY BEAST-THERAPY
@Egg&After
The magazine for new dragon mothers

Dear F. S-B (Argyll),

Are you absolutely sure your egg didn't get
mixed up with an egg from another species?
A crocodile egg, for example?

I have never heard of a baby dragon that didn't like gasoline . . .

Dr. Aunt CLB-T (Hon.)

Strega-Borgia
StregaSchloss
Argyll & Bute
Scotland

To: Dragony Aunt (Ms.)

What *are* you suggesting? I speak for myself and
Miss F. S-B in demanding that you retract your remarks
vis-à-vis the "egg" and its parentage. Miss F. S-B's egg
is certainly *not* a crocodile egg.

For your information, I strongly disapprove of interspecies
fertilization.

Yours indignantly,

T. S — B

T. S-B (crocodile, Argyll)

DR. AGONY AUNT
THE CENTER FOR LEGENDARY BEAST-THERAPY
@Egg&After
The magazine for new dragon mothers

Dear F. and T. S-B (Argyll),

Apologies for any offense caused. Regrettably, I suspect your baby
son is a runt/a genetic throwback/or was gestated within range
of decaying radio-isotopes.

Or . . . is this whole correspondence a hoax?

Yours cordially,

Dr Aunt

Dr. Aunt

Slander, Defame & Grabbit Attorneys-at-Law
The Old Vaults
Litigants Close
Auchenlochtermuchty
Argyll

Dr. A. Aunt
c/o *Egg & After*
Suite 34001, Nutmeg Towers
Canary Wharf
London

Publication of defamatory material impugning character and proclivities of T. & F. Strega-Borgia

Dear Sir/Madam:

My esteemed clients Tock Strega-Borgia Esq., Master Nestor, and Miss Ffup Strega-Borgia have brought to my attention a copy of your publication (July bumper edition) in which they were distressed to discover that their names, reputations, legitimacy, and intellectual capabilities had all been mentioned in a disrespectful, nay, slanderous manner. Not wishing to further impugn the good name of Strega-Borgia, my clients wish me to convey to you the terms under which they are prepared to "forgive and forget."

In the first instance, my clients demand that you print a fulsome apology to them in your magazine in a type size no less than 48 point, and spanning no less than one full double-page spread. This apology to be printed in the "mega holiday read" August edition.

Second, my clients are desirous of some form of material compensation to allay the considerable mental anguish caused them by your devastating attack on their good name. I would suggest that a sum of one hundred and fifty thousand pounds would suffice.

Finally, my clients would like to stress their direct connection through a blood tie to a large Italian clan, better known as the Mafia. It hardly needs to be said that some of these relatives would be inclined, if informed about your recent "indiscretion," to take more than a passing interest in slanderous journalists writing about Family members.

Capisce?

Yours sincerely,

Dormi Piscatelli

Sr. Dormi Piscatelli w.s. ("The Shark")

Blatta orientalis

Kiss of Death

Titus decided that if there were a button to press that would cause his sister to reincarnate as a cockroach, he would push it without a moment's hesitation. He stood outside her bedroom door, seething, as he read the notice taped to the oak paneling:

PANDORA'S ROOM
entry is absolutely forbidden to any of the following:
brothers
dweebs
possessors of smelly pits & dog's breath
one-celled amoebas with memory of goldfish
smug, rich jerks
the terminally plug-ugly
the criminally insane
and *especially* the vertically challenged over 12 yrs.

Titus, all of the above describe you, so bog off.

Yours Cordially, Pandora Strega—Borgia
Pandora's Room
StregaSchloss
Argyll
Scotland
United Kingdom
Europe
Western Hemisphere
Earth
The Universe
The Galaxy

"Just because I'm about to inherit *all* Grandfather Borgia's money and you're broke doesn't mean you have to be so aggressive." Titus's voice bounced off the door and down the landing, but brought no answering response from within. He pressed his mouth up to the keyhole and tried again. "Some people just can't handle other people's good fortune, *can they, Pandora?*"

Over his head, dangling from the cornice, Pandora's pet tarantula, Tarantella, gave out an exasperated *"Tchhhh."* Titus looked up and shuddered. There was something about the scuttling nature of spiders that revolted him. This one in particular, with her swollen abdomen, gave him nightmares. Titus loathed the entire spider race with a deep and abiding passion. Their gross hairiness, their appetite for flies, their—

The tarantula grinned widely, as if reading his thoughts. "Like it?" she inquired, puckering up her lipsticked mouth parts into a pout. "It's a new one. Now, what's it called . . . ?"

2

Tarantella rummaged under her abdomen with one hairy leg and produced a minuscule lipstick. "Let me see . . . 'Blood-Lust.' Mmm-hmm. Come on, Titus, I know you find me irresistible, give us a kiss. . . ."

With a barely stifled shriek, Titus fled downstairs. Trembling, he burst through the kitchen door and was immediately assailed by a stench that defied description. The beasts were already at breakfast and, judging by the state of the kitchen, had been eating for several hours. Sprawled across the kitchen table, Ffup, the teenage dragon, had her vast head buried in her talons.

"Don't say it," she warned, gazing down at Titus with her vast golden eyes. "Just *don't* say it, right? I've been up *all* night with that wee horror, and now he sits there, wolfs down forty-eight Miserablios, three boxes of Ricey Krispettes, and then does a major dump, downloading the lot into his pants. I tell you, pal, I'm not cut out for this motherhood stuff. I *hate* changing diapers, and . . ." The dragon paused, peered under her baby's high chair, and whimpered, "Yup, just as I thought, it's a shovel job."

"Spare me the details," muttered Titus, edging past Ffup and patting her offending infant on his scaly little head. "Phwoarr, Nestor, you *stink*, don't you?"

The baby gazed up at Titus and grinned gummily, clapping his tiny wings above his head and lashing his snake-like tail back and forth by way of greeting. This had the unfortunate consequence of launching most of the contents of his overloaded diaper into orbit.

"Stop. Stop. STOP!" wailed Ffup. "Oh, yeurrrch. I can't handle this. . . . *Knot!* KNOT? Come *on*, help me out here."

Emerging from the pantry with a sheepish grin, Knot the

yeti shuffled across the kitchen to stare hopefully at his fellow beasts. The yeti's perpetually unsanitary fur was clotted with fetid lumps of food that had somehow failed to make the journey to his mouth. He wrinkled up his fur in the general area of his nose, sniffed deeply in sincerest appreciation of the odors in the kitchen, and sighed in happy anticipation.

"Nestor has a wee something for you," muttered Ffup, burying her nostrils in a coffee cup. "Freshly laid, still warm . . ."

"Give me strength," gagged Titus, turning his back on this revolting inter-beast exchange.

"Mmm-yummy," observed Knot, dipping an experimental paw in the puddle under Nestor's high chair. Titus moaned softly and closed his eyes. Knot sniffed, unrolled his lengthy spotted tongue, and sampled a little morsel. "Naww," he pronounced, at length. "Bit overripe, that one. Nope. Don't fancy it much."

"Don't be so picky," said Ffup. "Be a gent. Help me out. Just close your eyes and think of Gorgonzola. Pleeeeease?"

Knot wiped his paw on his tummy and scratched his armpit thoughtfully. "If you don't mind, I'll pass," he mumbled, clearly uncomfortable at the prospect of letting Ffup down. "I'm not really too hungry right this minute."

"Well, I'm *starving*," said Pandora, arriving in the kitchen by way of the door to the herb garden. "Phwoarr. Urghhh. What's that *stench*?"

"Here we go again," sighed Ffup, glaring at her baby son. "See what you've done?"

"'Morning, all." Pandora kicked off her rubber boots and came over to warm herself beside Titus at the range. "Are we all pretending that there isn't a vast pile of dragon poo on the floor over there, or is someone going to clean it up?"

"Ffup is," said Titus. "Aren't you, Ffup?"

"What? And ruin my manicured talons?" squeaked the dragon. "You can't be serious. These took me *ages*." Hoping for female sympathy, she extended one paw for Pandora's inspection. Each of her seven talons was painted a lurid sugar-pink. "Pretty, aren't they?" Ffup smirked, examining her paw with satisfaction, turning it this way and that, all the better to catch the light.

Mrs. Flora McLachlan, nanny to Titus and Pandora, entered the kitchen with their baby sister, Damp, in her arms. Smelling something truly awful and assuming that it was about to be her breakfast, the little girl buried her face in the nanny's shoulder and gave a little moan.

"Good heavens, is that the time?" Mrs. McLachlan peered at the mantelpiece clock in dismay. "My bedside clock isn't keeping very good time, and the alarm didn't go off." Then, as she became aware of the odor in the kitchen, she added, "Ffup, dear, I'm sure you're aware that Nestor needs a diaper change. D'you think you could stop admiring your manicure, stir your stumps, and do it before your mistress comes downstairs for breakfast?"

Ffup gave two snorts of flame and slowly heaved herself out of her chair. "Do I *have* to? That's so *unfair*. Why do I always have to clean up after him? It's so *boring*."

"Ffup—" said Mrs. McLachlan in a tone of voice that offered no recourse to argument.

Ffup looked up and met the nanny's eyes, which had shrunk

5

down to two little slits of menace. Ffup was immediately galvanized into action. "Rrright away. Where's that shovel? Rrrrubber gloves on . . . *snap*. Antibacterial spray . . . *squirt*. Scrape poo out from between flagstones on floor . . . *splat* . . ."

"The high chair, too, Ffup," said Mrs. McLachlan, one eyebrow raised.

"Yup. Yuzzm. Your wish, my command. Breathe through mouth . . . *gasp*, remove infant dragon to kitchen sink . . . *squelch*, remove diaper . . . ah. Um. Yes. Perhaps you guys might care to have breakfast somewhere else?" Ffup suggested, as her infant slid out of her grasp and landed among the unwashed dishes in the sink. "Apply gas mask . . . *urrrrgh.*"

"What have you been feeding that poor child?" demanded Mrs. McLachlan.

"Oh, *that*?" said Ffup, breathing through her mouth as she unzipped Nestor's onesie. "I couldn't be bothered to cook last night, so we just polished off the remains of a couple of boxes of chocolates and some tinned peaches in syrup we found at the back of the fridge—"

"Those weren't *peaches*," groaned Mrs. McLachlan. "They were raw *eggs* for the cake that I was going to bake for this afternoon. Twenty-four eggs, Ffup. No wonder that poor wee mite's got an upset tummy. It's about time you faced up to the responsibilities of motherhood and grew—"

"What cake?" interrupted Titus. "Is it one of your chocolate meringue cakes? Oh, please make one of them! I'm so hungry I could eat at least six slices. Make a *huge* one. Use thirty-six eggs. Use a hundred. You're such a brilliant cook. I've never tasted cakes as good as—"

"What a crawler you are, Titus," said Pandora, regarding her brother with disgust. "Just listen to yourself. Slurp, slurp. Grovel, grovel."

"Shut up, Pan," muttered Titus. "This is for your benefit, too, you know."

"No, Titus, it's for your stomach's benefit, don't you know?" Pandora slapped her brother's midriff and tutted. "I know you're about to become a plutocrat, but there's simply no need to become a bloated one."

"Do you think, sister mine, that we might possibly, just once, let a day go by without reference to my impending vast inheritance from Grandfather Borgia? The millions that will allow me to live a life of unimaginable luxury while you, you poor thing, will only be able to watch and drool. Mind you, right now you're not so much drooling as spraying me with vitriol—I mean, anyone would think you were jealous or something. . . ."

"Oh heck, no," Pandora replied, examining her fingernails with apparent fascination. "Not in the least jealous, just a little peeved, is all. . . . After all, what possible difference could it make to me when you get your hands on your millions? It's not going to change anything important between us, is it? I mean, it's not going to make me think you're any less of a dweeb, or more intelligent, or less plug-ugly. And"—she delivered her final thrust with deadly precision—"from the moment those millions become yours, you're never, ever going to be sure if we all put up with you because you're one of us, our very own Titus, or because you're filthy rich."

Pandora turned on her heel and stalked out of the kitchen, banging the door behind her. She stormed along the corridor and across the great hall to the staircase, then took the stairs two at a time in order to reach the safe haven of her room before her feelings engulfed her. Stumbling across the moth-eaten rug, she flung herself facedown on her bed, emitting a strangled shriek. Downstairs, the grandfather clock chimed the hour, the half hour, quarter past the hour, thirteen, and then, apparently embarrassed at its own excesses, gave an asthmatic wheeze and fell silent. That was part of the problem, Pandora thought, thumping her pillow with both fists. If only she could turn the clock back and undo the past. Specifically, three months past, when Titus discovered that he was the chosen benefactor of their grandfather's vast hoard of money. Since then it was as if an invisible barrier had sprung up between her brother and herself. Everything was about to change, and probably not for the better. And yes, of course I'm jealous, thought Pandora, grinding her teeth. I'm turning a deep and unflattering shade of green at the prospect of Titus becoming a millionaire and me still having to make one measly week's pocket money last for a whole seven days.

"It's so un*fair*," Pandora wailed out loud. "Why did Grandfather leave it all to *him*?"

Time, Gentlemen, Please
(A.D. 127: Northwestern Argyll)

n filthy nights such as this, Nostrilamus was prone to curse the fate that had brought him to the Celt-infested wilds of Caledonia. Not only were the natives malevolent, woad-daubed savages, but the climate was hostile beyond belief, prompting the centurions under his command to ship many scrolls between Lethe and Ostia, begging the folks back home to send hides, blankets, and fleece-lined cloaks; in short, anything to prevent native Romans from freezing to death in Caledonia. An icy rain had greeted Nostrilamus on his arrival at the port of Lethe. It had dogged his passage across the country for the seven days it had taken him and his legion to reach this crude tavern on the northwestern shore.

To Nostrilamus's further discomfort was added the fact that his armor had rusted, his leather breastplate was currently sprouting some ghastly form of Celtic fungus, and he spent each miserable day frozen to the bone, wrapped in his useless green cloak. His hideously expensive green cloak, which the maker had assured him would easily withstand whatever the weather cared to throw at him. On contact with a mild drizzle, said wonder-cloak had begun to leak copious quantities of green dye, causing Nostrilamus's exposed limbs to turn the gangrenous hue of a plague victim on the point of expiry. In daylight, women and children took one look at him and ran away screaming. This, he decided, was no bad thing. In his new appointment as Malefica of Caledon, Nostrilamus regarded it as his duty to inspire fear and loathing in the native population.

Removing his helmet and stooping to enter the tavern, Nostrilamus noted that the room had fallen into respectful silence on his arrival. Even better, he was early, for the appointed table by the fire was empty. Peeling off his damp cloak and hurling it at the tavern-keeper, he raked the crowded room with a slitty-eyed glare. Judging by the insignias on their breastplates, the tavern's clientele were drawn from the ranks of Legion XII of Draco Inflatus, and judging by the vast quantities of liquor being drunk, they were just as homesick as he was.

The tavern-keeper bowed low before Nostrilamus—not quite low enough to indicate complete subjugation, but pretty well spot on for a respectful, if reluctant grovel. "*Ave*, Caledon," he muttered. "Welcome. Did you have a booking? As you can see, we're pretty full tonight, but I'm sure we can find a space for such an important person as yourself—"

"That one," said Nostrilamus, indicating the table beside the fire. "I'll take that, and a flask of Caoil Ilax for starters."

The tavern-keeper paled. Pointing with a quivering finger to a small scrap of vellum fixed to the table with a wax seal, he wrung his hands apologetically. "*Reservatus,* my esteemed Caledon. Reservatus, I'm afraid. But I'm sure we can squeeze you in at another—"

"You are mistaken," stated Nostrilamus, pushing past the trembling tavern-keeper and tearing the vellum off the table before hurling it in the fire. "This table is no longer 'reservatus,' it's taken. Now quit dithering and bring me the Caoil Ilax."

Behind him, the vellum burst into flames, causing Nostrilamus to be briefly haloed in red fire. The tavern-keeper gave a frightened squeak of terror and fell to his knees. His voice wobbled and his eyes became round orbs of terror.

"I beg you, Caledon, do not take that table. It is reserved for one, and one only."

At that moment the door to the tavern blew open, and the temperature plummeted, far below zero. Once more, silence fell in the crowded room. In the dim light of the lantern at the doorway, Nostrilamus could see a figure wrapped in a cloak, wreathed in coils of mist that rolled and twined around its feet. Cleaving a path through the legionaries, the figure arrived at the table by the fire and threw a strange black object onto it. Prostrate on the floor, the tavern-keeper gave a strangled sob.

"What a time I've had getting here," the cloaked figure complained. "Traffic was just *awful*. Been waiting long? Hang on a tick, I'll just turn this thing to mute. We don't want any interruptions, do we?" And seizing the black object, he pressed it with his index finger, causing it to emit a high-pitched note.

Lowering his gaze to where the tavern-keeper lay on the floor, the cloaked figure sighed. "Don't just lie there, man," he commanded. "Take my cloak, fetch my colleague here a drink, and bring me a goblet of the usual."

"B-b-brimstone and v-v-vitriol?" the tavern-keeper quavered, staggering to his feet.

"On the rocks." The figure shed its black cloak with a sinuous shimmy and slid into the seat opposite Nostrilamus. With an obsequious bow, the tavern-keeper backed away, and in the background the noise returned to a normal roar.

"And so, to business." The figure stretched its legs closer to the fire and turned its gaze on the silent Nostrilamus. "First—introductions. Tonight, you can call me Astoroth, Second Minister of the Hadean Executive, with special responsibility for pacts and soul harvests. You summoned, and here I am."

Despite his proximity to the fireplace, Nostrilamus shivered. This had all seemed like such a good idea back in Rome. Now he wasn't quite so sure. Meeting Astoroth's gaze across the table, Nostrilamus suppressed a scream. The minister from the Hadean Executive regarded him implacably through a pair of deep-red eyes. Eyes in which Nostrilamus saw himself twice reflected, naked of both clothes and skin, a skeleton burning in an unquenchable fire. . . .

"Now don't get all hysterical on me, pal," Astoroth advised, hooding those awful eyes and stirring the embers of the fire with an outstretched foot. Frozen with dread, Nostrilamus saw that the minister's foot was not only unshod, but ended in a cloven hoof.

"Too late to press rewind," Astoroth advised, the sound of his voice resembling the noise of fingernails being dragged across slate. "I'm not some sort of minor demon, a genie that you can just stuff back in the bottle. . . . Have you mortals no concept of the amount of paperwork involved in setting up this kind of deal?"

Taking Nostrilamus's silence for understanding, Astoroth continued, "Right. Pay attention. Seeing as how this is your first time, I'll go through the contract with you before you sign it at the bottom. Here, take my knife and open a vein while I explain. . . . "

Numb with fear, Nostrilamus obeyed, using the minister's outstretched knife to cut a deep nick in the skin of his left wrist. Blood welled up and began to drip from the wound. He tried to concentrate on the words.

". . . and in return for vast wealth, in a currency of our choosing, the Hadean Executive merely requires a small favor. To wit: you get gold, salt, gems, myrrh, et cetera, and on your death, we harvest your soul. Simple, huh?"

The strange black object on the table beside Astoroth began to quiver and twitch, as if it had a life of its own. Ignoring this, Astoroth produced a scroll covered in dense rows of script in a foreign language, which he unrolled in front of Nostrilamus. His tapping forefinger indicated a space at the foot of this document.

"Sign here. Excuse me for one moment while I take this call. *Such* a bore. I do apologize—" He plucked the vibrating object off the table, pressed it to his ear, and did something that caused it to light up and emit a tiny note like a mechanical birdcall. "Yes, *what?*" he barked, pointing with ill-disguised impatience at the scroll. Miming the action of writing, he turned his attention back to the black object. "I'm in a meeting. What d'you mean there's a couple of problems? You want an extra clause

13

added in? Consider it done—the client's putty in my hands. Now, what else? I can hardly hear you, you're breaking up. . . . Who? What awful mistake? The Chronostone has gone AWOL? Of *course* I know what it looks like. D'you take me for a complete moron? When I chose the trinkets for this job, there's no way I would have mixed up the Chronostone with that bunch of tacky baubles." Astoroth stared into the flames, trying to drown a growing sense of foreboding in a tide of bluster. "I'm not a cretin, you know. Don't get your asbestos knickers in a twist. The Boss probably dropped it in the Pit. It'll turn up."

Using an index finger as a clumsy tool with which to scrawl his signature in his own blood, Nostrilamus tried hard not to eavesdrop. Astoroth's black object had not only lit up and made noises like a bird, but now it appeared to have its own voice. A tiny voice that repeated the word "Chronostone" with dismaying clarity. Each time the voice spoke, Astoroth appeared to flinch, until finally he removed the black thing from his ear and regarded it with loathing.

"Lost the signal. Infernal things. And bad news all round, I'm afraid . . . especially for you." He crossed one leg over the other and frowned at Nostrilamus.

Mystified, Nostrilamus smiled nervously. He hadn't a clue what the minister was on about, but he had a sinking feeling that none of it augured well.

"Change of plan," Astoroth said. "I've been told to add a codicil to your contract. Terribly sorry, but it can't be helped. Security reasons, close a few loopholes—that sort of thing. . . ." He bent over the signed document and breathed on it. Where there had been rows of dense script was now blank paper.

Licking the end of his finger as if it were a stylus, Astoroth began to use his own spit to redraft the contract. The words smoked as they branded themselves onto the paper.

The tavern-keeper reappeared at the table, bearing their drinks on a wooden board. Turning the contract back round for Nostrilamus's signature, Astoroth took his drink from the trembling landlord.

"A toast," he said, extending his goblet at arm's length.

"Apologies, M-M-Minister," the landlord stammered. "I'm fresh out of bread for the t-t-toa—"

"Not *that* kind, you stupid imbecile," Astoroth hissed. "A toast to the future. To the future harvest of souls—"

"Um, yes. I wish you'd given me some w-w-warning, Minister. The boats haven't been out for a while. I'm out of fre-fre-fre-fresh—soles."

"Give me strength," Astoroth muttered, rolling his red eyes upward. "Drink up, Caledon," he commanded, adding darkly, "You're going to need it." He pushed the contract toward his companion and bid the landlord fetch his cloak.

Seeing Nostrilamus peering in utter incomprehension at the newly written contract, Astoroth pointed to his amendments. "It's paragraph three, subsection thirteen, clause seven you might want to have a wee squint at. Specifically, the line beginning, 'The soul of the undersigned and that of all male firstborn descendants thereof shall be forfeit from now until eternity—'"

"WHAAAAT?" squealed Nostrilamus.

Astoroth drained his goblet and smacked his lips with evident relish. Smoke began to leak from his nostrils, ears, and mouth.

"Sign it, Caledon," he commanded, each word propelling gouts of yellow sulfurous smoke from his mouth, like a bad case of spectral halitosis. "And get a move on. Time is money." He stood up and turned to where the tavern-keeper stood holding his cloak. This movement afforded both mortals the ghastly sight of a long, snake-like protrusion whipping round the minister's calves, swiftly and mercifully obscured by the folds of his cloak—but not before it became apparent that the minister from the Hadean Executive was in possession of a forked tail.

Nostrilamus signed. Drawing scant comfort from the fact that at least *he* wouldn't be around to see the damage wreaked on his unborn descendants by this pact with Hades, he consigned all their souls to perdition. Right now, he would have signed his grandmother into slavery, if it guaranteed getting rid of this cloven-footed, fork-tailed, brimstone-swilling obscenity.

As if reading his thoughts, Astoroth tutted mildly, then purred, "Been a real *pleasure*, actually." Tucking the contract into his cloak and holding out a small roll of vellum, he said, "You'll find the money hidden in the Forest of Caledon. Here's a wee map to pinpoint exactly which of the eighteen thousand and twenty-one oaks I've hidden it under. Oh, and before I forget, take some reinforcements with you, dear boy. . . . I've heard tell that the natives are none too friendly. *Ave*, Caledon. Abyssinia, toodle-pip—I'll . . . be . . . back."

With this last threat, he sauntered straight across the tavern and out through the door into the darkness.

Friendly Fire

Such is the voracious nature of the West of Scotland gnat that whole communities have been known to spend their entire summer indoors, thereby avoiding offering up their bodies for insect consumption. Thus it was with the Strega-Borgia family, every year without fail. Returning to StregaSchloss with the morning papers and milk, Latch the butler had vanished, bearing a bottle of calamine lotion and a wire brush in the hope of calming down his new crop of gnat bites. Ten minutes later, the sight of their butler, bleeding and calamine-encrusted, made the Strega-Borgias vow that they would rather set their hair on fire than brave the infested air of Argyll.

Imprisoned in the kitchen, Damp sat at the table, watching as Mrs. McLachlan put finishing touches on a three-tier chocolate meringue cake. When the nanny's attention focused on something outside the kitchen window, Damp stretched out her hand to sample a fingerful of cake. The door swung open and Damp's mother, Signora Baci Strega-Borgia, swept in, a tide of black silk swirling round her from her shoulders to her feet. The overall impact of her costume was somewhat marred by the ragged holes that marched across the brim of her ceremonial witch's hat, the topmost pinnacle of which was dented beyond repair. Oblivious to the sight of her baby daughter's hand poised over the cake, Signora Strega-Borgia dragged her hat from her head and groaned.

"Oh, just look at that! What a *mess*. And Flora—that's the first guest arriving now, isn't it?"

Mrs. McLachlan turned round from the window and gazed at Signora Strega-Borgia. Damp immediately stuffed her hands into her pockets and swallowed the evidence.

"Very nice, dear," the nanny said, as if seeing one's employer in full-on witch's costume were an everyday occurrence not worthy of comment. "Perhaps *not* the hat, though. Not quite up to scratch. And yes, your first guest is dropping out of the sky, even as we speak. . . ."

Puzzled by this, Damp slid off her chair and wobbled across to the window. Walking was a recently acquired skill, and the baby still preferred the safety of the crawl or even the bottom-shuffle if the terrain was perilous. Mrs. McLachlan plucked her off the floor and held her up to the window.

"Look, pet—here comes one of Mummy's friends. What a *most* unusual way to travel . . ."

From the wicker gondola suspended below the giant hot-air balloon, the aerial view of StregaSchloss and its surroundings was truly breathtaking. The land rolled in sinuous folds from the peaks of Bengormless down to a wooded plain, which curved round the Strega-Borgias' home before sloping gently into the clear waters of Lochnagargoyle.

Sadly for the arriving guest, the dizzying rate of her descent afforded little time for admiring the view. Ariadne Ventete's first sight of StregaSchloss was through a hail of crisped insects that had expired in the flame of the gas burners keeping her hot-air balloon aloft. She aimed for the garden, sweeping over the fifty-six chimneys of StregaSchloss, heading for the meadow that lay between the house and the sea loch. To slow her rapid approach, she tugged on the chain that opened the vent of the burners and was immediately engulfed in another wave of carbonized gnats.

Accompanied by a sound like a cappuccino-maker, the vast panels of pink balloon silk were for one glorious moment illuminated against the sky.

One of the three beasts sprawled across the stone steps of StregaSchloss was seriously impressed by this short display of firepower.

"Now, *that's* what I call fire." Sab the griffin dug his elbow into the ribs of his companion, who responded with a snort.

"I could do that sort of squitty piddly little flame with my eyes shut," replied Ffup, regarding the descending balloon with disdain. "You non-dragons are always impressed by anything bigger than a candle. Check it out—no staying power—just one feeble wee puff and then nothing, nada, zilch, zippety-doo."

On the dragon's lap, Nestor gave a flatulent *parrrp*, followed almost immediately by an acrid stench.

"Is that what I think it is?" hissed Sab, glaring at the small creature. "Has your offspring filled his diaper *again*? Honestly, if he's not downloading into his pants, he's spitting it up over your shoulder." The griffin gave a fastidious shudder and stood up.

Oblivious to the slander, the baby beast wriggled in Ffup's lap, popped a knobbly talon into his mouth, and closed his eyes with a happy snuffle.

Ffup gazed down at her baby son, as ever amazed at how much life had changed since the infant had hatched on the stroke of midnight of the new year. Gone were the freedoms she had enjoyed for the previous six centuries. Now, with this little creature to look after, Ffup's sleep was interrupted several times every night with infant wails, and as for freedom . . . that was just a distant and fading memory. In consideration of this, Ffup spat rebelliously into a flower bed and gave a fiery snort from both nostrils.

Overhead, the balloon sank lower, its gondola just grazing the treetops, its passenger leaning over the side with a mooring rope dangling from one hand. Down by the loch, Tock the crocodile emerged from the water and lolloped toward the meadow. Knot crawled out of the loch behind him, and made his way effortfully over the pebbles of the foreshore.

"Well, *that's* an improvement," observed Ffup, picking up her baby and ambling forward to assist in tethering the balloon.

"Taking a bath once a year does seem rather inadequate, don't you think?" said Sab, making his way down the steps to the rose-quartz drive. "Give Knot two weeks and he'll stink again."

The yeti shook himself, thus ridding his fur of several gallons of loch-water. Each vigorous shimmy was accompanied by a loud slap as potato peelings, coffee grounds, apple cores, chicken bones, and bacon rinds flew from his fur in a swinging arc across the meadow.

"Could someone grab this rope and tie it to a tree before I land on your *dog*?"

The balloonist made shooing noises at Knot and hurled out a length of rope from the gondola. Insulted at being referred to as a mere dog, the yeti pointedly turned his back on the balloon and began to pick lice out of his wet fur and transfer them to his mouth. Ahead of him, Tock shot across the meadow to assist in the landing, his stumpy crocodile legs flattening the grasses, sending clouds of gnats boiling up into the sky in his wake.

The beasts watched impassively as the gondola rocked and bounced, its passenger thrashing and flailing ineffectually with one hand, the other clutching the mooring rope.

"Hurry it up, would you?" she yelled, an edge of panic creeping into her voice. "I'm being eaten alive here."

Watching this drama from the gnat-free zone of the kitchen, Signora Strega-Borgia felt compelled to help. After all, it had been her idea to offer StregaSchloss as the venue for a study week with her classmates from the Institute of Advanced Witchcraft. Therefore it was her responsibility to look after her guests as a good hostess should. Mrs. McLachlan was busy washing chocolate meringue cake off Damp's legs, hands, and face; Latch was winding himself into rolls of bandages after an over-enthusiastic exfoliating session with a wire brush; her husband, Luciano, had driven Titus and Pandora down to the village to spend their pocket money; and so it fell to her to extend a warm welcome to this first guest. Signora Strega-

Borgia opened the kitchen door, nearly tripping over the hunched figure of Marie Bain, the StregaSchloss cook, who was laboring under the weight of a tray laden with what looked like inflated sea slugs.

"Mmmm. Yummy," lied Signora Strega-Borgia, trying to edge past without inhaling. "Gosh, Marie, how, um . . . inventive."

The cook frowned and shrugged modestly, causing the sea slugs to quiver revoltingly. "Ees doll mads," she muttered. "For the Seenyora's veezitors."

"Super," gasped Signora Strega-Borgia, hoping she could squeeze past into the great hall before she had to draw breath.

"Ees verr hard to cook, zis." Marie Bain propped the tray against the kitchen door handle and sniffed wetly. "Ees no vine leafs, zo I use nettles instead. Ees no mince lamb, zo I find some ox-liver in freezer and use zat. Ees no meurrrnt in z'erb garden, zo—"

Trying to stem this ghastly tide of culinary horror, Signora Strega-Borgia interrupted. "Golly. Heavens. How resourceful, Marie. But goodness, must dash, guests arriving—" She pushed past the cook and bolted along the corridor to the great hall, but not before she heard Marie say, ". . . zo I find ze citronella and use zat instead . . . ," followed by a resounding crash as the tray slipped off the door handle and mercifully tipped its entire contents over the floor.

Citronella? Signora Strega-Borgia shuddered. Citronella was what the family used as their last bastion of defense against the gnats. Citronella was the evil-scented oil with which one slathered one's skin prior to braving the infested air of Argyll. The little bottle of citronella oil was still in its accustomed place in a niche by the front door, but Signora Strega-Borgia found it to be empty. She opened the door and looked across the drive to where the balloon hovered at head height above the meadow, surrounded by beasts, all yelling helpful instructions to the passenger in the gondola, who was obscured by clouds of insects and clearly in need of some help.

"Hold on!" called Signora Strega-Borgia, shrouding her head in a length of black silk to keep the gnats off her face. "I'm coming. Don't panic!"

To Ariadne Ventete, the vision of Signora Strega-Borgia hurtling across the meadow toward her was not comforting. Maddened by gnat bites, deafened by yelling dragons and griffins, utterly confused by waving crocodiles and giant sulky dogs, she assumed that she had stumbled into a Caledonian version of Hell. Furthering this impression, she saw the figure— swathed in deepest black, lacking only the skull and sickle of popular imagery—of the Grim Reaper, racing across the meadow to greet her. Raising her wand above her head, Ariadne stammered out what she fervently hoped was the correct incantation to ward off her fate.

With a flash and an accompanying crash of thunder, the hapless balloonist was instantly surrounded by a vast circle of fire. The beasts took several leaps backward out of harm's way, and Signora Strega-Borgia tripped over a trailing length of black silk and fell flat on her face. Then came an immense crack as all eighteen ropes suspending the wicker gondola under the balloon charred, blackened, and snapped. With a shriek, Ariadne plunged to the ground as the balloon, free of all restraint, shot up into the sky.

The Coven Cometh

The sight of a vast pink tent-thing ascending through the air over Lochnagargoyle caused Signor Luciano Strega-Borgia to floor the accelerator and race for home. In the rear of the car, Titus and Pandora pressed their faces to the windows and gazed out in awe. Sadly, their father was less impressed.

"For heaven's sake, Baci," he hissed, swerving perilously along the bramble-clad track that led from the village of Auchenlochtermuchty to StregaSchloss. "What madness is *this*?"

"Yup," said Titus, inwardly wincing. "That looks like one of Mum's dodgy spells."

"Giant pink pants floating across Lochnagargoyle?" groaned Pandora. "How *embarrassing*."

Their car drew closer to StregaSchloss, a break in the trees allowing them a brief view of the waters of the loch. In the distance they saw a ship in full sail, with its wake cutting a perfect line through the reflection of the floating balloon. The sails filled with wind, and a line of white foam was etched in the wake. Titus could just make out a skull and crossbones flying from the top mast.

"What an amazing boat . . . ," murmured Pandora. "Wonder where it's going?"

Their view of the loch was again obscured by a clump of densely planted chestnut trees. Signor Strega-Borgia stopped in front of a car parked across the ornately carved bronze gate that barred the drive to StregaSchloss.

"We appear to have a visitor," he remarked, pulling on the hand brake and opening his window. The car ahead was a shiny black convertible with its roof firmly closed. The driver's door gaped open and a woman could be seen peering through the gate with the aid of opera glasses. She turned to greet them, smiling uncertainly as she tucked a tendril of her unruly black hair behind one ear.

"It's locked," she said apologetically, indicating the gate. "And I'm afraid I was expected at the house by . . ." She paused, rummaged in a pocket of her leather jacket, and produced an exquisitely fashioned silver pocket watch, at which she peered through her glasses. "Oh *dear*. Ten minutes ago."

"It's not locked," said Signor Strega-Borgia, opening his car door and stepping out to explain. "It's just jammed shut. Look, I'll show you."

"Thank you *so* much," said the woman, peering in at Titus and Pandora through the windows. "I'm sorry. How *rude* of me—let me introduce myself. I'm one of Baci's colleagues from the institute—name's Hecate Brinstone, but most people call me Heck. . . . And you must be Luciano, Titus, and Pandora. Baci has told me so much about you."

Signor Strega-Borgia hauled open the rusty, screeching gate and secured it to a stone pillar with a frayed bit of baling twine.

"There," he said. "Not locked at all. Just showing its age like most things in these parts." He held out his hand to Heck and smiled. "Welcome to StregaSchloss."

It was at this precise moment that they all became aware of a distant whinnying sound. Around where they stood, the tops of the chestnut trees whipped and tossed, as if being bent aside by some colossal force.

"What the—?" Signor Strega-Borgia threw himself full-length on top of the astonished Heck just as something rocketed past overhead, displacing so much air that for an instant their ears popped—and then it was gone, leaving broken twigs and leaves swirling behind. Titus craned forward in his seat to afford himself a better view.

Thundering toward StregaSchloss came thirteen ink-black horses, their eyes blinkered, their hooves thirty feet above the drive. Steam poured from their nostrils with the effort of pulling a windowless carriage behind them, its wheels spinning wildly out of control. Climbing slowly to his feet and helping Heck to stand, Signor Strega-Borgia brushed dust from his clothes and squinted into the distance. As the carriage neared StregaSchloss, they could all hear the horses scream as they slowed to take the curve onto the rose-quartz courtyard in front of the house.

"*What* a show-off," muttered Heck, picking twigs and leaves from her hair. "She threatened to pull a stunt like this."

Pandora opened her door and climbed out gingerly. "What was *that*?" she asked, pointing to StregaSchloss, where the carriage had pulled up in front of the house, still at treetop height, the peaks of Mhoire Ochone eerily visible *through* the bodies of the horses.

"That was Fiamma d'Infer and her precious hearse," Heck stated, investing each word with as much contempt as she could muster. "Fiamma, our very own rich witch, heiress, society beauty, ex-model, ex-musician, ex-sculptor, and probably, if she keeps on with her dangerous practices at the institute, ex-witch as well—"

"Look—the boat!" interrupted Pandora. "It's dropped anchor opposite the house. And there's an inflatable dinghy tied up at the jetty . . . it must belong to another of Mum's guests."

"Yup," agreed Heck. "That belongs to Black Douglas, our only male classmate—used to be a publisher on one of the big London papers, but he decided to chuck it and enroll at the institute. Nice boat . . ."

"Who are all those people on board?" Signor Strega-Borgia's voice betrayed just the faintest hint of apprehension.

"I can't see too well," said Heck, glasses pressed up against her nose, "but I imagine that'll be the rest of our class. . . ." She sighed. "And as usual, I'll be last to arrive."

"How many students did you say were in your class?" Signor Strega-Borgia batted a cloud of gnats away from his face as he spoke.

"I didn't say, but in total there are one hundred and sixty-nine—thirteen groups of thirteen."

"Honestly, I do wish your mother was a little less vague about

27

arrangements sometimes." Signor Strega-Borgia addressed the retreating figure of Pandora, who was heading back to the car in an attempt to avoid the gnats. "She told me she'd invited a *few* colleagues over for a *couple* of nights' study leave."

"Oh dear," said Heck, her eyes sliding away from Signor Strega-Borgia. "Um, not exactly. My impression was that Baci has invited all twelve of us over here for about a week's study leave, actually. . . ." Her voice trailed off and she added, "But we could put up at the local hotel if you don't have enough room."

In front of them lay the turreted mass of StregaSchloss, its ninety-six rooms, wine cellar, dungeons, and sprawling attic looking as though it could easily offer hospitality to a small country without feeling too stretched. Signor Strega-Borgia sighed. It would be churlish to turn Baci's colleagues away. Undoubtedly there was ample room for all the guests; there was probably enough food; Latch would manage to scrape together a quantity of linen and bedding to ensure sweet dreams for everyone, but—

Pandora had reached the car and discovered that Titus had activated its central locking system. He was stretched out across the backseat, headphones clamped to his ears, eyes shut, arms flailing as he played an imaginary set of drums in time to some internal rhythm. In an attempt to draw his attention to her gnat-bitten plight, she yelled, "Open *up*—I'm being devoured out here—*Titus!*

"TITUS! Open. The. DOOR!" Pandora scratched frantically with one hand, hammering the windshield with the palm of the other. Titus's eyes sprang open and he abruptly stopped playing air-drums. A puzzled expression crossed his face as he opened the door for his sister. He removed the headphones from his ears and frowned at them.

"Weird," he muttered, looking out of the window to where Heck and his dad stood. The student witch met his eye and winked. Just once, but unmistakably a wink meant just for Titus.

"What's weird?" asked Pandora, flopping onto the seat beside him.

"My CD stopped in mid-track," said Titus, "and just for a second or two, I could hear a woman saying, 'Open the car door, Titus—your sister's waiting'—and then the music started up again."

"Big deal." Pandora waved a dismissive hand in Heck's direction. "She's a *witch*. They're all witches. They'll all be pulling weird kinds of stunts while . . . while . . ." Her voice trailed off and she blinked, rubbing her eyes and frowning. With a wave, Signor Strega-Borgia began to walk back to their car, and Heck climbed into hers and closed the door.

"*What?* While what?" demanded Titus. "I *hate* it when you just trail off in mid-sentence like that."

"Did you see that?" squeaked Pandora. "Her car—that black thing—it just changed into a pumpkin, just for a second, a pumpkin pulled by rats. . . ."

"I don't know if I'm up for this," groaned Titus. "All Mum's classmates, all of them probably as incompetent as Mum, every last one of them trying to outdo the rest. We'll be falling over cauldrons and being stabbed by pointy hats while they're houseguests. They'll all want frogs for breakfast—they'll take over the washing machine with endless black robes needing laundering—the fridge will be stuffed full of tincture of maggot and bottles of newts' eyeballs in brine—the house'll stink of brimstone and candle wax—"

As Heck started her car, a puff of small black bats emerged squeaking and chittering from the exhaust. Seeing this, Titus slumped back in his seat and rolled his eyes meaningfully. Signor Strega-Borgia did not seem inclined to be cheerful either. The remainder of the drive to StregaSchloss took place in uninterrupted silence as the three Strega-Borgias individually contemplated the current invasion of their home by twelve proto-sorcerers.

Slightly Damp

Left to finish licking the contents of a mixing bowl in the kitchen, Damp decided to explore. She slid off her seat and teetered off along the corridor, still clutching a sticky wooden spoon. In the great hall beasts galloped back and forth, ferrying steamer trunks, hatboxes, suitcases, cauldrons in aluminium flight cases, and assorted items of designer luggage up from the shore of Lochnagargoyle to the interior of StregaSchloss. Strange grown-ups wandered in and out of the house and, to Damp's delight, no one paid her the least bit of attention. Laboriously she crawled upstairs, stopping to peer through the banister rails at the activity below.

Latch staggered through the front door bearing Ariadne Ventete in his arms. Since he was still heavily bandaged and caked in flaking calamine lotion, he bore an uncanny resemblance to the leading character in *Return of the Mummy*, an effect not lost on Ariadne. She had taken one look at the butler's eyes twinkling at her through bloodstained bandages and promptly passed out.

Unobserved, Damp continued up the stairs till she reached the second floor. Ahead, the corridor branched off in four different directions. Damp sucked her wooden spoon as she considered which way to go, then caught a glimpse of movement out of the corner of her eye. Ambling down the sunny corridor that stretched along the south face of StregaSchloss was a large rat holding an open picture book. It read the story to itself under its breath. Curious, Damp crawled closer to see what the rat was reading. The illustration on the book's cover was of a girl asleep in a bed surrounded by roses.

No, don't tell me, Damp thought, nibbling her wooden spoon to aid concentration, let me guess. I know I *know* that one— *Cinderella?* No. Hasn't got a glass shoe. *Snow White?* No. Girl hasn't got black hair and isn't sleeping in a glass box-thing. . . . *Goldilocks?* Nope, no bears . . . Wait a minute, it's—it's—"

"*SLEEPING BEAUTY!*" Damp yelled in triumph.

Multitudina looked up from her book with a squeak. "Is *that* how you pronounce it? No wonder it wasn't making much sense. I thought it was *Sleeping Boaty*. . . . Oh, sigh. That's what comes of being an Illiterat—" And dropping the book in disgust onto the floor, the rat scuttled off down the corridor and disappeared round a corner. Following this intriguing rodent, Damp found herself outside a door that was half-open, warm spring sunshine spilling through the gap. She pushed the door wide and crawled into the room to reconnoiter. In the middle of the room the shapes of furniture could just be discerned under their shrouds of dust sheets. The carpet had been rolled up and the curtains removed for storage—but despite being unlived-in, the room felt warm and welcoming.

Crawling across the bare floorboards to the windows, Damp sneezed, sending a cloud of dust dancing upward. Caught in a beam of sunlight, the dust sparkled as it was sent spiraling to the ceiling, catching Damp's attention. She batted at it with her wooden spoon, making it dance and swirl. Engrossed, the baby narrowed her eyes and looped her spoon in wild circles in the air, faster and faster, in wider sweeps, more and more, and . . .

"Pretty!" Damp cried, as suddenly the air was full of roses—masses of them—their pink and cream blossoms suspended in the sunshine, with only the odd falling petal obeying the dictates of gravity. Delighted by this, Damp stood up and waved her spoon extravagantly round her head like a demented conductor. More roses appeared—wine-red, icy white, pink streaked with gold. Amazed at the effect she was having, Damp laughed out loud, her spoon spinning in acrobatic loops and spirals, her bare feet dancing on a soft carpet of fallen petals whose perfume drenched the still air. Backing into a sofa hidden beneath its dust sheet, Damp tripped and sat down abruptly, her spoon clattering across the floor. Damp crawled over to retrieve it. She grasped it in one chubby fist and, unconsciously reversing the direction of her loops and swirls, began again. It quickly became apparent that this was not having the desired effect: to Damp's dismay, the roses began to wither and rot. Shriveling into black shapeless masses, the once-perfect blooms began to drop a shower of beetles, slugs, and caterpillars onto the floor. In a panic, Damp waved her spoon faster, as if by speeding up she could somehow undo this unwanted

decay. To the baby's utter horror, the blackened roses began to quiver and twitch, their leathery petals assuming a new shape entirely. With a wail of terror, Damp recognized what the flowers were turning into—

Outside, bending over a table on the front lawn, Marie Bain and Mrs. McLachlan were laying out the best china for afternoon tea. Hearing a distant but familiar scream, Mrs. McLachlan looked up at the house. Unable to see Damp at any of the windows, she was, however, alarmed at the sight of hundreds of bats squeezing out of a half-open window on the second floor. Without hesitating, she sprinted across the lawn and up the stone steps, bolted through the front door—sending hatboxes rolling across the hall—and took the stairs three at a time. She arrived breathless and shaking in the room where Damp had crawled shrieking under a dust sheet, still hanging on to her spoon. The nanny plucked the screaming baby up in her arms and ran out into the safety of the corridor, slamming the door shut behind her.

"Och, pet," Mrs. McLachlan whispered, stroking Damp's trembling shoulders. "What *have* you done?" With a furtive look to make sure that there was no one around, she bore the child off to the nursery. Locking the door behind her, she carried Damp to the rocking chair, brushed aside a pile of darning lying folded on the seat, and, with a huge sigh, slumped down with the baby on her lap. Since her employment as nanny at StregaSchloss nearly a year before, Flora McLachlan had been dreading this moment. A true witch herself, Mrs. McLachlan had recognized Damp as one, too, from the first moment she had held the baby in her arms. Hoping to postpone the day when Damp discovered her own latent powers, the nanny had encouraged the adult Strega-Borgias in their mistaken assumption that the only witch at StregaSchloss was Damp's mother, the wildly enthusiastic but truly incompetent Signora Strega-Borgia. Mrs. McLachlan had long acquaintance with the necessity of hiding her own considerable gifts under the sensible, unflappable guise of a boring old nanny. Now she considered how best to disguise Damp's newfound gift for sorcery—and how to protect the baby from inadvertently alerting beings from the darker end of the magical spectrum to her presence.

"Heavens above, my wee pet," she whispered, stroking the child's soft hair. "How are we going to keep you a secret?"

Mrs. McLachlan was used to keeping things hidden, but she suspected that Signora Strega-Borgia would be unable to remain silent about Damp's abilities for very long. Moreover, to allow Damp to develop her true potential powers, it was vitally important that the baby received instruction from a true adept, and *not* from a well-intentioned amateur like her mother.

Damp looked up at her beloved nanny with a truly woebegone expression. Her lashes were stuck with tears in pointy clumps, and she sniffed, rubbing her eyes with a fist. Sitting back in the rocking chair, Mrs. McLachlan began to rock, patting the baby in her arms, the rhythm calming the nanny as much as it soothed the child. After a few minutes, she gently removed the wooden spoon from Damp's unresisting hand.

"No more wooden spoons for you, pet," she said, smiling at the baby. "In fact, anything remotely resembling a wand has to be put away out of your reach. Like Sleeping Beauty and the spindle—one slip and we're doomed."

Mud and Diamond
(A.D. 130: Uncharted depths of northern Scotland)

nder a dripping canopy of leaves in the heart of the Forest of Caledon, Nostrilamus picked the remains of last night's roasted hind from between his teeth and snarled at the laboring legionaries.

"Can't you lot work any faster? A bunch of eunuchs armed with toothpicks could dig faster than *that*. Come on, put your backs into it!"

Exhausted and dispirited, the legionaries doggedly sank their rusting spades into the mud and gritted what few remaining teeth they possessed. Hollow-cheeked and prematurely gray, the men bore little resemblance to the bronze musclemen they had been when they left the sun-kissed shores of Italia, full of hope and eagerly anticipating the adventure of a posting in Caledonia. It had been three long years since they had arrived here, spades in hand, to begin this idiotic treasure hunt. Three interminable years of rain, mud, and misery. Sleeping in leaky tents, eating only what they could catch in the forest, waking every dawn to the sound of rain, and fueled on little more than acorn porridge, the legionaries began to suspect they were digging their own graves. As if that wasn't bad enough, the depressed Romans had to endure dragon attacks—which came with no warning and inevitably proved fatal.

"*Hold it!*" Nostrilamus left the shelter of his tree and limped toward them, his emaciated frame barely able to support the weight of his rusty armor, his boil-encrusted ankles spattered with mud from the trailing hem of his once-fine woollen cloak—now a tattered rag that gave scant warmth and served only as a reminder of how far he had fallen from grace. "There. That there. What is it?" Nostrilamus, the once autocratic Malefica of Caledon, wheezed like a set of leaky bellows as he peered into the muddy pit in which his men stood, knee-deep in icy sludge, picking fitfully at the walls of mud that rose above their heads, their battered shovels hardly equal to the task. With a clawlike hand, Nostrilamus pointed to where he could just see a shard of metal glinting in the surrounding rocks and clay. Despite prolonged burial in mud, its silver color seemed undamaged, and it was this that had drawn his eye. On shaking legs he climbed down into the pit and waded over to where his men stood propped on their shovels, praying to Jupiter that *this* time they'd struck pay dirt.

There had been numerous false alarms along the way: the half-buried weapons and armor of their deceased predecessors, peeled of their inedible shell of breastplates and helmets and devoured whole by the dragons like some soft-fleshed Italian delicacy. Astoroth's vellum map, which Nostrilamus had used

37

to try to locate the demon's treasure, had long since disinte-grated in the perpetual drizzle, but by then, having pored over it so often, the legionaries could have redrawn it in their sleep. They had dug so many holes in the hope of finding treasure that the floor of the Forest of Caledon looked as if it had been struck by a meteor shower. So the legionaries betrayed little excitement as their commander scrabbled with his fingernails at the earth surrounding the outcrop of gleaming metal.

"Yes. Yes. Yessss!" Nostrilamus hissed. "This is *it*! Toadflax, get over here and dig, but *carefully*, man—damage it and I'll have you posted to Siberius."

The chosen Toadflax sloshed forward, shovel raised to shoulder-height, and began to pick tentatively at the mud, exposing more of the strange silver metal. Beside him, Nostrilamus flapped excitedly, like a moth-eaten bat in the terminal stages of dementia. As each shovelful of mud was removed, the shape of a metal casket was revealed. Sweating with the effort, Toadflax dropped his shovel into the slurry at his feet and hauled on a corner of the casket. Making a sucking sound, it slid effortlessly out of its muddy cradle, its weight propelling the legionary backward with a grunt of surprise.

"Up here!" commanded Nostrilamus, scaling the wall of the pit with an agility at odds with his ravaged appearance. "Under the tree, quickly."

Curious to see what manner of treasure this was, all the legionaries scrambled out of the pit and gathered round their leader. Toadflax laid the casket on the ground with something approaching reverence. His brow furrowed in concentration, he pointed to where a series of marks were embossed in the metal.

"Begging your pardon, Caledon, but what's that then? Those weird symbols on the lid? What's it say? You being schooled in the interpreting of symbols, not like us dumb squaddies."

Nostrilamus cleared his throat and leaned over the casket. Must be a name, he guessed, racking his brains in an effort to recall the alphabet used by the native Caledonians. "Sih, Ah, Mih, Sih, Aw, Nih," he pronounced at length, peering intently at the metal and adding, "Ih, Tih, Eh—S-a-m-s-o-n-i-t-e. Never heard of him. Must be the previous owner. Well, hey, who *cares*? It's mine now." Prying the lid apart with the edge of his sword, he inhaled sharply.

So absorbed were they all in the sight of the jeweled contents of the Samsonite suitcase that they completely failed to notice the vast shape that had tiptoed up to stand behind them. The vast shape with an even vaster appetite . . .

Wallowing comfortably in a scented pool five hundred miles away from these events in the Forest of Caledon, Astoroth heard the unmistakable sound of his cell phone ringing. Apologizing to his fellow bathers, he wrapped a linen towel around his hairy thighs and clip-clopped off to answer it, his forked tail undulating behind him. Plucking his cloak from the astonished slave in charge of the cloakroom, he headed for the privacy of the vomitorium to take the call.

"Excellent," he whispered, grinning into the mouthpiece. "What took him so long? Three years, for pity's sake! What a *moron*—he had the map, after all." Listening to the voice on the other end, Astoroth was momentarily distracted by the sight of a portly tribune who staggered into the vomitorium and, oblivious to the demon's presence, leant over a hole in the floor and emptied his stomach of all contents. The laurel crown on the man's head fell off into the pool of regurgitated food, and sank without a trace.

"Rrrevolting," muttered Astoroth, adding into the mouth-piece, "can't wait to be relocated in a more civilized time zone. Look, I have to go. Walls have ears and all that jazz. Does this mean I'm in line for promotion? It was I who did the deal with Nostrilamus and descendants, after all. Surely *that* counts for something?"

From the other end came an outraged roar, causing the demon to turn pale and blurt, "It said nothing in *my* contract about retrieving the Chronostone. Why are you picking on me? I've never even *seen* it. What does it look like?" Across the room, the tribune was fishing for his laurels in what appeared to be an open sewer. Gritting his teeth, Astoroth whispered, "You're dropping me in the poo here. Are you one hundred per cent positive it's been muddled up with the gems I planted for my new client?" Trying desperately to rein in his thoughts, the demon groaned. Even if he set off on horseback immediately, he'd *never* make it up to the Forest of Caledon in time to find the suitcase. That meant hanging around in this hideous time zone till Nostrilamus popped his clogs and had a soul ripe for harvest. . . . By then, the Chronostone could be *anywhere*. Still, the demon reasoned, anything was better than crawling back to the Hadean Executive with the happy tidings that he, Astoroth, had somehow managed to lose the Boss's most prized possession. With this in mind, he pleaded with the voice on the other end of the line, "Look, I'll try and get it back before anyone notices. For my sake, *please* don't let the Boss know it's, ah . . . missing, or he'll relocate me as a cockroach in Moscow. . . ."

Night fell in the Forest of Caledon. Helmets lay abandoned in the ferns, swords littered the mud, and a watery moonlight picked out the battlefield where Nostrilamus's legionaries had failed to defend themselves against the dragon attack.

Drawn, not by the smell of unwashed humans, but by the brilliant light that poured out of the excavated casket, the dragon had stood statue-still behind the legionaries, watching as each rope of pearls, each little leather pouch of rubies, emeralds, and sapphires had been plucked from the hoard—until at last, at the very bottom of the pile, Nostrilamus came upon the single stone whose brilliance made all the other jewels seem dull and tawdry by comparison.

At that point the dragon cleared her throat and announced her presence. "I'll have *that*, squirt," she growled, stepping forward to claim the egg-sized diamond. "I've been hunting for yon earring for eons. Pass it over," and extending a massive, taloned paw, she shouldered through the terror-stricken circle of legionaries.

If only they hadn't put up such a *fight*, she thought, patting her vast belly with faint regret. Italian food was *so* fattening. She'd let the scrawniest one go, watching in amusement as he ran screaming into the forest, gemstones spilling from his pockets, sheer terror giving his feet wings. Self-preservation overcoming his greed, Nostrilamus had abandoned the most precious treasure of all without a backward glance.

41

"Silly boy," the dragon whispered, reclining in her roost at the top of a Scots pine and reaching up with one talon to check that her long-lost earring was safely in place. It dangled from her ear, each facet of the diamond-like stone catching the moonlight and sending sparkling reflections dancing across the clutch of eggs beneath the dragon's belly. With no desire other than self-adornment, the dragon had no idea of the immense power currently decorating her ear. In its time, the gem had been given many names—Precious, Pericola d'Illuminem, Ignea Lucifer—names spoken in many tongues and in as many countries across the world as it was traded, passed on, inherited, and fought over. It answered to one name only, however, and that was Chronostone, the Stone of Time.

Scary Biscuits

fternoon tea on the lawn had evolved into supper, and despite the gnats and the slight chill in the air, the Strega-Borgias and their guests still sat outside round the table. The light in the sky had faded to a dusky lavender, so Latch had hung several lanterns from the lower branches of a flowering cherry tree. Tock and Ffup had combined their swimming and fire-lighting skills to send a flotilla of candles set on lily pads floating serenely across the moat. Black Douglas produced a three-quarter-sized violin from a small case and, tucking the tiny instrument under his beard, proceeded to draw from it a haunting melody. Round the table conversation ebbed and flowed, the music weaving in and out of the voices like an endless ribbon. Even Mrs. McLachlan relaxed her hawk-like watch over Damp and, closing her eyes, sighed with deep contentment.

"They played that tune at our wedding, didn't they, darling?" Signora Strega-Borgia said to her husband, wishing to somehow lighten his mood. Luciano was not for cheering up, however. The hideous prospect of a week of wall-to-wall houseguests stretched out interminably ahead of him, and he declined to reply.

"Oh, Luciano, surely you remember this bit. . . ." And hoping that music might reach the parts that her words were failing to touch, Signora Strega-Borgia began to sing in harmony with the violin. *"Ae fond kiss, and then we sever. . . ."*

Walking across the lawn with a lit candelabra in each hand, Latch stopped abruptly. That song . . . His eyes filled with tears as the music tugged at his memory. In childhood, his mother had sung the same melody to soothe him to sleep. . . .

Even Titus for once failed to be embarrassed by his mother's behavior. He'd always loved the sound of her singing and here, looking at the candlelit heads round the table, he knew that they, too, were caught in his mother's spell. All except Fiamma d'Infer were swaying in time to the music—but she alone sat rigid, her mouth curled in a sneer. Across the table, Damp appeared to be conducting Signora Strega-Borgia, using an unlit candle as a baton. . . .

Mrs. McLachlan suddenly snapped out of her reverie. Something had dropped into her lap and was scrabbling back up on the tablecloth. Peering down, she found a small gingerbread man, one of a trayful she'd baked that morning—now no longer inert cookie dough, but fully alive and, alarmingly, very vocal.

"*Nya*-nya-nya, *nyaa*-nyaa, you can't catch *me*!" it squeaked, adding somewhat redundantly, "I'm the Gingerbread Man." As if to underline this, the animated biscuit ran a lap around the table, vaulting over wineglasses and clearing knives and forks with one bound. Sensing the disturbance, Signora Strega-Borgia trailed off in mid-song and looked to Mrs. McLachlan for understanding.

"Must be weevils in the flour," muttered the nanny, reaching out to catch the running figure as it sped past her outstretched hand.

"I *don't* think so. . . ." Fiamma d'Infer expertly speared the Gingerbread Man on the end of her fork. To Mrs. McLachlan's horror, she brought the squealing little figure up to her mouth and, with a vicious smirk, bit its head off.

Damp dropped her conductor's candle and screamed. Instantly Mrs. McLachlan was by her side, plucking the baby off her seat and hugging her tight.

"Poor Damp. What on earth happened?" cried Signora Strega-Borgia, not having witnessed the beheading of the biscuit. Consequently she was somewhat in the dark as to why her youngest daughter was weeping. Mrs. McLachlan, hoping to avoid explanations, sought distraction. "Now, Damp, what have I told you about candles?" she chided, adding, "They're hot, hot, *burrrny*." Since the candle Damp had been holding bore no evidence of ever having been lit, this statement might have caused some confusion had it not been for the appearance of Marie Bain at the head of the table.

The cook's shadow stretched crookedly across the tablecloth, and a strange volcanic rumbling came from the vast coffeepot she was clutching with both hands. She listed across the lawn, each step causing a hissing brown fountain to erupt from the spout. Signor Strega-Borgia stood up. "Are you sure you can manage? Here, Marie, let me——" But before he could take the pot from her, the cook lunged toward the table and dropped the pot in the middle with a muffled shriek.

"Ees hot," she said, somewhat unnecessarily, since the tablecloth round the coffee pot was turning brown and beginning to smell like burnt ironing. "Now we haff coffee," she said, making this simple statement of fact sound like a threat. She locked eyes with Black Douglas and demanded, "Meelk? Zoogir?" then tilting the pot at a dangerous angle, slopped a quantity of brown fluid into a nearby cup.

"What *is* that stuff?" Titus whispered as his father sat down again. "It doesn't smell anything *like* coffee. . . ."

The hapless Black Douglas, victim of Marie Bain's slitty-eyed scrutiny, brought the cup to his lips and took a tiny sip. For a split second his eyes registered shock, but just as quickly, realizing the cook was still monitoring his every gesture, he forced his stunned facial muscles into an approximation of a smile. "Mmm-hmm. Excellent," he lied, reaching for the sugar bowl and spooning several heaped teaspoons of what he fervently hoped was brown sugar into his cup. Sweat broke out on his forehead and all the color drained from his face. Marie Bain smiled grimly and turned her attention to Signor Strega-Borgia, pouring out another cupful. Mrs. McLachlan hastily stood up, forestalling the cook's attempts to do the same for her. "No, thank you, dear. I must get this poor wee mite to bed," she said, shifting Damp onto her hip. "Say good night to everyone, pet," and she swiftly bore the baby off across the garden.

Much to Mrs. McLachlan's dismay, a figure slipped away from the table and intercepted her before she could reach the house.

"I didn't get a chance to say good night to the child," said Fiamma d'Infer, stepping in front of Mrs. McLachlan and blocking her path. Damp gave a small howl and clung like a limpet to her nanny. But Fiamma persisted, standing too close and staring intently at the baby.

"What a *special* little girl," she purred, reaching out to curl a finger under Damp's chin and bring the baby's head up to meet her gaze. Damp immediately squeezed her eyes tightly shut.

"I think she's a wee bit too tired to be sociable, don't you?" said Mrs. McLachlan briskly. "Come on, pet, let's run your bath."

Fiamma was not to be put off so easily. "Oh, but I have some absolutely heavenly stuff for your bath, my dear. Mmmm, yellow bubbles with green glittery stuff in them—you would just love it, wouldn't you?"

"She's got sensitive skin," hissed Mrs. McLachlan, hugging Damp protectively and attempting to step around this dreadful woman.

"That's not *all* she's got." Fiamma's voice developed an edge as she whispered, "I'm sure you know exactly what I'm talking about, *Mrs*. McLachlan."

The nanny shivered involuntarily. This ghastly woman *knew*. Somehow she'd worked it out. . . . Mrs. McLachlan felt short of breath, as if she were about to faint, almost as if hands were gripping her throat and squeezing—

"Look at me," Fiamma commanded, bringing the full force of her will crashing down on top of the nanny. "Look. At. Me."

To Mrs. McLachlan's horror, she felt as if invisible hooks were dragging her chin upward. Damp was keening—a high, thin sound that the nanny had never heard her make before;

she sounded as if she were in agony. Fiamma d'Infer laughed mockingly. "Look. At. Me," she repeated, the words echoing weirdly, as if spoken down a well.

"Heavens, do you have to be *quite* so demanding?" said a familiar voice from overhead. Giving a languid flap of her giant wings, Ffup glided down from the roof to land beside Mrs. McLachlan and peer at Fiamma with some confusion. "Okey-dokey, I'm here. I'm looking at you, seeing as how you asked, but, um . . . have you done something I should notice? Your hair? Your eyebrows?" The dragon frowned. "Nope, not the eyebrows. New makeup? You've had a nose job? Face-lift? Botox injections? Oh, come on, ladies, help me out here!" Realizing that no verbal clues were forthcoming, Ffup tried to fill up the silence with inane chatter. "So—where's the party? What's the haps, chaps? Why so glum, chum?" And with a little snort of flame, she dug Fiamma d'Infer in the ribs with her elbow, causing the woman to lose her balance and lurch into Signora Strega-Borgia, who had come running at full speed up to the house.

"Ooops, sorry, Fiamma," she gasped. "I've just realized what that awful coffee was made out of. Do excuse me for a minute, I must make sure that poor Marie doesn't make another pot." And without further explanation she fled indoors.

Taking this as an opportunity to escape, Mrs. McLachlan followed her employer inside. She ran upstairs to the nursery and locked Damp and herself in the bathroom. Not that one wee lock is any protection against that *fiend*, she thought, pulling Damp's dress off over her head and bending down to remove the baby's socks and shoes. She reached over and turned on both bath taps, finding the sound of running water strangely comforting, as if by its very domestic nature it could somehow wash away the terror of the previous five minutes. Whatever Fiamma d'Infer is, Mrs. McLachlan decided, she is most certainly *not* a student witch. As if she could read her nanny's thoughts, Damp wriggled round in her lap and peered intently into Mrs. McLachlan's face.

"Not like it," she stated. "Nasty nasty yuck lady."

"Absolutely," agreed Mrs. McLachlan. "Stay away from her, pet. She's verrry, very dangerous."

"Hot, hot burrrny?" the baby asked, her brow furrowed with the seriousness of the question.

"Very," said Mrs. McLachlan, pouring a capful of bubble bath into the stream running out of the cold tap. The bathwater turned a delicate rose-pink, and the air filled with the fragrance of strawberries. Damp sighed happily and laid her head against Mrs. McLachlan's comforting chest.

Out of earshot of the guests on the lawn, Signor and Signora Strega-Borgia were having a hissed conference in the kitchen.

"Baci, you can't be serious. You mean to tell me that we've just been drinking coffee brewed from rodent droppings?"

"Um . . . not *exactly* rodent droppings, darling. Don't worry, they were just freeze-dried guinea-pig droppings that I'd stored in an old coffee jar. An understandable mistake—"

"An understandable mistake for Marie Bain, perhaps, but I'm not angry at *her*. How was she to know? It's *you* that's responsible. What were you thinking of? What sort of lunatic stores feces in her kitchen? And why?"

"It was for a tincture, Luciano. I didn't think—"

"That's the problem in a nutshell. You *never* think." Unable to stop himself, Luciano launched into Italian opera mode. His chest swelled, his eyes glittered, and his gestures grew wildly expansive. Shamefully aware that he was behaving badly, he listened in horror as he heard himself continue, "You didn't *think* about your family when you invited all these weirdos to stay. You didn't *think* how we'd feel having our house taken over by incantation-muttering witches. You didn't *think* about our health when you filled our house with jars of biological hazards. I'm going to bed before I break out in boils from another of your exercises in magical incompetence."

There was a crash as the kitchen door banged shut, and then came the thunder of footsteps stamping upstairs. Unobserved in the china cupboard, tucked away in a corner of the kitchen, Tarantella rolled her eyes and applied another coat of lipstick to her already alarmingly pink mouthparts. The tarantula peered out at where Signora Strega-Borgia sat sniffling and dabbing her eyes at the kitchen table. Such trauma and fuss, Tarantella thought. Far better just to eat one's spouse when he starts getting lippy.

Night Moves

Sitting bolt upright and fully dressed on her bed, Mrs. McLachlan was waiting for the household to retire. Given that twelve guests currently roamed the corridors of StregaSchloss, this was taking longer than usual. Water coursed along ancient copper pipes as toilets were flushed and baths drawn. The traffic of feet up and down stairs had gone on for hours. After a prolonged wailing session, Nestor had finally succumbed to slumber in his corner of the dungeon, allowing his fellow beasts to catch some sleep before the baby dragon woke for the four o'clock feed.

When all had been quiet for half an hour, Mrs. McLachlan stood up, checked that her bedroom door was locked, and took a small rolled-up rug out from its hiding place at the bottom of her wardrobe. Placing this in the middle of the bedroom floor, she unrolled it, carefully untangling its tattered fringe. The rug was ancient, woven by some unknown hand hundreds of years before, and now its silk threads were faded and worn, their complex pattern of interwoven stars and spirals nearly invisible with age. Drawing her bedroom curtains back and opening the window wide, Mrs. McLachlan looked out at the meadow beyond, noting with satisfaction that all was quiet and still. Patting her pocket to confirm that she had the magical Soul Mirror safely stowed away, she drew a deep breath.

"Right," she said to herself. "Time for lame excuses and apologetic groveling . . ." And crouching down to kneel on the floor, she crawled across onto the rug feeling faintly foolish. She maneuvered herself carefully into the middle and wriggled into position, keeping one hand firmly on the floorboards. Closing her eyes and taking a deep breath, she snatched her hand off the floor and grabbed a handful of the fringe at her feet. The rug rippled and flapped, as if giant gusts of air were circling beneath it. Then, with a shudder, it rose swiftly into the air and hurled itself and its passenger through the open window at an indecent speed, causing Mrs. McLachlan's hair to come unpinned and stream out behind her.

She arrived at the library with minutes to spare. Placing her hand on the ground, she slid gingerly off the rug and rolled it up, tucking it under her arm as she pushed her way through a small bronze-paneled door.

"We're just about to close," the librarian informed her, taking in the nanny's disheveled appearance and emitting a faint *tut* as he saw what she was holding out to him.

"I *wondered* when you were going to bring that back," he said, drawing down his thick black brows till they joined in a furrow above his nose. "What's the excuse this time?"

Mrs. McLachlan sighed. The problem with borrowing things from the library was remembering to return them on time. "I'm so sorry," she said simply. "I'll try to do better in the future—it's just I'm so busy, it's quite hard for me to find a moment. Actually, I almost forgot I had this."

The librarian ran a handheld scanner across the returned artifact and pursed his lips. "Six *months* you've had this. I'm going to have to impose the maximum fine. There have been plenty of other wannabe mind readers wanting to borrow it. The soul mirror is one of our more popular items. . . . Take a seat while I dig out your file."

Mrs. McLachlan sank into a low chair and watched, as the librarian clip-clopped across the floor to place the returned object carefully in one of the glass-fronted cabinets that lined the walls. The library consisted of this one stone-walled room, dotted here and there with small tables and deep, comfortable chairs. A fire glowed dimly in a large marble fireplace, and the room was lit by tall beeswax candles. Tiny oil-burners on the tables gave off the mixed scents of myrrh, rosemary, and juniper, and the calming sound of running water came from a lion's-head fountain in a corner by the door.

There wasn't a single book to be seen.

Remembering why she was here, Mrs. McLachlan cleared her throat and said, "Actually, I'd like to borrow something else."

The librarian ignored this, busying himself with accessing her records on a wall-mounted screen. He was completely naked, as centaurs tend to be, but as a concession toward his role of librarian he wore a metal collar round his neck inscribed with the word ALPHA and had woven his chest hair into a single braid that swung heavily down to his hooves.

"I need a shield," Mrs. McLachlan continued, her voice betraying some of her concern about the dangers of Fiamma d'Infer.

"They're all out on loan." The librarian swished his tail for emphasis. "Terribly popular at the moment, shields. Last year it was laser lances, year before—"

"A Quikunpik, then," Mrs. McLachlan interrupted, getting up and crossing the floor to stand beside the librarian. "Surely you've got one of those?"

"I'll look." The little centaur scrolled down the list of items owned by the library until he came to the Q's. "Quark-espresso, Qualmudes, Quibbles, Quick-ees . . . Ah, here we are, Quikunpik. Nope, sorry, it's not due back until tomorrow."

"Well, what *have* you got?" said Mrs. McLachlan with a faint edge of desperation, her eyes rapidly trawling the display cases around her. Her gaze fell on a small silver clock the size of a pocket watch, which appeared and disappeared with each passing second. Tick—there it was; tick—there it wasn't. The effect was oddly mesmerizing, and her thoughts drifted pleasantly for a few seconds until, recalling the urgency of her visit here, she gave a small shiver and turned back to face the librarian.

"What does that little clock do?"

"It's an update on our old Time Flies™—remember those horribly inaccurate bluebottles that dumped you at various unpredictable points in time? Such a pain . . . Anyway, this is the new and improved version, 24-hour clock with state-of-the-art Moebius drive, infinitely pre-programmable for accurate entry and exit. It's known as the Alarming Clock."

"Not the most reassuring of names," murmured Mrs. McLachlan, her attention caught by the flickering device as it winked into being and promptly disappeared again.

"I imagine they called it 'alarming' because of the size of the instruction manual." The librarian sighed, producing a large paperback book of similar dimensions to the telephone directory for Mexico City. "Now don't be put off," he warned, passing this tome to Mrs. McLachlan and opening the display case to remove the Alarming Clock.

Mrs. McLachlan waited, leafing idly through the pages of dense print and wondering when, if ever, she would have time to get to grips with the complex volume of instructions. The librarian passed her the Alarming Clock, logged the withdrawal into his computer, and escorted Mrs. McLachlan out.

"Sorry to rush you," he said, opening the door onto the night. "Normally I'd prefer to go through the instructions with you, but I simply haven't enough time. Just remember two things: always carry spare batteries wherever you go and, when you leave your destination, be it in the past or the future, be sure *never* to take anything back with you. No extra luggage, no tourist tat, and no souvenirs. . . . And a warning. If you're late bringing this back, it'll be a *far* more severe punishment than a mere fine."

A chill gust of air blew through the library door, causing the twin shadows cast by the centaur and the nanny to dance in the flickering candlelight.

"Good luck." The librarian stepped aside to let Mrs. McLachlan pass. "Bon voyage . . ."

Weirdm@il

The following dawn, returning to StregaSchloss after a dip in Lochnagargoyle, the beasts halted at the edge of the meadow, somewhat perplexed by the sight that greeted them up ahead. Several figures lay on the lawn, their contorted bodies rendered ghostlike by the early morning mist that wrapped round their twisted limbs and hung damply above the grass, dotting everything at ground level with chilly dew. Strange grunts and occasional roars of pain disturbed the silence, demonstrating to the watching beasts that all the figures were alive, even if horribly injured.

"What d'you think *happened* to them?" Sab whispered, at a loss for what to do next.

"They weren't there when we left the house," Ffup said, raising a pawful of lurid pink talons to scratch the top of her head. "Whatever it was must have taken place while we were down at the lochside."

One of the figures heaved itself into a sitting position and, much to the beasts' confusion, dragged a leg over its head and curled it round the back of its neck. With a wail of agony, it toppled over and lay facedown on the grass.

"Oh, the poor thing," groaned Ffup, turning away in horror.

"Come on, guys, we'd better go and see how we can help." Tock lolloped ahead, disappearing into the meadow, his passage marked by a thrashing trail of green as he trampled the grasses under his paws.

But when the beasts arrived on the lawn, far from being greeted as welcome agents of rescue, they found themselves being rudely rejected as unwanted gate-crashers. The contorted bodies belonged to seven of the houseguests, none of whom were even remotely grateful for the arrival of the beasts—who stood panting in their midst, offering help, medical aid, and the possibility of ambulances.

"Do bog off, would you?" Ariadne Ventete muttered as Knot attempted to pat her consolingly on her back. "Eurrrch. I *loathe* dogs. Don't let it breathe on me."

Tock ambled over to where Black Douglas lay on his stomach, his legs twisted up over his spine, his head straining painfully backward till it touched his feet.

"Bad luck," the crocodile murmured sympathetically. "Can I get you anything? Some Tylenol? Aspirin? Would a massage help? My back goes like that sometimes—"

Black Douglas collapsed suddenly, his legs crashing down on the grass, his face following seconds later. His shoulders shook and he emitted little sobbing sounds.

"Oh lord," Tock breathed, aghast. "Guys, get over here. I think we're about to lose this one."

Black Douglas rolled over onto his back and opened his eyes.

"Yup," said Tock sadly. "I'll try and do some lifesaving stuff here, but while I'm busy giving mouth-to-mouth, one of you run and call an ambulance." Sab obediently bolted off to the house, leaving Ffup and Knot to watch in admiration as Tock bent over Black Douglas. The crocodile took a deep breath and grabbed the man's face between his front paws.

"Listen, Tick," Black Douglas growled. "One kiss and you're history." He sprang upright and elbowed Tock aside. "Pin back your ears, reptile. We're not ill, not injured, and definitely not in need of medical assistance. We. Are. Practicing. Yoga. Understand?" Seeing the total lack of comprehension on all the beasts' faces, he seized Tock and rolled the alarmed crocodile onto his back. "Relax," he commanded. "You're dreadfully tense. Look, you're clenching your jaw. . . ."

"Help," mumbled Tock. "Mnnng . . . urk . . . aaowww!"

"There," said Black Douglas, grabbing the crocodile's tail and expertly twisting it into a loose knot. "Now we'll just ease your legs over your back, like so—"

"Nooooo," wailed Tock. "I'm not designed to bend that wayyyy—OH-NOOO-AAAOWWW!'

"That's what all beginners say," said Black Douglas disgustedly. "Just relax, you great wuss—it only hurts because you're fighting it."

"Too right, I'm fighting it!" howled Tock. "Knot, Ffup—*do* something. HELP MEEEE!"

Knot shuffled up and leant over until his furry face was next to Black Douglas's. "Read my woolly, unwashed lips," he said firmly. "Put the crocodile down."

"Yeah," added Ffup, leaning over Knot's shoulder and grinning menacingly. "Or else—"

Sensibly deciding that now was perhaps not the best time to win the beasts over to the joys of yoga, Black Douglas released the moaning crocodile and got to his feet. "No hard feelings?" he said, holding out a hand to Tock.

"No hard feelings?" squeaked the crocodile. "I've no hard *anythings,* thanks to you. You've turned me into jelly, you brute. I don't think I'll ever walk again." And followed by Knot and Ffup, Tock limped off across the lawn toward the solace of StregaSchloss.

Seeking to avoid his mother's eccentric houseguests, Titus had forgone breakfast. He was closeted in the map room, hunched over his laptop, and close to despair.

"Come on," he begged the lit screen in front of him. "Please? Don't do this to me."

An internal chittering sound alerted Titus to the fact that the laptop had, not surprisingly, failed to respond to his spoken pleas. Onscreen, a dialogue box popped up bearing the glad tidings:

> Mail could not be received at this time.
> An error type h:ex//yt occurred.

Titus laid his head on the keyboard and groaned. This was just so not fair, he decided. For weeks now his laptop had been playing a perverse game of hide-and-seek with his e-mail. Time after time, he'd log on, attempt to download his e-mail, and up would come several dialogue box variants on a theme of: YOUR MAIL? EH? WHAT MAIL? WHO ARE YOU, ANYWAY, DEMANDING

MAIL? COME TO THINK OF IT, WHO AM I? AM I A COMPUTER? WHAT IF I'M JUST A LITTLE LUMP OF EXPENSIVE GRAY PLASTIC? AM I GOING TO CRASH?

In vain, Titus had tried to reassure his neurotic computer that indeed it was a mega-machine, a brain the size of planet Earth and enough processing power to launch a spacecraft into orbit, if required. But back would come the message that his laptop was currently enjoying the cyber-equivalent of door shut, lights off, and fingers jammed firmly into ears.

He tried once more, sidling sneakily up to the SEND AND RECEIVE menu, trying to make sure the laptop was looking the other way before he brought his index finger slapping down on the ENTER key. To Titus's relief, little clicks and whirrs came from inside the machine, not the chittering noises that usually preceded a fit of the cyber-vapors. Waiting impatiently for something to happen, Titus shivered. The map room at StregaSchloss was situated in the oldest part of the house, built beneath the central courtyard and dating back to the fifteenth century. Here no daylight shone and the walls were six feet thick, which might have accounted for the deep chill that permeated the air. Titus could see his breath forming clouds in front of his mouth, and condensation beaded the laptop's screen.

"Hurry it up," he complained. "I'm beginning to get frostbite—" Behind him, the hammered brass lights on each side of the fireplace dimmed, flickered, and went out.

"Oh *great*," muttered Titus. "A power cut—just what I need." In front of him, automatically switching to battery power, the laptop sprang to life. Apparently overcoming whatever had previously ailed it, the computer began to download Titus's mail. Loads of it. Faster and faster it came, each message bigger than the last, byte piling upon byte, the computer barely able to sustain the flow.

"Whaat?" Titus squeaked as his in-box filled up, overflowed, and mail still kept on coming. After what seemed like hours, the flood slowed to a downpour, then a drizzle, and finally, with an exhausted beep of protest, the last one dropped into his in-box.

TO WHOM IT MAY CONCERN was the subject, and H_EX@DAEMON.NET was the sender.

"What *is* this?" Titus whispered, hoping that he hadn't been sent a virus. No alerts sounded from his computer, and finally curiosity overcame caution and he clicked it open. To his extreme frustration, it was written in purest computer gobbledygook. Ignoring this, Titus clicked on the little paperclip icon above the undecipherable message in order to open its accompanying attachment.

Immediately, he wished he could turn the clock back and undo what he'd just done. "No . . . no . . . *Stop!*" he wailed as his computer greedily devoured the virus-laden attachment, dragged it, gloating and slobbering, into its hard drive and, with a strangled squawk, went down. The screen turned black, and a wistful little dialogue box informed Titus

```
Connection terminated
Hard drive erased
A pox on the house of h_ex@daemon.net
```

Titus slumped back in his chair. This was just too awful to contemplate. How could he have been so dumb? And how was he going to tell his father that he'd accidentally erased the hard drive? The noises now coming from the inside of the laptop sounded prohibitively expensive. Titus reached over to turn the computer off and put it out of its misery, but his hand halted quiveringly above the ON/OFF key. His mouth fell open and he blinked rapidly, noticing several things simultaneously: his keyboard was covered with frost, the screen was glowing a deep and poisonous green, and, incomprehensibly on a dead computer, a new dialogue box was telling him

YOU HAVE MAIL

The thought crossed his mind that his laptop was haunted, but dismissing this instantly, he pressed ENTER.

To: Titus@stregaschloss.co.uk
From: pbs@amartin.co.uk
21/02/XXXX

Dear Mr. Strega-Borgia:

As per your faxed instructions of 28/07/XXXX, we are pleased to inform you that your new car will be delivered to your home address in approximately six weeks' time. Please do not hesitate to contact us if you have any further requirements, and be assured that we will contact you closer to the delivery date to receive your final instructions.

Yours sincerely,
Piers Brooke-Shepherd
Senior Managing Executive (Sales)

Aston Martin Limited
London WC1 1AM
e-mail: pbs@amartin.co.uk

Mystified, Titus watched as this message was replaced by another.

Titus,
are we still on for sat? cant remember if
you're back from ny late frid or sat a.m.
dyou need a lift from the airport? let me
know.
lots of love,
M

Frowning in total incomprehension, Titus watched helplessly as this was replaced by

Get rid of it. Don't take it. It will consume the taker. Destroy it for it will destroy all who seek to possess it. Somehow the Borgias have to break the chain. You'll never know how much I regret . . .

Totally alarmed by the tone of this last message, Titus stood up, shivering uncontrollably. From a long, long way off came the sound of mocking laughter. Unnerved, Titus glanced at the screen. White fingers of ice were running across it, reaching out to obscure the words that Titus saw, just before his courage failed him entirely.

Help me please

Hel h
Ex

The laughter changed to a hissing repetition of one word.
Over and over, increasing in volume and menace, Titus heard
himself summoned, *Titusssss . . . Titusssssss . . . Titussss . . .*

He clutched at his throat, a feeling of suffocation overcoming him. In the dim light from the screen he saw the walls of
the map room begin to move and shift, in and out, like a giant
stone heart beating all around him.

Stumbling back out of the map room, Titus fled. He crashed
blindly along the flagged passageway, hardly able to breathe for
terror and, coming to the stone steps that led up to the kitchen
corridor, fell to his knees and began to scrabble upward.

"Ah . . ." came a familiar voice. "Splendid. My brother in the
full-on grovel position. Heavens, Titus, what brought *this* on?"
Standing on the steps above him, Pandora looked down to where
he knelt, tear-stained and in desperate need of a handkerchief,
incoherently gibbering an explanation for his distraught state.

"Map r-r-room. Mail. Got loads of mail. Horrible . . . It's
dead, but it was *working*. Got to help m-m—"

Pandora tutted. "Tell me, Mr. Strega-Borgia, have they
changed your medication recently? Forgotten to take it, perhaps? Ughh—don't wipe your nose on *me*."

"Pandora. Listen to me, please. Something awful's going on
down there." Titus gestured behind him, down into the gloom.
"Come and see, you have to believe me. My computer—"

Aghast, he saw Pandora was shaking her head and walking away. He scrambled to his feet and followed, temporarily delayed by a trio of his mother's guests, who were attempting to roll a vast, pockmarked cauldron along the narrow corridor leading to the kitchen. Consequently, by the time Titus over took Pandora, she was halfway up the main staircase.

"What's wrong with you? Why are you ignoring me?" he demanded, blocking her way upstairs.

Pandora regarded him with scientific detachment, as if he were some undistinguished species of slug, too common to merit more than a cursory glance. "It was the word 'computer' that did it," she sighed. "Titus, when will you ever get it through your pointy little head that I'm not interested? I simply don't understand your complete obsession with modern technology. Look," she explained, "I like computers almost as much as you like spiders. I came to find you because there's more 'mail' for you downstairs." She attempted a smile. "A letter. From the lawyers handling Grandfather Borgia's estate. I guess it won't be long now, will it?'"

Titus drew a deep breath. Obviously Pandora was becoming quite obsessed about this money stuff. Himself, he couldn't care less. The prospect of his forthcoming inheritance made him feel as if he were observing his whole family down the wrong end of a telescope. Their petty quarrels and concerns all seemed so far away. He shook himself and gritted his teeth. Even his own temporary . . . upset, over something so stupid as a malfunctioning laptop, was beginning to fade and dwindle. Family squabbles? Just buy another house and leave home. Computer breakdowns? Toss it in the bin and order up a better one. He sneered at his sister and stepped aside to let her pass.

"Thanks for your support, Pandora. Really appreciated your concern for my welfare. Next time I think I've seen a ghost, I'll go find a saber-toothed tiger for sympathy and moral support." Feeling victorious but oddly empty, Titus spun round and sauntered slowly downstairs, this time for the comforts of the kitchen.

The Comfort of Cobwebs

Tight-lipped and willing the prickling behind her eyes to stop, Pandora crept forlornly upstairs to the attic. Windows set into the walls of the many staircases afforded her ever-higher aerial views of the land surrounding StregaSchloss. At last she came to the top floor, a part of the house inhabited by Latch, his bachelor accommodation located at the end of a low-ceilinged corridor. Lined up outside his bedroom door were several pairs of highly polished brogues, and the distant sound of running water and someone whistling a tune indicated that the butler was indulging in his perpetual quest for cleanliness.

Pandora tiptoed across the corridor to the steep wooden staircase that climbed up to the attic. Judging by the footprints in the dust-covered uppermost treads, no one but she had ventured to the top of StregaSchloss for some time. Trying not to sneeze, Pandora crept upstairs and pushed the heavy trapdoor open above her head. She crawled in and closed it behind her, lowering it carefully back into place with hardly a sound. The attic had long been her refuge, since—despite her best efforts to deter casual visitors with notices pinned to her door—every resident of StregaSchloss ignored all warnings to keep out of her bedroom, and after a cursory knock would walk straight in. However, in this vast attic, you could have hidden a battleship under the piles of dust and clutter, and no one would have been any wiser.

Ropes of spider silk festooned the rafters, except those below a recently mended section of roof, where the ferocious blasts of a midwinter gale had scoured that area clean, blowing cobwebs away and bleaching the surrounding timbers a pale and ghostly white. Averting her gaze from the new flooring that replaced a section where two unfortunate strangers had plunged to their deaths, Pandora headed for the dustier and more congenial parts of the attic, climbing over open sea-trunks, teetering piles of old books, rolled-up carpets, one unused set of bagpipes, and finally, under one of the dusty windows, she slumped onto a faded bolster, its worn fabric warm in the morning sun.

Determined not to give Titus the satisfaction of seeing her cry, Pandora was now able to give way to her real feelings. In the solitude and quiet of the attic, she curled into a little ball and wept. She cried for herself and for her lost brother, who despite being under the same roof might as well have been on the moon as far as she was concerned. Propped up against a rusty birdcage, home of a long-deceased cockatiel, was an old picture book, one that Pandora had loved as a young child—the gilt of its title long gone, the cover somewhat chewed and worn. The irony of seeing *The Snow Queen* reappear after all these years was not lost on Pandora. A new wave of tears engulfed her as she remembered the tale of a brother and sister frozen apart by the evil Snow Queen, the brother saved from his icy fate by the tears of the sister who loved him. Gerda and Kay, Pandora thought, the names coming back to her as if she were sitting in the old nursery hearing it read to her again, over Titus's protests. Back then, she remembered, he used to wear overalls. . . . The vision of her brother as a four-year-old caused her to smile through her tears. . . .

. . . blue denim overalls with a big rusty blotch on the bib from when he'd had a spectacular nosebleed after she'd pushed him off his tricycle. He'd been about to plunge into the moat, the moron, and her one concern had been to stop this from happening, but he thought she'd done it on purpose to hurt him. . . . His nose was always running back then. And the nursery was in a different room, a blue room with big windows on the second floor. A beautiful room, always sunny, always warm and safe. Mummy said Titus had even been born there. . . .

"Was I borned there?" Pandora demanded, gazing up into her mother's face, uncomfortably aware that her diaper was growing somewhat damp.

"You weren't borned," Titus snorted, looking up from a Lego tank that he was steadily chewing apart, his chubby fingers unable to separate the slippery little bricks he needed for building a tractor. *"You were made in a hostiple,"* he added cuttingly.

"No I wasn't," Pandora yelled. *"I wasn't wasn't wasn't!"*

Titus turned his back on this outburst with a four-year-old's disdain. Picking up the Lego tank, he brought his jaws down on a particularly stubborn wheel.

"Pandora, darling, don't—"

"WASN'T WASN'T WASN'T, SO THERE!"

"That's enough now, don't shout—"

To Titus's alarm, the wheel sprang off its axle and flew into his mouth. He gasped, his indrawn breath vacuuming the little plastic disk back to lodge suffocatingly in his throat. His nose, permanently blocked with mucus, allowed the passage of no air whatsoever. Eyes bulging, he instantly turned purple with the effort of trying to breathe.

"HOBBLE, HOBBIBLE TITUS!" Pandora bawled, falling off Signora Strega-Borgia's lap with a banshee shriek and crawling toward where Titus sat with his back to her, quietly asphyxiating.

"Pandora. For heaven's sake, calm down. NO! DON'T DO THAT!"

Pandora raised both of her chubby little fists and brought them thudding down on her brother's back. With the sound of a champagne cork being popped, the wheel shot out of Titus's mouth and flew across the nursery floor. Signora Strega-Borgia sprang to her feet just in time to catch her son as he toppled backward, his face a deep blue but thankfully able to draw in great lungfuls of air. . . .

It had been a close call, Pandora thought, recalling the many other times she'd hauled her brother back from the brink. . . . But now, for some reason, she had an uneasy feeling that Titus was in far graver danger than ever before. In the past they had quarreled, sometimes with devastating unkindness, both of them retreating to their separate bedrooms to lick their wounds . . . but after a recuperative sulk they'd always effected some sort of repair. This was different though—nastier, more bitter, and prolonged. . . . This time, it seemed as though neither of them had any idea how to even begin bridging the chasm that separated them.

A shadow fell across the floor, and Pandora looked up to the rafters, where a giant tarantula hung swinging back and forth on a skein of spider silk.

"Tarantella?" Pandora whispered, barely able to see through tears.

"Absolutely," came the languid drawl from above. "Tell me, O leaking one, is this a Robert-the-Bruce moment, or am I talking out of my fundament?"

"Excuse me?" Pandora said, watching as Tarantella glided down from the rafters and sashayed across the floor to where she lay clutching her bolster.

"Robert the Bruce," the spider prompted. "Ancient biped, big hair, especially on his face. Come *on*, you know this stuff. Stuck in a cave with a blunt razor and a helpful spider? Already hacked his chin to pieces in a misguided attempt to obtain a smooth shave—?"

"Um, actually, that's not the version of events that I know," said Pandora.

"Whatever," Tarantella said dismissively, consigning the incorrect contents of many history books to the oblivion she so patently thought they deserved. "So, legend has it he's sitting there, freezing in his woolly skirt, peering at his blunt razor, chin a mass of cuts and scrapes, beard still attached. He's totally depressed, gazing at his reflection in a puddle, and the cave's resident spider, name of Apocryphylla, drops down in front of his face. She says, 'Check this out, bog-breath,' and proceeds to spin a web right in front of his eyes. So he goes, 'Eurrrgh! Spiders!' or something along those lines and reaches out to wreck the web. . . . You *are* listening, aren't you?"

"I'm fascinated," said Pandora truthfully. "Do go on."

"With a patience that future generations of spiders can only admire, Apocryphylla trucks off to a distant corner of the cave and begins again, this time spinning a web of such Celtic intricacy that despite himself, Bob is deeply impressed—"

"Bob?" queried Pandora.

"Oh, do keep up," chided Tarantella. "Bob the Brute, Robert the Bruce. Anyway, he watches as my talented relation creates an ephemeral masterpiece—"

"And?" prompted Pandora. "What happened?"

"Well, it's a bit of a gore-fest from now on in. Not for the whole family. . . . So, the web's hanging there, testament to Apocryphylla's powers of endurance, and Bob turns to her and demands to know what it all means. 'Means?' she says. 'You want philosophy as well as beauty? It means, O woolly-skirted one, that if at first you don't succeed, due to some unshaven cretin failing to appreciate your true genius, then you have to try, try agggg—' She meant to say 'again' but, insulted by being addressed so disrespectfully by a mere spider, Bob the Brute brought his massive fist down upon her fragile body, and then got on with trying to have a shave."

"Oh, how *awful*," breathed Pandora, ashamed of her common humanity with this monster.

"Don't give it a second thought," said Tarantella cheerfully.

72

"Listen up. How's this for divine justice? Bob cuts himself shaving—draws the razor across his own throat and—shock, horror—hits a vein and collapses on the floor of the cave gargling horribly, lifeblood leaching across the et cetera. Regrettably, for him, a scant six feet away, and sadly unreachable by a man in extremis, is the only thing that could have stanched the flow of blood and thus saved his life—"

"The *cobweb*?" asked Pandora, eyes shining.

"The cobweb," said Tarantella. "A simple and effective remedy against hemorrhage. Used since time began to assist in the healing process."

"Poor Apocryphylla," said Pandora. "What a waste."

"Indeed," said Tarantella crisply. "But tell me, what brings you dripping up in my domain? Not a need to shave, I trust—you are hirsutely underendowed enough as it is."

"It's Titus," said Pandora, as a wave of gloom swept over her. "I don't know how to make things right with him again. He's so distant—"

"Not distant enough," muttered Tarantella. "Even Betelgeuse would be too close for comfort. Still, there's no accounting for the eccentricities of human nature. You came up here to consider how best to deal with the problem of your brother?"

"Something like that," mumbled Pandora, imagining what horrors lay ahead. What would the tarantula suggest? Bite him? Wrap him in spider silk and hang him up to dry . . . ?

"My advice, for what it's worth," Tarantella began, grinning widely at Pandora, "is try again. Try to win him back. Take him a peace offering: some daddy longlegs' legs, a sun-dried bluebottle." Seeing Pandora shudder at these suggestions, Tarantella amended her menu somewhat. "No? Perhaps not . . . How about some cake? A cup of tea? In my experience, you have to *feed* the male of the species before attempting to converse with it. So. Feed him and then attempt to make friends. And"—the tarantula ran a little black tongue over her lipsticked lips—"if *that* fails, then just go ahead and eat him. That way he can't answer back. Byeeeee." Winching herself upward on a spinneret, Tarantella vanished abruptly into the shadows.

Alone again, Pandora smiled. Odd as the conversation had been, it had also been enormously comforting. As cobwebs heal wounds, the company of Tarantella had soothed her hurt feelings. She stood up and leant against the window seat, breathing onto a pane of dirty glass and wiping it clean with her sleeve. Down below, way off in the distance, she could see the masts of Black Douglas's beautiful boat anchored off the shore of Lochnagargoyle. Dwarfed by distance, tiny people dotted the lawn, and she could just make out the figure of Mrs. McLachlan hanging out sheets to dry on the line. Beside her, Marie Bain was slowly pegging out several tentlike black corsets and shrunken stripy stockings, the cook's body language clearly indicating that she regarded guest laundry as a task not within her job description.

From the attic window they all looked so small and insignificant, but as Damp wobbled across her line of vision, Pandora was reminded of how very dear they were to her. Just because she couldn't reach out to touch them right now didn't change how she felt about them. It depended on one's viewpoint, she decided. Titus was still her brother, and nothing would change that; just because he appeared to be as far away as one of the tiny figures below didn't mean she would never reach him again. Cheered by this thought, Pandora crossed the attic and lifted the trapdoor to go downstairs.

"Tarantella?" she called over her shoulder. "Thank you for your advice. I'll try the stomach route to his heart—it's bound to succeed."

Down the Hatch
(A.D. 145: Becalmed somewhere off northeastern Caledonia)

The war against the Celts had been one of the most bloody campaigns ever waged in military history, illustrating what happens when vast empires attempt to crush the life out of small but determined guerrilla tribes. Death came to the pristine shores of Nova Caledonia as each high tide surrendered its grisly flotilla of Roman corpses, which provided rich pickings for the flocks of hooded crows blowing in on the December gales.

Captain of a warship engaged in an attempt to recapture the port of Lethe, Nostrilamus had been mortally wounded when an iron vat of boiling pitch exploded on deck and embedded long shards of metal in his legs. Now he lay in his stateroom, his skin the color of tallow, his injured limbs a stinking mess of putrefaction. Visitors to his sick bay had to hold vinegar-soaked sponges to their noses in order to withstand the stench, and even the ship's surgeon refused to attend his patient, preferring to take his chances on deck in the mercifully clean-smelling gales that threatened to capsize their craft. Even these winds were unpredictable. Yesterday the warship had wallowed in peaks and troughs larger than herself but today, becalmed south of Aberdonium, the wind had vanished at dawn, turning the surface of the water into jaundiced glass and causing the sails to hang limply from the masts. Surfacing briefly from his delirium, Nostrilamus ordered the oars to be used and, exhausted by the simple effort of giving a command, sank back on his befouled bed of pelts as the great drum began to beat the rhythm for those slaves unfortunate enough to live below decks.

*Heave—thump—heave—thud—*faster—*crack—heave—thump* it went. And just audible below the rhythm of the drum came the sound of groans and sobs as the oarsmen strained and struggled to overcome the dead weight of the ship and, by their efforts alone, force it into motion. In this creaking, claustrophobic underworld lit by smoking oil lamps, the slave-master held dominion. He strode up and down the passage between the rows of manacled oarsmen, flicking a lead-tipped whip over the shoulders of those he judged to be working at less than a killing pace. From time to time a deadly fatigue would overcome a slave, and he would slip from his place to fall under the oars with a scream of terror.

"*Thump—heaaave—thud—heaaave—thump—heaaave—*you guys have no sense of rhythm whatsoever." The slave-master strode up to the drummer and tapped him on the shoulder. "I *said,*" he yelled above the din, "where's your sense of rhythm? Can't you do a bossa nova? A tango, then, how about a tango?" Seeing the look of sullen incomprehension on the drummer's face, the slave-master sighed. "Oh, all *right.* A dashing white sergeant? Strip the willow? Oh, give me *strength*—come on, guys, lighten up a bit. . . ."

Thump—heave—thud—heave—thump—heave.

With an exasperated *tsssst*, Astoroth turned his back on the slaves and their drummer and climbed up through a hatch onto the deck. Squinting in the daylight, he drew in a deep breath of fresh air. Not much longer now, he reminded himself. Find out where Nostrilamus hid the Chronostone, collect same, dispatch him, harvest his soul—and head back to the Hadean Executive with the joyful tidings that the plan was now in place and he was long overdue a promotion from the dreary task of being Second Minister with a special responsibility for pacts and soul harvests. He was heartily sick of shunting back and forth through time, enduring the massive discomforts and perils of centuries without flush toilets and antibiotics. . . . When I'm promoted, he decided, strolling past the galley where the unappetizing smell of the lunchtime broiled dormice wafted through an open hatch, I want to be forever in the twenty-first century, with endless access to wealth, magnetic good looks, and nonstop room service. . . . His thoughts were interrupted when the rank meatiness of the odor of lunch was suddenly overlaid by something infinitely more unpleasant—a foul miasma of decay that intensified with each step that Astoroth took toward the stateroom, where Nostrilamus, the once powerful Malefica of Caledon, was fighting his last battle with the foe none could vanquish.

Astoroth paused, taking a small square of muslin from his pocket and sprinkling it with oil of vetiver from a tiny flask kept on a chain round his neck. Crumpling the scented muslin in his hands, Astoroth sniffed it and then folded the cloth into a triangle and fashioned himself a rudimentary face mask.

Thus attired, he moved forward through the press of legionaries grouped outside the stateroom. As the door was opened for him by a gagging slave, those on deck were engulfed in an odor so vile that all save Astoroth were driven to retch and rush for the ship's rails. Propped up on pillows, Nostrilamus appeared to be mercifully unaffected by his own effluvia. The dying man was utterly engrossed in writing a will, absentmindedly batting blowflies away from his face and apparently unperturbed by the mass of maggots that squirmed in the cyanotic flesh of what had once been his legs. Livid lines of red ran upward from the wounds, arrowing toward his heart—harbingers of his approaching death from blood poisoning. Nostrilamus's breath came in ragged gasps, each inhalation an effort of will, each rattling exhalation ticking off the moments till his heart stilled. Without raising his eyes to the intruder, Nostrilamus spoke, his voice contemptuous, a far cry from his ambitious younger self, a wiser man now than he'd been all those years ago in a tavern in Caledonia.

"You again," he whispered, laying down his stylus and passing the engraved wax tablet to the slave by his bedside.

"Payback time." Astoroth crossed the room to stand over Nostrilamus, the Malefica of Caledon, ignoring the dying man's slave, who bore the waxen will and testament outside, closing the door quietly. "One thing, Caledon," the demon murmured. "There seems to have been a mistake—the hoard of treasure in the forest contained something that was never meant for human possession." He bent over his victim and tried hard not to breathe too deeply. "I want it back," he said, in a voice intended to sound utterly menacing, but which emerged as faintly desperate.

With the hypersensitivity of one standing on the edge of the abyss, Nostrilamus realized that his tormentor was not in control of the situation. Moreover, he clearly recalled the day he had uncovered the treasure. In that strange metal trunk there had been wealth beyond his wildest dreams, but the thing he remembered above all was the gemstone, as big as a plover's egg, that sent light spinning upward from where it lay buried at the bottom of the hoard. The last time Nostrilamus had seen it, before fleeing for his life, the precious stone had been dangling from the ear of the dragon that had devoured all his legionaries. He felt his heart miss a beat and the chill creep up from his ruined legs. The room seemed to dim slightly and he knew that the end was almost upon him.

"Come on, you moron," Astoroth muttered. "Where did you hide it? *Tell* me where it is." With a deplorable lack of bedside manners he grabbed the dying man and shook him. "Tell me *now* or I'll—"

Nostrilamus laughed in his face, his last puffs of breath causing the demon to recoil in disgust. "Or *what*?" he gasped, the rattle in his chest more apparent. "What're you going to do to me that hasn't been done already? Kill me?" A hideous clotted bubbling came from him as he choked out his valediction. "Do your worst, Minister. You can't always get what you waaaaa—"

In his fury at being outwitted by a mere human, Astoroth nearly forgot to harvest the departing soul. Halfway to the door he remembered and spun on his heel just in time to see a small soot-black thing flutter out from the dead man's mouth. In truth, Nostrilamus's soul looked more like an animated prune than the luminous anima of popular mythology, but for all that it was still a soul. With one strike, the demon plucked it from the air, and, pausing briefly to savor the moment, swallowed it whole.

"Right," he growled, flinging open the stateroom door and pushing past the waiting legionaries. "I'm out of here."

"Master?" said a centurion. "What news of Caledon?"

Astoroth had gained the side of the ship and was scrambling onto the handrail, hampered only slightly by his cloak. Far below, the oily water rolled and heaved, the surface broken here and there by drowned ribbons of bladder wrack. Balancing carefully on the rail, Astoroth rose to his feet, his arms outstretched against the sky, cloak billowing dramatically behind him, as he considered how best to break the news to the crew.

"*Vale*, CALEDON!" he roared. "I regret to inform you that your leader has popped his clogs!" Silence greeted this announcement. The legionaries frowned at him in some confusion. With a sigh, Astoroth rephrased his announcement. "The management is sorry to inform you that your boss has bought the farm . . . turned up his toes . . . shuffled off this mortal coil—" Frowns deepened, and a mutinous grumbling rose from the rear of the crew. Sensing that all was not going smoothly, Astoroth changed tack abruptly. "For what it's worth, guys, my advice is to forget trying to take over the world by battering the Caledonians into submission. Trust me, there's an easier way to achieve world domination. Just go home now, bury your dead, invent pizza, and learn how to play football. . . ." Laughing insanely, the demon overbalanced, and, with hardly a splash to mark his passing, was swallowed by the sea.

The Ablutions of Astoroth

Clasping a black leather toiletry kit, Fiamma d'Infer was first up to use the guest bathroom. At this early hour the corridors and passageways of StregaSchloss were deserted, and outside the world was silent. From the nursery the witch could hear the sleepy burblings that heralded Damp's awakening. Hobbling slightly, Fiamma slipped into the bathroom, closed the door behind her, and turned the key in the lock. She dumped her kit on the marble-topped washstand, checked the bath for spiders, and extravagantly turned both bath taps on full. Taking a small flask and cotton balls from her kit, Fiamma began to remove her makeup, which was somewhat the worse for wear after a night's sleep. What she uncovered with each application of cotton ball was a far older face than the one currently on display to her colleagues from the Institute for Advanced Witchcraft. As each layer of paint came off, a network of lines and connected liver spots was revealed, until at last she gazed on her naked face in the mirror.

"Eughhh," she remarked pleasantly, reaching up to unpin her long red hair and hurl it across the room. Wigless, makeupless, she resembled an ancient tortoise. Adding to this impression, she reached inside her mouth, groped around, and removed a set of teeth, which she placed carefully in the sink. Lacking the support of her teeth, Fiamma's lips collapsed inward and her face began to lose definition. Worse was to come: bending down, she seized her left foot and twisted it sideways with enough force to break her ankle. The foot unscrewed with the grim sound of bone grating on bone, and revealed itself to be a prosthetic device designed to conceal the fact that Fiamma's leg ended in a cloven hoof. She attacked her other foot with similar results, then placed both false feet in the sink alongside her teeth. Disrobing entirely, she squatted on the edge of the bath and proceeded to extrude a grotesque forked tail from some internal cache located deep within her stomach.

"What an *effort*," she complained, turning off the taps and flopping into the water. She had no sooner settled comfortably in the bath than a muted ringing came from the direction of her toiletry kit. "Give me a break," she muttered, as she climbed out of the bath and leapt across the floorboards to retrieve her cell phone from its hiding place.

"What?" she whispered. "It's *not* a good time right now." Aware that even in summer one cannot stand around in Argyll in a state of naked wetness without courting frostbite, she climbed back into the bath and continued, "No . . . No, I haven't found it yet, but I know it's here somewhere. Yes, the clocks are all out of kilter. . . . Yes, I *know*, the signs all point to it being close at hand, but it's just not that easy to find a stone the size of an egg in the middle of an estate in Argyll. Have you any idea just how big this house *is*? Or indeed how much *stuff* these guys have been hoarding over the centuries? Do the words 'needle' and 'haystack' sound familiar?"

Fiamma leant back and listened as the voice on the other end droned on. Idly, she gazed up at the ceiling, noting the parlous state of the cornices and the sloppy housekeeping that allowed ropes of cobweb to crisscross the plasterwork.

"I am aware that I'll be reincarnated as a head louse if I mess this one up," Fiamma murmured. "All too aware. However, that simply isn't going to happen. I can guarantee that there's as much chance of that as Hell freezing over. You see, I've stumbled on something while I was digging around here. Mhmmm, it's a real treasure. An infant magus. Mmmm-hmmm, lucky old me. Very small, somewhat undeveloped, unaware of its latent powers . . . Yes, I *know* it's appallingly hazardous to attempt to harvest the soul of one such, but if I can somehow win its confidence—" To mask the sound of her voice, Fiamma reached forward and turned on the hot tap, which, being connected to the dodgy StregaSchloss plumbing, obliged with a cacophony of splutters and clanks before it disgorged a gout of peat-stained water.

"No, no, I'm not breaking up, it's just my mud bath," she continued. "Listen, you have to trust my judgment here. I'll get the Boss's precious Chronostone back, harvest the last male soul as per the agreement, and—as a bonus—I might be able to up the ante by harvesting a baby magus. Now, tell me *that* isn't going to make those red eyes glint? Put a point in your tail? Not to mention put me in line for a major promotion coupled with a meteoric pay raise . . ."

Crouched in a corner of the ceiling cornice, Tarantella was absentmindedly grooming her abdomen while eavesdropping on this one-sided conversation. Clouds of steam billowed up from the bath, causing the tarantula to glare down at the bath's occupant.

"Hey, you down there. Yes, *you*. Do you have to use quite so much water?" She dropped vertiginously floorward on a skein of silk and bounced to a halt a scant hand's-breadth away from Fiamma's nose. "I mean, *look* at me," Tarantella continued, giving a vigorous shudder to dislodge droplets of water vapor beading her furry abdomen. "Anyone with half a brain would know that spiders *hate* water, and here I am *covered* in it, thanks to yauuuuk——" A miniature tidal wave knocked Tarantella out of the air and swept her in a bedraggled tangle into a corner of the bathroom. Half-drowned, unable to pry apart her water-logged legs and escape, the tarantula could only watch helplessly as the witch climbed out of the bathtub and bore down on her, still muttering into her cell phone. Frantically, Tarantella struggled against the film of water coating her limbs, aware that for once she would have been far wiser had she kept quiet. A foot shot out, its horny yellow hoof missing Tarantella's body by a fraction, but brutally amputating one of her legs in an attempt to consign her to oblivion. Tarantella's eyes widened in pain and terror, but she made a supreme effort to survive by dragging her body behind the waste pipe of the toilet. There, drifting in and out of consciousness, she inspected the damage. Extruding a lumpy length of spider silk, she gathered this into a sticky bundle and used it to plug the gaping wound where her leg had been.

Overhead, a loud crash followed by a shriek signaled that Fiamma's hoof had made contact with the unforgiving porcelain of the toilet.

By now, Tarantella was in too much pain to care. The spidersilk dressing was soaked with blood, and she hadn't the strength to replace it.

"Eughhh," moaned Fiamma from somewhere above. "My poor hoof . . . No, not you, you idiot. Look, I'll phone you back. I've got to take care of something at this end. . . . Yes. Catch you later." There was a beep as she switched off the phone. Then her voice dropped in pitch to a growl, causing Tarantella to cast around for a refuge—only to face the chilling realization that there was nowhere to hide.

"Right, spider. Eavesdropping on Executive business is a crime punishable by death. Lipping off to a Minister, ditto. Ignorance is no excuse. In short, you're legless, clueless, and about to be lifeless—"

"And you're hairless, toothless, and, it has to be said, charmless," observed a voice, close to where Tarantella lay.

"Yeah," agreed another voice. "Bog off, baldy. Pick on something your own size."

Just before a pink mist settled over Tarantella's vision and bore her off to oblivion, she recognized the voices of StregaSchloss's free-range rodents, the Illiterat Multitudina and her educated daughter, Terminus. Before Fiamma could make good her threat to kill Tarantella, the rats hoisted the unconscious tarantula onto a stretcher improvised from a sheet of toilet paper and carried her away out of danger through a gap in the baseboard.

Thwarted, Fiamma's face contorted into something resembling a malignant walnut. Behind her, the bathroom mirror cracked from side to side, sending a lethal shower of glass cascading onto the floor. In the bath, water bubbled and hissed, turning a bilious yellow and emitting a feral stench. Underfoot, the floorboards rippled and bowed as if the wood had turned into a liquid that allowed a glimpse of something swimming below its surface. Then, as suddenly as it had appeared, Fiamma's rage vanished. The floor stilled its tidal motion, the bathwater returned to post-ablution grunginess, the mirror shards re-formed into an unbroken looking glass, and Fiamma looked within and found her reflection pleasing. Reabsorbing her tail, and replacing her makeup, hair, teeth, and feet, she strained to hear the sound that had caused her flash of temper to evaporate. The sound came again and she smiled. There it was: Damp in the distant nursery, her infant voice raised in song, greeting the day, with each note ringing pure and true.

"Such *untapped* potential," Fiamma confided to her reflection. "Such *latent* power." The demon licked its lips and gazed into the mirror, its foul mind looking out at the world through eyes that had changed shape and color countless times as Astoroth reincarnated himself for the express purpose of harvesting souls down through the centuries. The Borgia Inheritance was, thankfully, his final task as Second Minister for the Hadean Executive. Second Minister? The demon spat on the floor. Frankly, the Boss's dominion over Hades was way past its sell-by date. With the Chronostone plus the power of the baby magus's soul, well . . .

"Just watchhh me now," Fiamma hissed, snatching up her toiletry kit and striding out of the bathroom, leaving the faintest whiff of sulfur in her wake.

The Illegitimate Dragon

It had long been Damp's habit to greet each new day with a song to her pajamas. The infant had only recently discovered that she could undo the snaps on her nightwear with one sharp tug, and since then it had been her pleasure to strip herself of both pj's and diaper and hurl these over the bars of her crib. This was invariably accompanied by an enthusiastic rendition of "There Was a Princess Long Ago," punctuated by gales of infant mirth as each layer of clothing sailed out of Damp's crib and onto the nursery floor.

Damp had just reached the verse where she was describing the princess's accommodation:

and she lived in a big high towel,
big high towel,
big high—

THUD . . . and Mrs. McLachlan woke to the sound of

Damp's diaper landing wetly on the floor. This morning there was also a heavy slapping from the other side of the nursery door, accompanied by a determined scratching, as if something were attempting to claw its way in.

"NESTOR!" roared the nanny. "Stop that at *once*. You know you're not allowed up here. . . ."

Silence from behind the nursery door. Mrs. McLachlan groaned as she hoisted herself out of bed. This was becoming all too wearisome, she decided, padding across the floorboards to open the door and ascertain whether the baby dragon had obeyed her dictates. He hadn't, but pity moved Mrs. McLachlan to step aside and allow the little beast access to the warmth of the nursery. Nestor crept across the floor and curled up in a woebegone ball at the foot of Damp's crib, with his head pillowed on her discarded pajamas.

"This is *ridiculous*," muttered the nanny, pulling a purple woollen dressing gown around herself and carrying Damp off to the bathroom. Moments later, with Damp washed and dressed, Mrs. McLachlan shepherded both infants downstairs for breakfast.

The kitchen table bore witness to the hasty satisfaction of several appetites: cereal bowls lay abandoned, an almost empty milk bottle sat unhygienically on the warming plate of the range, an empty glass coffeepot floated in the scum of last night's dirty dishwater, and the butter was pockmarked with specks of charred toast. The door to the kitchen garden was ajar, and from outside Mrs. McLachlan could hear the distant groans and shrieks that indicated the morning yoga class was in session. As she washed cereal bowls, the nanny noted with disgust that Ffup was outside, practicing yoga with no thought for her infant's welfare.

"Selfish beast," she muttered, crashing crockery onto the draining board with uncharacteristic force. Ever since Nestor had hatched at StregaSchloss last Hogmanay, Mrs. McLachlan had hoped that Ffup would knuckle down to the responsibilities of single parenthood and attempt to raise her baby son in a manner befitting a dragon. Regrettably, this had not been the case. . . . While there was no doubt that Ffup adored her child, it was also true that she worshiped herself in equal measure; the teenage dragon spent many more hours preening her wings, painting her talons, improving her waistline, and gazing in the mirror than she spent nurturing Nestor. Moreover, Mrs. McLachlan thought, as she stirred a pot of porridge at the range, it was perfectly obvious that Nestor was never going to grow up to be a pedigree dragon. The Strega-Borgias appeared to be united in a conspiracy of silence on the subject of who, exactly, Nestor's absent father might have been, but one look at the baby—with his redundant wings (too small), deep blue scales (should *really* have been muddy green), occasional lack of fire-breathing ability (even as an infant, he should have been lighting candles with one hiccup), and—most significantly of all—his vast, overgrown tail that the family all affected to ignore . . . well, *really*! Mrs. McLachlan dropped a large pinch of salt in the porridge pot and snorted loudly.

As she decanted the steaming oats into three bowls and sat down to have breakfast with Damp and Nestor, she was suddenly struck by a distant memory from countless decades ago, long before she became nanny to the Strega-Borgias. . . .

... a vast, frozen loch, across which she fled with a group of women, all escaping some nameless horror. The turning year brought the coldest winter in living memory. The ice that formed a skin over every loch in Scotland had been measured in finger-widths at Hallows Eve—hand-spans by midwinter—and by Candlemas, no spade or pick could penetrate the iron-hard cover on every body of water from Roxburgh to Sutherland. Without fish to supplement their meager winter diet, whole communities of loch-dwellers found themselves facing starvation. Far from celebrating Candlemas, the hitherto God-fearing congregations plundered their churches and ate the candles. Rumors abounded of desecrated graves, gutted crypts, and other horrors too hideous to mention. In the perceived absence of divine mercy, the lochside people turned to old religions and darker practices.

The fugitive women had sought shelter in a tiny hamlet on the shores of a frozen loch. Huts and houses huddled next to a sheet of ice beneath which, it was rumored, swam enough fish to feed the entire population of Scotland for centuries to come. In gratitude for the hospitality shown to her by the people of the hamlet, Flora McLachlan had resolved to rescue them from starvation. At first light she had slipped away from the press of sleeping bodies huddled round the ashy fire and walked out onto the ice. . . .

Near the shore the wind had scoured rutted circles in the ice, but farther out all was still, save her breath rising in misty clouds above her head. Faced with the impossibility of breaking the ice herself, she resolved to awaken the Sleeper, even though she would, in all probability, perish in the attempt. But how to make the creature rise from *a sleep of several centuries past? Should she weave a spell of warmer waters, fish-full salty southern seas, to melt the frozen skies of the Sleeper's underwater world? Murmur a lullaby of rocking rivers to bear the lonely beast in its tidal ebb and flow? Tempt him awake with tales of the mackerel mountain and the herring hill that rims the salmon stream? Cruel to wake this creature, who slept to heal a broken heart, who created the loch from tears, and who closed his eyes believing that this world held no love for him—the Sleeper, whose kin had long crumbled to dust. Flora knew, even as she whispered the words that would awaken him, that with his dawning consciousness would come the knowledge of all that he had lost and all the loneliness to come. . . . She almost faltered in her resolve, but beneath her feet, from fathoms below, came a faint cry like a rabbit in a snare. Slipping on the ice, Flora began to run, her frozen feet betraying her as she skidded and stumbled toward the far-off shore. Behind her, the cry rose to a desolate keening that hurt the ears of all who heard. The sound rose in pitch as, with a deafening crack, dark lines zigzagged across the ice. Still the sound of some creature in mortal agony grew and swelled to fill the air. The ice suddenly fractured along the cracks and Flora leapt from floe to floe, trying to find her way back to solid ground.*

Only once did she turn back to look, to catch a glimpse of that lonely, awful shape—mouth agape, as it howled its outrage at a world that had broken its centuries of mindless, forgetful slumber for no better reason than the survival of a handful of loch-dwellers with a desperate need for fish.

A handful of loch-dwellers, thought Mrs. McLachlan as she raised a spoonful of porridge to her mouth, whose idea of grateful thanks to their savior was to attempt to burn her at the stake for witchcraft. . . .

"HOT, HOT BURRRRNY!" wailed Damp, hurling her porridge spoon across the breakfast table. Beside her, Nestor's mouth dropped open in a howl of outrage at the singular *lack* of hot, hot burrrny in his bowl. Abruptly hauled back to the present, Mrs. McLachlan found herself giving silent thanks for the good fortune that had brought her here to StregaSchloss, where being accused of practicing witchcraft was a sincere compliment. . . .

Time Out

On her way downstairs for breakfast, Pandora paused outside her parents' bedroom, crossing her fingers in the hope that they had settled their differences over the vexed question of the houseguests, and were even now sitting up in bed, planning the day ahead and admiring the view through their bedroom window over coffee and croissants. A wail and a crash from behind their door told a different story. Signor Strega-Borgia, unpredictable of temperament and with a fondness for yelling matched only by a habit of hurling china around to underline his point, was in full operatic flow. Approaching footsteps and an increase in volume signaled to Pandora that he was about to storm through the door in front of her, and if she didn't want to be accused of eavesdropping, she'd better make herself scarce.

She fled down the corridor, leaping over several pairs of pointy lace-up boots that had been placed outside bedroom doors by a few of the more demanding houseguests on the mistaken assumption that Latch would attend to their polishing. Reaching the nursery, Pandora slipped behind its open door and hid, chewing her fingernails as she heard her father stamp past, muttering to himself in unintelligible Italian. Pandora slumped on the floor beside Mrs. McLachlan's bed and laid her head wearily on the quilt. Downstairs the front door slammed shut and footsteps crunched across the rose-quartz drive. Minutes later, Pandora heard the car starting up and correctly deduced that Signor Strega-Borgia was off to inflict his bad mood on the nearby village of Auchenlochtermuchty. The sound of running water and clanking plumbing meant that Signora Strega-Borgia had taken refuge in the shower. Not for the first time, Pandora wished her parents would get a grip on themselves and stop fighting. Their battles were always about such stupid things, and this latest skirmish over the appearance of rodent droppings in the coffee was just so childish and immature that Pandora would have felt embarrassed for them had it not been for her own current war with her sibling. . . . She debated whether to go and wake Titus and put Tarantella's plan into action by bringing him breakfast in bed. Brilliant plan, Pan, she congratulated herself, checking the bedside clock to make sure that it wasn't too early to rouse the slug-a-bed. The digital display read 20:02, which by Pandora's calculations was about twelve hours fast, since she had a rough idea of the time from the light filtering in from outside, the amount of birdsong audible from the garden, and the sound of activity coming from downst—

The alarm clock vanished. Pandora blinked, and there it was, back again, still reading 20:02. She hardly had time to draw a breath before it vanished again.

"What?" she gasped as it reappeared, its palindromic numerals still visible on its face. Pandora sat up and reached out to touch it as it disappeared once more, reappearing one heartbeat later, reassuringly solid under her fingertips. However, the time remained unchanged and Pandora watched and waited to see what would happen when the numerals advanced to 20:03. The clock blinked in and out of existence for several minutes, but according to its own mysterious internal reckoning, time stood still.

Wondering if it was broken, Pandora picked it up and turned it over in her hands. For such a small artifact it was ridiculously heavy, and being made of metal, it felt cool to the touch. On the rear of the clock were two small knobs: one was pretty obviously the ON/OFF switch. But the function of the other knob was less clear, since the only clues to what it did were two opposing arrows and letters embossed into the metal thus:

$$P < > F$$

Wondering what language was being used, Pandora assumed that this must be the knob to turn in order to reset the display on the clock face. At first the knob resisted any attempt to turn it, until Pandora pulled it toward her, whereupon with a small click it rotated easily under her fingers as the display ran backward. Reaching 08:02, Pandora clicked the knob back into place and immediately wished she hadn't bothered.

The floor underneath her vanished and the walls of StregaSchloss fell away. Still reflexively clutching the clock,

Pandora found herself spinning sickeningly in midair. No sooner had she registered this fact than she crash-landed on something hard and extremely unfriendly to human flesh.

"AOWWWW!" she wailed, trying to work out which bit of her hurt most. Attempting not to move too much, she looked around and found that she was inside what appeared to be a gigantic pit made from twigs and branches. Overhead she could see daylight through a filigree of leaves, but all around and underneath her were mud, dirt, and woven twigs. It was not unlike being at the bottom of a vast hedge. Pandora stood up carefully, tucked the clock in the back pocket of her jeans, and looked around properly. The floor at her feet was littered with bones—and when she caught sight of the hedge-pit's one inhabitant, an egg the size of a rugby ball, she realized that not only was she in all probability unwelcome, but she was also trespassing.

It's a *nest*, she thought, gazing in horror at the egg, and whatever laid *that* isn't going to be too thrilled to find me here when it gets home. The nest was far too well constructed to allow her to force an escape through its walls or floor, so Pandora began to climb up and out, hanging on to the twigs and branches and wedging her feet into the mud and dirt that had been used as a primitive form of insulation. Bark and dirt rained down on her head as she scrabbled for handholds, and jamming her feet into the walls caused a continual fall of debris to patter down onto the floor of the nest and its sole occupant. After what felt like a lifetime, Pandora pulled herself over the rim of the nest and, dreading what she was about to see, peered over the edge.

"Whaaaat?" she groaned, stunned by the bizarre familiarity of the view below her. There was Lochnagargoyle up ahead, and there behind her were the peaks of Bengormless. "But . . . but—" squeaked Pandora, clinging to the dusty rim of the nest—but what on earth was she doing six hundred feet above ground, perched in what appeared to be an ancient Scots pine—and where had StregaSchloss gone?

Steeling herself to look down, she saw a thin spiral of smoke coiling up from the floor of what appeared to be virgin forest. Gone too were the gardens, the meadow, the icehouse, and the road to Auchenlochtermuchty. Below lay an almost unbroken canopy of leafy green, dotted here and there with little patches of dun-colored earth. It was as if StregaSchloss had never existed. Pandora trembled as she clung to the nest, her thoughts in disarray, but with a vague fear beginning to take shape in a corner of her mind. This isn't exactly a nest, she thought, watching the smoke drift up from below; the correct name for what I'm currently gate-crashing is a "roost." A dragon's roost, she reminded herself, trying not to scream. She peered again at the source of the smoke, leaning out over the edge in order to obtain a better view down through the treetops. On the forest floor were two figures; the smaller of the two reassuringly human, the other, with its telltale wings and spiny tail, unmistakably a dragon. Despite the Strega-Borgias' long and happy association with dragon-kind, the presence of gnawed bones on the floor of the roost tended to indicate that this particular dragon might not regard eating humans as a breach of etiquette.

This is ridiculous, Pandora thought. It's just not possible to be in the nursery one moment and in the blink of an eye to find myself . . . She closed her eyes and opened them again. Wide. Blinked twice and then, reaching carefully behind her, pulled Mrs. McLachlan's alarm clock out of her back pocket. There it is, she told herself, and . . . there it isn't. The time was still 08:02, but in one of those flashes of understanding when whole new synaptic pathways open up and one's brain undergoes a crash and rapid reboot, Pandora understood. It's not two minutes past eight, you numpty, she thought, it's eight hundred and two, as in the *year*, not the *time*, and to get back home, all you have to do is reset the numbers. . . . A shadow fell over her and, looking up, Pandora realized that time was about to run out. She pulled out the knob on the back of the clock and began frantically turning it clockwise. A blast of hot air singed her eyelashes as she looked up into the eyes of the builder of the roost and, in all probability, the mother of the egg.

"NOT *ANOTHER* YIN!" it roared, affording Pandora a memorable view of rows of lethal yellow teeth, behind which waved a set of fireproof tonsils. "Youse wee pests must've been breeding like *bunnies*," it observed, adding, "I thought I'd got rid of youse dwarves years ago." The dragon shut its mouth with a clash and glared down at Pandora, its massive wings slowly folding behind its back with a leathery creak. Hissing clouds of steam came from its nostrils as it reached up with one taloned leg to claw at something behind its head—the vast diamond stud in its ear catching the sun and sending a cascade of reflections dancing around the roost.

"Must be time for a snack," it remarked, patting its distended belly. "Me, I like mah toast well done, can't abide it *raw*," and reaching out to grab Pandora, it demonstrated the ease with which it intended to grill her.

Without a moment's hesitation, Pandora hammered the knob home. In a blaze of fire she spun through the air until, with a jarring crash, she landed on cold, unforgiving stone. Opening her eyes, the first thing she saw was the alarm clock, which read 16:50. . . . Groaning, she stood up and realized where she was. This is *StregaSchloss*, she thought. This is my home hundreds of years before I was born. For some unaccountable reason this realization made her feel achingly lonely. I miss my *family*, she thought, stifling a moan—and trying not to make a sound in case something worse than dragons awaited her. It's like they're *dead*, she thought, or like *I* am. Officially, I don't exist. Awash with self-pity, she gazed around. It was indeed StregaSchloss, but a very different StregaSchloss to the one so familiar to her that she could have sleepwalked round it. The first thing she noticed was the lack of light. The reason for this soon became apparent: the windows had shrunk down to narrow little slits glazed with panes of glass of such bottle-bottom thickness as to allow little light to pass through. In the fireplace a half-charred tree trunk had replaced the more familiar oil-filled radiator that routinely warmed the nursery, and on the floor in front of the fireplace an all-too-real bearskin had been substituted for the rag rug that two generations of Strega-Borgias had admired while having their diapers changed.

The walls were unpainted rough-hewn stone, and the door to the corridor was a substantial chunk of iron-studded raw timber, still oozing sap. The sound of loud voices and heavy footsteps came from nearby, causing Pandora to cast around for somewhere to hide. Unhelpfully, the room was almost empty, save for a large table upon which sat a globe—remarkable only for its wildly inaccurate depiction of all major landmasses—several rolls of paper tied with ribbon and sealed with wax, and a small metal box.

The door rattled as someone on the other side thrust a key into the lock. Snatching up the alarm clock, Pandora positioned herself behind the door and, squinting in the gloom, began to reset the time. The door swung open and the voices were now distinct. Three men, Pandora guessed, praying that they wouldn't shut the door and discover her cowering behind it, armed with nothing more than a clock. To her relief, she might as well have been invisible for all the attention they paid her. The focus of their intentions was the metal box on the table.

"The key, Malvolio," one of the men said, obscuring Pandora's view of the table.

"I have it here," said another voice, presumably Malvolio's. "Do you take me for a simpleton?"

"Use it then, the barbarians are upon us," said a third voice, gruff and urgent in its delivery. There came a pause, and Pandora bent her head to peer at the numerals on the clock, looking up as the first man spoke, his voice filled with wonder.

"It is as foretold in the prophecy . . . the Pericola d'Illuminem . . ." His voice trailed off, replaced by Malvolio's, who murmured, "Some call it the Dragon's Bane, others from across the water tell it as Man's Desire—"

"Yes, yes, a thousand pretty names," interrupted the gruff voice, obviously unimpressed by his companions' knowledge. "How came you by this—this *jewel*, Malvolio?"

"My grandmother traded it with the dragon-kind."

Sneaking a glimpse from behind the door, Pandora saw the three men silhouetted round a source of light far stronger than the feeble rays that shone through the window. She noted irreverently that the men, dressed for battle, were thus wearing enough metal to qualify them for inclusion in a dragon's larder under "canned goods."

"*Traded* it?" laughed the gruff voice, scorn dripping from every syllable. "Pray tell, what could that toothless hag possibly possess to trade for such a treasure?"

"In truth, certainly not her woman's charms," muttered the other man, spitting on the floor by way of emphasis.

"My grandmother," said Malvolio, with commendable self-restraint, "is a sorceress, and as such has the healing powers. The dragon-guardian of the—the *jewel*, as you call it, had a baby to fend for, a mate too stricken with melancholy to be able to feed his roost, and, most importantly, a broken wing."

"Hence the trade?" said the gruff voice.

"Indeed. My grandmother healed the dragon's wing with her sorcery, and in return was given the treasure. Which, in her wisdom, she has passed on to me for safekeeping during this troublesome time. . . ."

Pandora was riveted by this exchange. Malvolio di S'Enchantedino Borgia was one of her earliest ancestors, and the sorceress he referred to could only have been Strega-Nonna—future denizen of the large freezer chest at StregaSchloss, in which she would lie, cryogenically frozen, awaiting advances in medical science. . . .

There came a repeated booming crash from outside, a noise

that resounded through the stone walls and caused the three men to clutch their swords in alarm.

"The siege is over! Our defenses are breached!" yelled the gruff voice. "We must flee for our lives!"

"Hold fast," Malvolio commanded. "We dare not risk being found in possession of the stone—"

"But, but—if it were to fall into the wrong hands . . ."

"Perish the thought. We must leave it hidden within these walls and pray that we are spared and might one day return to retrieve it."

"But where, Malvolio? Where can you hope to hide a gem more radiant than the sun itself?"

"In the company of others such as itself," Malvolio stated obliquely. "In the chandelier above the great hall—come, follow me now." He spun round to face the door, his face turning ashen as he saw Pandora gazing at him in wide-eyed horror.

"By all that is holy!" shrieked Malvolio, crossing himself rapidly. "Begone, shade!"

Pandora didn't hesitate. Bringing her thumb down hard on the knob, she vanished.

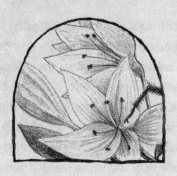

A Death in the Family

The faraway chink of rattling china and the growing suspicion that he was not alone roused Titus from the worst night's sleep he'd ever endured. Tossed from one nightmare to another, he had spent the hours before dawn clutching his pillow, wide-awake and determined to remain so, lest the dreams return to fill his sleep with their hideous blend of visceral horror and homely domestic detail. Moreover, he was denied the mindless comfort of computer games, ever since his laptop had formed a dark alliance with something so vile that just to think about it brought Titus out in a cold sweat. As the sun had begun its slow ascent over Lochnagargoyle, he had fallen into a deep and mercifully dreamless sleep that now, as he unglued his face from the pillow, made him too slow-witted and thickheaded to appreciate the generosity of the gift Pandora was offering him. He struggled to a sitting position, rubbing sleep from his eyes, and yawned widely.

"'Morning, Titus." Pandora placed a laden breakfast tray on top of a pile of computer manuals on the bedside table and crossed to the window to fling open the curtains.

"Urrrrrgh. It's too *bright*," Titus moaned, feeling his pupils contract painfully. Pandora ignored this, returning to the bedside to pour a cup of tea and pass it to her brother. "I've made you twelve slices of toast, there's a pile of scrambled eggs in that dish, along with eight slices of dry-cured bacon, two roasted tomatoes, four hot croissants, two of Mrs. McLachlan's raspberry muffins, warmed, and some freshly squeezed orange jui—"

"Whoaaa," Titus interrupted. "What's going on? Why are you doing this? You *never* bring me breakfast in bed. Yesterday you treated me like I was something you'd stepped in and now—" He waved his hand over the banquet steaming seductively by his bed.

"Eat up, Titus, before it gets cold," Pandora replied mildly.

"Have you poisoned it? That's why you're so keen, huh? You're hoping to stand there, cackling over my twitching body, and then rush off to inform my lawyers that due to my unforeseen demise, you're next in line to inherit Grandfather's millions . . ." Titus prodded a perfectly grilled piece of bacon with his fork and sighed. He couldn't keep this up. The breakfast smelled like heaven, sunshine poured into his bedroom, and Pandora looked as if she was about to burst with excitement.

"Paxshhhh?" he mumbled through a mouthful of croissant, spraying his quilt with crumbs.

"That's why I'm here," Pandora said. "I wanted to say sorry for being so . . . unhelpful the other day."

"Mmmfle," said Titus indistinctly. "But I was being pretty

foul too. Gloating and rubbing it in . . . after I'd stopped trying to tell you about the weird e-mails."

Pandora reached out for a slice of toast. Suddenly she was *starving*. "If I promise to listen properly this time, would you tell me again and in return I'll tell *you* what I've found in Mrs. McLachlan's bedroom?"

Titus laid down his fork with a shudder. Since reading the haunted e-mails he had endeavored to put as much distance between them and himself as possible. Attempting to pull down a psychic shutter and forget what he'd seen was proving to be impossible, and last night's nightmares had more than demonstrated the futility of trying to resist. To his embarrassment he realized he'd picked up his fork again and was gripping it like a weapon. Using it to spear a tomato and pop it whole into his mouth, Titus found himself dribbling juice and seeds down his chin as he began explaining what he thought had happened in the map room.

Ten minutes later they stood shivering in front of Titus's laptop. The map room, untouched since Titus had fled from it the day before, looked so ordinary that for a moment he wondered if he'd dreamt the whole thing. It was cold, but then the subterranean map room was always cold, which was why the family rarely ventured into it, preferring the relative comforts of the library or kitchen or any of the other ninety-four rooms on offer inside StregaSchloss. Here the walls were lined with maps that dated back to times when such charts were drawn and colored by draftsmen whose apparent disdain for measurements, geography, and general accuracy brought a whole new meaning to the phrase "artistic license." The older maps sought to disguise their inaccuracies with embellishments designed to draw the eye away from their lack of cartographic correctness. Strange sea serpents boiled out of oceans, lochs bore intricate legends of "here beye monsteres," and round exquisitely limned mountain peaks, dragons flew in tight formations. The most beautiful of these maps hung over the empty fireplace in a massive gilt frame. As family history had it, this had been drawn on vellum by an ancestor whose passionate love of hot-air ballooning explained the relative accuracy of his drafts-manship.

While Titus attempted to resuscitate his ailing laptop, Pandora peered at the perfect postage-stamp-sized rendering of StregaSchloss and surroundings, noting the presence of a formal garden leading down to what must have been Lochnagargoyle. Unable to make out the tiny words written below those indicating the Kyle of Mhoire Ochone, she turned round just in time to see the laptop spring back to life.

Titus flinched and turned in his seat to clutch at her arm. "It's still *there*," he said, the pitch of his voice betraying the suffocating terror that had overtaken him as the computer rebooted.

"What does that wee envelopy thing mean?" asked Pandora, adding, "The one that's flashing on and off?"

"It—it—it's telling me there's more," groaned Titus. "*More* mail. Please, Pan, let's go. Leave it. This was a really bad idea. . . ." But even as he spoke his fingers were automatically straying to the mouse pad, and before he could stop himself he'd moved the cursor on top of the envelope icon and pressed

ENTER.

YOU HAVE MAIL

the dialogue box informed him, this information immediately replaced by another dialogue box stating that the laptop was helpfully downloading not only the incoming mail but also an application that would assist in deciphering it.

"I feel sick," whimpered Titus, closing his eyes and trying to stand up.

"Oh look—isn't that clever, Titus, what's it doing now?" Immune to her brother's feelings of dread, Pandora was glued to the image appearing on the screen. "It's a film clip," she said, nudging Titus with her elbow. "Move over, I can't see properly."

Onscreen a title bar scrolled past with the words "Forthcoming Attractions" in a Gothic font.

"Wha—?" Titus's mouth fell open as the screen filled with an image at once vaguely familiar but also utterly alien. "The Auchenlochtermuchty cemetery," he said, his voice flat and colorless. "Like my dream from last night—"

The title bar vanished, and the sound of tires on gravel filled the map room. Transfixed, Titus watched as onscreen . . .

. . . a line of black cars drew up at the gates to the Auchenlochtermuchty cemetery and halted, engines idling, while the driver of the first vehicle negotiated with the gatekeeper. Removing his woolly hat, presumably out of respect for the dead, the old man looked up at the darkening sky.

"It's gaunny chuck it doon," he observed, throwing his

weight against the rusty iron gates, pushing them open with agonizing slowness to the accompaniment of a threnody of squealing metal. This done, he latched them open against stone pillars and stood back, head bowed, allowing the funeral cortege access to the graves.

"Awfy sad, yon," he muttered to his shoes. "Poor wee bairns, left withoot a faither . . ."

"Gosh, Titus," Pandora breathed. "Aren't computers just *amazing*?"

The first car rolled past, bearing its cargo of two funeral directors and their boxed client. In its wake, one of the many wreaths of white lilies piled on top of the coffin bounced out of the hearse and onto the road. The gate-keeper sneezed and casually wiped his nose on his sleeve as the second car edged through the gates.

Onscreen, the image cut to the interior of this vehicle.

"Disgusting old man," muttered a woman sitting in the rear. "Here, give him this, would you?" She produced a tissue from a box on her lap and passed it to the driver. Sitting back in her seat, she glared out of the tinted glass windows at the rows of tombstones that stretched ahead of her up the hill, those farthest away merging with the gloom of a midwinter afternoon sky. Sitting beside her, a younger woman gave a stifled sob and began to weep in earnest.

"Oh, for heaven's sake, Damp, pull yourself together."

"DAMP?" shrieked Pandora, pulling back from the laptop as if it had sprouted fangs. "Then . . . then that old bag must be m-m-meeee." Stuffing a fist into her mouth, she glared at the screen and muttered, "I can't believe this is really happening, I mean this *is* just a film, isn't it?" In the absence of a reply from Titus, she fell silent and watched in stunned horror as the film clip rolled on.

Pandora pulled a handful of tissues from her box and thrust them at her sister. "You'll set us all off, and then the whole day will just turn into one long blub-fest. . . ."

The sobs redoubled as Damp pressed a soggy wedge of tissue to her face and gave way to grief.

"Oh, come on," Pandora insisted. "We have to be strong for Mum. How d'you think she feels? Or Dad?"

The sobs turned into gasps interspersed with little howls. Pandora tapped the driver's shoulder.

"Pull over here for a moment, would you?" she said. "My sister needs a minute or two to compose herself."

Obediently, the driver parked beside a pitted marble angel whose outstretched hand pointed skyward, either indicating the direction of heaven, or pointing out the fact that it was probably about to start raining.

Pandora reached across the rear seat and took her sister in her arms. "Hush, now," she whispered. "Hush, Damp. No more tears. Save them for later. . . ." Pandora lifted Damp's chin and gazed into her sister's red-rimmed eyes. Gently she tucked a stray wisp of hair behind Damp's ear and smiled bravely. "You're a mess, girl," she said, bending down to look in her handbag. "Let's see if we can do a quick repair-job before Mum sees you."

Pandora found a small lipstick and passed it over to Damp along with a tiny mirror. Damp sniffed deeply, rubbed her eyes with a gloved hand, and peered miserably at her reflection.

"I look like death warmed over," she remarked, somewhat tactlessly. "Honestly, Pan, I really think that soon—I mean, after all this is over"—she waved a hand in the general direction of the serried ranks of tombstones and then uncapped the lipstick—"once the estate is settled and we find out how much we're going to inherit, I'm definitely going to see that dear wee man in Harley Street about a face-lift—"

"The plastic surgeon?" Pandora's voice rose to a horrified squeak. "WHAAAAT? But you're, you're only—"

"Thirty-one," said Damp, snapping the cap on the lipstick and handing it back to her astonished sister. "Yup. Time flies. Should have had it done when I was twenty-seven, but, hey—it's pointless thinking about the past."

"But, Damp—" Pandora gasped. "Plastic surgery—that's for babes, bimbos, fluff-brains. I mean, speaking personally, the very thought of going under the knife just to knock a few years off my age fills me with disgust."

"Precisely," snarled Damp, uncrossing her long, silk-clad legs and unfolding herself from her seat to open the door. "And that's why you look every one of your forty years, sister dear."

"Oh ughhh. URRK EURCHHHHH!" wailed Pandora. "*Forty?* FORTY? I can't cope with much more of this. . . ."

Damp flung open the door and climbed out on the gravel path, turning back to watch as Pandora staggered inelegantly toward her.

"Don't look at me like that," said Damp. "I'm not something nasty that you just found growing mold at the back of the fridge. I'm merely telling you the truth. You look sad, Pandora. Sad and old and wrinkly."

"OF COURSE I LOOK SAD!" yelled Pandora. "I'm about to bury my brother, for heaven's sake. How d'you think I should look? RADIANT?"

A fat tear plopped onto her tweed coat and was instantly absorbed in the fabric.

"Titus?" Pandora's voice shook. "Can we stop now? I think I've seen enough."

Beside her Titus looked as if he'd been turned to stone. White marble, to be precise. Onscreen a familiar figure appeared and the hideous film clip continued.

Mrs. Flora McLachlan emerged from a third car and hobbled across the gravel to where the sisters stood glaring at each other through teary eyes.

"I'm ashamed of the pair of you," their old nanny hissed. "Bickering and squabbling like a pair of vixens—today, of all days."

Damp blushed and mumbled an apology, offering her weeping sibling a soggy tissue.

"Mummy!" A miniature version of Pandora lunged from the rear of the third car and hurled herself at her parent.

"Now, dear." Mrs. McLachlan patted Pandora's shoulder. "Wipe your eyes and look after your wee girls while I help your mother." A second little girl emerged from the car, tripped over a marble flower urn, and fell onto a crumbling gravestone with a wail of dismay.

"Oh lord—" Pandora spun round, alerted by the loud howls coming from her daughter. "Rose, poppet, Mummy's coming. . . ."

Little moans escaped from Pandora's lips as she absorbed this unwanted snippet of information with glassy-eyed horror. Twins, she thought, TWINS? But I *never* want to have children, I've *always* said that. . . .

"Clumsy, isn't she?" confided the first little girl, slipping her hand into Damp's gloved one and gazing adoringly at her aunt. Behind them, Pandora picked up the sobbing Rose and bore her off in Mrs. McLachlan's wake.

"Where is Uncle Titus?" continued the child, tugging Damp's hand to gain her attention. "Can we see him? Is he in that box? Is he sleeping? Mummy says he's going to heaven, but how will he find the way? Mummy used to say he was awful at reading maps—"

"It's a Borgia failing," sighed Damp. "Come on, Lily, let's go and find Grandma, shall we?"

Minutes later, a small group of mourners stood at the ornate metal gate to the family crypt, shivering as they watched the pallbearers coming toward them with a coffin on their shoulders. Behind them came Signor and Signora Strega-Borgia, followed by Damp and Pandora. Around the crypt lay banks of lilies, waiting for the time when all the living had gone, leaving the dead to wither along with their flowers. Pandora stumbled and retraced her steps to where one of her shoes lay embedded, its heel stuck in a grassy hummock.

Mrs. McLachlan's eyes began to water uncontrollably as she saw the three little figures of Titus's bereaved children running across the graveyard in the wake of their mother, Mercedes Strega-Borgia. Titus's glamorous widow was currently loping across the grass toward the crypt, trailing furs and pearls and arriving in a cloud composed of equal parts aggression and hysteria.

The widow gathered her sons about herself and glared at the assembled mourners. Mercedes's eyes were suspiciously dry. Moreover, her immediate concerns appeared to be more materialistic than spiritual, as the occasion demanded. To wit:

"—and if you vultures think you're going to see one penny of my husband's estate, you can think again." Mercedes waved her bejeweled hands for emphasis.

"Oh, per-lease," hissed Damp. "Spare us. I hardly think that now is the time to be discussing Titus's money."

Signor and Signora Strega-Borgia made no comment. Shrouded in deepest black, their pale faces bore witness to the fact that they were living through every parent's worst nightmare, coming here to this depressing Scottish graveyard to bury their only son. Swathed in black organza,

Signora Strega-Borgia clutched her husband's arm for support. Lily and Rose, dimly sensing that this was not a Happy Day, began to whine.

A gray drizzle began to fall at the same moment as a tiny member of the family emerged from the crypt. Tarantella, tarantula extraordinaire, paused on the stone step, produced a microscopically small lipstick from some hidden part of her anatomy, and raked the family with a withering stare.

"Oh, come on," she said. "Cheer up. It's not the end of the world. . . ." She paused, applied a smear of lipstick to her mouth, and waved a few legs in the direction of the leaden sky. "Sure, it's raining, and that is pretty hideous, but as for this"— she scampered out of the crypt, scaled the leg of one of the pallbearers, and leapt onto the lid of Titus's coffin—"it's not as if he's going to be all alone. There's five hundred or so of my children down there in the crypt, just waiting for him, and they'll make sure he's comfy. . . ." With a hairy leg, Tarantella pointed back into the crypt, where, dangling from cobwebs, the whole interior appeared to be alive with grinning spiders.

"But, but—" Pandora gasped, "Titus hated. . . ."

The image on the screen froze, the millions of spiders halted in mid-dangle, Pandora's face caught for all time with her mouth open, the soundtrack playing, as if stuck in a rut, *"hated, hated, hated, hated . . ."* the incessant repetition removing all meaning from the word until, as Titus and Pandora simultaneously stood up to leave the map room, to their ears it sounded more like *"fated, fated, fated, fated . . ."*

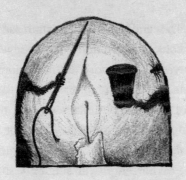

Under the Weather

Signora Strega-Borgia turned off the shower and wrapped herself in a towel. Wiping steam off the bathroom mirror, she gazed at her reflection with a critical eye, then, picking up the hairbrush, began the ritual of readying herself to face the morning. Halfway through getting dressed, she was hit by a wave of nausea so strong, she barely made it to the sink in time.

"Oh dear," she whispered, turning on the cold tap and opening the bathroom window to remove the sour smell of vomit. "Oh dear. Oh dear. Oh dear . . ."

Luciano was right, she thought: storing rodent droppings in a coffee jar was foolhardy, horribly unsanitary, and probably the cause of her current malaise. Recovering slightly, she pulled on a black linen dress and slipped her feet into a pair of fuchsia-pink flip-flops. As she walked along the corridor to the stairs, she wondered if she dared risk breakfast, given the upset state of her stomach. Descending the main staircase, she caught the faintest odor of cooked bacon and nearly gagged.

Hoping to have a quiet word with Signora Strega-Borgia and raise her deep concern about the threat that Fiamma d'Infer posed to Damp, Mrs. McLachlan kept the kitchen door ajar and listened for the distinctive sound of her employer's flip-flops *shlepp-shlepp*ing downstairs. Peering into the corridor, she caught sight of her employer suddenly stopping halfway down the main staircase and clutching the banister. Puzzled, the nanny watched as Signora Strega-Borgia gingerly descended to the ground floor then—at high speed, considering her footwear—bolted out the front door to be abruptly sick over the stone griffin that graced the front steps.

"Oh *dear*," muttered Signora Strega-Borgia, propping herself upright on a stone pillar. She was dimly aware of the familiar engine sound of the family car, and she looked up from the besmirched statuary to see her husband pulling up on the rose-quartz drive, waving and mouthing something through the driver's window. Another wave of nausea forced her attentions back to the stone griffin, and when she next opened her eyes, it was to see Luciano bending over her, his eyes full of concern.

"*Cara mia*," he murmured, wrapping a protective arm around her shoulders and producing a clean linen handkerchief, which he used to wipe round her mouth. "You are unwell," he stated, somewhat unnecessarily, since Signora Strega-Borgia bent once again over the griffin, and provided ample evidence that this was indeed the case. Mrs. McLachlan appeared on the doorstep with Damp and Nestor trailing behind her.

"Oh, you poor dear." The nanny made soothing clucking sounds and patted her employer on the back. "Let's get you inside and I'll make you a cup of mint tea to settle your stomach." So preoccupied was she with her ailing employer that she failed to notice when Damp hauled a large golf umbrella out of the stand by the door and started to wave it around purposefully. It wasn't until Signor Strega-Borgia had picked his wife up in his arms and carried her inside that Mrs. McLachlan turned her attention back to Damp, just in time to see the little girl wave the umbrella in the direction of the boot cupboard.

"NO! DAMP! STOP—"

There was a crash, immediately followed by the unmistakable sound of breaking glass. The nanny groaned as she peered round the door of the cupboard. Where seconds before had been the family and their guests' collection of ancient Wellingtons, gardening shoes, rusting ice skates, muddy soccer cleats, tennis shoes, broomstick crampons, fork-toed mules, ceremonial high-heeled calfskin waders, and moldy hiking boots, now stood rows of gleaming glass slippers, in every size from infant up to adult. Broken glass littered the floor of the cupboard, where toppling piles of footwear had succumbed to the laws governing glass and gravity.

Firmly shutting the door of the boot cupboard, Mrs. McLachlan removed the offending umbrella from Damp's hands and tutted. "My fault, dear. I should have been paying attention. No umbrellas or shooting sticks for *you*, I think. . . ."

Plucking Damp up into her arms and calling for Nestor, she headed to the kitchen to make Signora Strega-Borgia's promised mint tea.

In the pantry, the rats Multitudina and Terminus were deciding how best to treat the recent amputee, Tarantella. The tarantula lay between them on a spotlessly clean tea towel, eyes closed, and utterly motionless as overhead the rats discussed her condition.

"Did you get the cobwebs?" Terminus looked up from her perusal of an ancient copy of *Allopathica for Arachnidae*, open at the section "A Disquisitione on the Mattere of Amputatione and Hydropathie."

"Check," muttered Multitudina, dipping her front paws into a stolen capful of dish soap. They emerged green and slimy and, wincing slightly, the rat began to rub them across the bristles of a toothbrush (also stolen).

"What on earth are you doing?" Terminus peered over the edge of her book and sneezed as a flurry of soap bubbles drifted across the pantry.

"Scrubbing up," coughed Multitudina, her head surrounded by a cloud of froth from the dish soap. "I'll be the surgeon, you can be the anesthetist. . . ."

Terminus returned to her studies, skipping forward from "Amputatione" to "Anaesthesiae" with some difficulty, since the pages appeared to be stuck together with dried blood. Minutes later she looked up in alarm to see Multitudina holding a lit match in one paw and an enormous darning needle in the other. Flickering shadows flitted over Tarantella as Multitudina held the needle in the flame.

"What are you doing *now*?" squeaked Terminus.

"One of the first principles of surgery," muttered Multitudina, her eyes narrowed in concentration, "is that everything has to be squeaky clean, so I'm sterilizing this needle with heat. . . ."

"Well, I'm going down to the cellar for some anesthetic," Terminus said. "Try not to burn the house down while I'm away. . . ."

Half an hour later, Tarantella regained consciousness to find that she'd died and gone not, as expected, straight to heaven, but to some dark and nightmarish place. By the light of a guttering candle she saw two rats bending over her, one wielding an enormous needle with a long piece of pink thread trailing out of one end, and the other rat inviting her to drink something out of a thimble.

"Drink?" she squawked. "Are you out of your tiny mind? I'm a *spider*. I don't *do* wet."

She attempted to struggle into an upright position, then suddenly something hard crashed into her head, and everything went mercifully black.

"What did you do that for?" Multitudina squeaked reproachfully. "You didn't have to *hit* her with the brandy bottle, just persuade her to drink some of its contents—"

"You're *way* too sensitive to be a proper surgeon," hissed Terminus. "Come on. Stop wasting time. She's unconscious now—you may as well get on with it. . . ."

Terminus slumped back on her haunches beside Tarantella, watching for signs of returning consciousness. She was desperately trying not to look as Multitudina's needle dipped in and out of the skin round the wound where Tarantella's leg had been so violently amputated. To distract herself from the grue-someness of the surgery, she returned to her reading matter, but the soggy crunching sounds coming from the operating table were hard to ignore.

At last Multitudina threw down her needle, bit off an extra-neous length of pink thread, and spat it on the floor. *"There,"* she said with considerable satisfaction. "Done." She stood back to admire her handiwork. Where previously had been a gaping wound, there was now a neat little line of pink stitches. She turned to look at Terminus just in time to see her draining the contents of the thimble.

"A toashhht," Terminus hiccuped. "To—um—to . . . *hic*—"

"You drunken slob. You're totally *legless,*" Multitudina said accusingly.

"On the contrary," gasped Tarantella, regaining conscious-ness in time to catch the tail end of this exchange. *"I'm* legless, and you, madam, are just plain *drunk.*"

Soggy Batteries

Titus and Pandora sat on the end of the jetty, staring morosely across Lochnagargoyle, listening to the gentle slap and suck of waves against the worn planks beneath them. Drifting down from the meadow came the voices of Signora Strega-Borgia's classmates practicing their craft. So immersed in thought were Titus and Pandora that they didn't even attempt to bat away the clouds of gnats feasting on their exposed skin. Overhead the sun beat down out of a clear summery sky, but down on the jetty the mood was closer to winter.

Titus shivered, the motion causing ripples to spread outward from where his feet dangled in the loch, his toes white and shriveled from prolonged immersion. Clearing her throat, Pandora broke the silence.

"Eughhh. That was just so horrible, wasn't it? And so *real*, too. I mean, how did they *do* that—make Mum and Dad look so old and Damp grown-up? Where could they find actors that looked just like *us*? And why? Why did they do it?"

"They?" said Titus. "*They?* What d'you mean? There isn't a film company on the planet that could do that. . . ."

"The special effects weren't *that* special, Titus. With makeup and latex masks and . . . and, well . . . anyway, it can't be *that* difficult to make a wee film clip and post it on the Internet."

Titus turned to face his sister and grabbed her by both shoulders. "That's *not* what I mean. Didn't you hear me in there? When the clip started I said, 'That's like my dream,' and it was. Word for word. Exactly like the nightmare I had last night. No one on earth could have done that and then made sure that I had my own up-close-and-personal, one-to-one premiere in my own head, in my own b-b-bed. . . ." He abruptly released his grip and turned away, shoulders shaking, brushing unwelcome tears away from his face.

"Oh, Titus, that's *awful*. . . ." Pandora shuddered, her arms suddenly covered in gooseflesh as the meaning of her brother's words sank in.

"Creepy, isn't it?" Titus was barely audible.

"I just don't understand what's going on." Pandora's voice was muffled as she gnawed thoughtfully on a fingernail. "You said you'd got other e-mails before that one, remember? One about a car, another from someone meeting you at a plane, and the last one, the really scary one that warned you—"

"Get rid of it," Titus interrupted. "The e-mail told me to get rid of it, give it away, burn it—whatever *it* is—then something about the Borgias having to break the chain. . . . Pan, I don't know what on earth any of that was about. None of it makes any sense to me at all."

A snapping sound from behind them made Titus and Pandora turn in time to see Ffup hurtling down the overgrown path that led from the meadow to the loch shore. The dragon's eyes were wide in alarm as she lolloped across the pebbly beach pursued by Fiamma d'Infer.

"Don't be such a wimp!" the witch panted, brushing aside the brambles and wild roses lining the path. "I just need a tiny bit of dragon's blood after all—" She stopped, realizing that she had been overheard. Fixing an insincere smile on her face, she waved at Titus and Pandora and spun on her heel to head back up to the meadow. Unaware that she was no longer the witch's quarry, Ffup was running flat out along the jetty, her massive weight causing its wooden planks to bounce up and down, threatening to catapult Titus and Pandora into the loch.

"Calm *down!*" yelled Titus, as Ffup bounded toward him. "Slow DOWN! YOU'RE GOING TO—"

With a tremendous splash, Ffup belly-flopped into the loch, displacing a tidal wave of a volume equal to that of a full-grown dragon, most of which landed on Titus and Pandora. Ffup rolled onto her back, paddling serenely with all four limbs, and emitting little snorts of steam from her nostrils.

"Gosh, did I do that? Heck, I'm really sorry," she gasped, uncomfortably aware that this was a somewhat inadequate apology for half-drowning one's mistress's offspring. "Can I help you dry off? Give you guys a quick blow-dry?"

"NO!" yelled Pandora, her recent experience of being roasted in dragon-fire reminding her that she still had Mrs. McLachlan's alarm clock in her back pocket. "Oh *NO!*" she wailed, leaping to her feet and recovering the clock from her wet jeans. "Oh, you *dumb* dragon . . . what have you *done?*"

"Don't know," mumbled Ffup, paddling across to the jetty, "but I have a feeling that you're about to tell me. . . ."

"Is that Mrs. McLachlan's clock?" Titus stood to look at the object in his sister's hands as Pandora fiddled with something on the back of the clock and frowned. Intrigued, Ffup dragged herself out of the water onto the jetty, her weight making it tilt dangerously to one side, causing Titus and Pandora to lose their balance and topple straight on top of the dripping dragon. Pandora's shriek turned into a bubbling splutter as the waters of Lochnagargoyle closed over her head. She surfaced seconds later, still clutching the alarm clock, with Titus clinging round her neck and underwater thrashings indicating that Ffup wasn't far behind.

"You *idiot*!" she yelled, treading water as she attempted to loosen Titus's grip. "Let go, Titus, you're going to drown us both. Relax—the water's not that deep. Put your hands on my shoulders and I'll tow you to shore."

Eyes squinched shut, twelve years and eleven months into his shameful career as a non-swimming aquaphobe, Titus clutched his sister's shoulders as instructed, and within seconds found his footing on the bottom of the loch. Behind them, Ffup surfaced in a cloud of steam and waddled onto dry land, trailing seaweed in her wake.

"I'm freezing," Titus moaned, crawling onto the beach and collapsing facedown on the pebbles with his eyes shut.

"Let's go back to the house . . . Oh *no* . . . I must have pushed the— Oh lord, what time is it?" Pandora peered at the clock. "Um, Titus, there's something I think you ought to know."

"*What?*"

"Don't throw a hissy fit. Just take a look around and tell me if you notice anything different."

"Pandora? What are you on about?" Titus sat up and opened

his eyes. His mouth dropped open and his voice rose in pitch to a squeak. *"What's going on? Where are we?* Pandora, where's . . . ?" He waved a violently trembling hand across the meadow to where the familiar turrets of StregaSchloss were horribly absent.

Under strict instructions not to open her mouth, Ffup trailed disconsolately through the rhododendrons behind Titus and Pandora. Mounting a clandestine reconnaissance operation with a vast mythical beast in tow was proving to be more difficult than anticipated, but the comfort of Ffup's protective presence outweighed her unsuitability as a spy. She crawled along the ground, complaining fitfully as her knees and elbows encountered sharp sticks and stones.

"My manicure's just ruined—I mean, look at my talons, the polish is all chipped," she whined as the group halted by the herbaceous border that used to surround the east wing of StregaSchloss. Squinting through the glossy rhododendron leaves, the dragon gave a snort of dismay.

"Who built that monstrosity?" she demanded, gazing in disgust at the glass-and-steel sprawl that stood in place of the architectural jewel that had been StregaSchloss. "And tell me this: how did they build it while we were having a wee dip in the loch? We can't have been gone more than ten minutes and look at it—it's massive."

It was, Titus agreed. Massive, overblown, and utterly without charm. In the midday sun its glassy walls threw back dazzling shards of light, searing the eyes of the group huddled in the bushes. Parked outside on the unchanged rose-quartz drive was a dented Aston Martin, a vintage Jaguar convertible, and a utilitarian Range Rover. A young man in khaki overalls crawled out from under the Aston Martin and swore loudly.

"Look at those *cars*," Titus whispered in awe. "Whoever lives in that house must be either rolling in it or have some very rich friends. . . ."

A large glass panel slid across the front of the house, and a portly figure emerged from the building.

"I bet that's the owner," Titus remarked, watching as the figure strolled across the drive to where the man in overalls was dropping wrenches into a toolbox.

"Shhh, I can't hear what they're saying," hissed Pandora, adding, "I wonder who he is?"

The figure under discussion bent over the side of the Aston Martin to examine something under the fender, thus exposing a vast acreage of tweed-clad bottom for inspection by the watchers in the bushes.

"He's got a major lard problem, whoever he is—look at the *size* of his—"

"Of his what?" prompted Pandora, as her brother fell silent and his eyes grew wide.

"Tell me it's not," Titus whimpered, his head sinking into his hands as he realized who he was looking at. Another figure appeared at the open glass panel—a woman, who shrieked in tones all too audible for comfort:

"Titus! For heaven's sake—you're going to be late for your appointment. Get a move on—you can take the Range Rover instead."

"Titus?" squeaked Pandora. "Is that man—is that . . . is that *you*? Grown up? Eurrrrch. What a chub, what a porky." Unable to stop herself, she added, "I always did say you had the appetite of an elephant—now you've got the dimensions of one, too."

"Let me see that clock." Titus glared at his sister as she produced Mrs. McLachlan's alarm clock for his inspection.

"Water must have got into it—that's not the right time."

"Titus, I told you: it doesn't tell the time, it tells you the year, dumbo. It's 2022—it's the *future*—*do* keep up."

"I want to go back," Titus said. "I don't want to see what happens next. I *know* what happens. That fat slob is going to die in nine years' time, and frankly, having seen what he's like, that's not a moment too soon. I can't take much more of this. I don't want to grow up if it means being like . . . like *him*. Please, Pan, let's go back. Now."

Something in his voice convinced Pandora that he'd really had enough. With a sigh, she pulled out the reset knob and turned it counterclockwise till the display read 20:02 once more. "Time travel made easy, huh?" she said, pressing the knob.

Nothing happened. There was no spinning sensation, no crashing out of control into the herbaceous border in front of StregaSchloss. Pandora checked the time. She pulled the knob back out, then pressed it back in again, and still nothing happened. Out on the drive, the obese Titus waddled toward the Range Rover and squeezed into the driver's seat. The loud woman disappeared into the glass building, and the man in overalls opened the hood of the Aston Martin and hunted for something in his toolbox.

"What's wrong?" Titus looked over Pandora's shoulder as she twiddled with the reset knob.

"I don't know. Maybe it's not working after its dip in Lochnagargoyle—"

"I can dry it off," Ffup suggested, giving a couple of snorts of flame by way of example.

"NO!" Titus and Pandora shrieked in stereo.

"You guys are way too picky," Ffup complained. "Could we quit futzing around and just get out of here? I need to get back home *now*. Nestor's due for a feed—*over*due, in fact—and he'll scream the place down if I don't get back pronto and do the needful."

Pandora looked up from tinkering with the clock and scowled. "Ffup, I can't get us back to StregaSchloss right now. Thanks to you bouncing us into the loch, the clock isn't working, and until I fix it, we're stuck here."

"AUGHHHHHH!" wailed the dragon, displaying a maternal streak hitherto absent from her behavior. "My poor *baby*. He'll *starve* without his mummy, he'll fade away to noth—"

"Stop being such a drama queen," said Titus. "Hush up, for heaven's sake. Mrs. McLachlan will feed your precious infant."

"Oh no, she won't," muttered Ffup, wrapping her front legs tightly round her ribs. "Not unless she happens to be a dragon."

Titus glared at Ffup. "What are you on about? Mrs. McLachlan feeds Nestor every day."

"Not with dragon's milk, she doesn't," Ffup insisted. "He's not properly weaned yet. Sure he'll eat porridge and Miserablios, fruit and other mush, but he needs his mum to give him the Real Thing. I mean, *look* at me. . . ." The dragon threw her front legs outward in a dramatic gesture designed to draw attention to the fact that Nestor's lunch was not only ready and waiting, but present in such abundance that it was dribbling down Ffup's chest.

"Stop, please," Titus begged, snapping his eyes shut and trying not to gag. "Spare me the details. . . . Trust me, there are some things that I simply don't need to know."

"Look, here are the batteries." Pandora removed four flat little cells from the underside of the clock and examined them. "I don't *think* they got wet when we fell in the loch. The clock's waterproof and there's a sort of silicone seal round the battery compartment. What a relief . . . I guess they must just be dead after all."

Titus sank his head into his hands with a small wail.

"What's the matter now?"

"Think about it, Pan. If the batteries are dead, how do you propose to replace them? We can't just amble down to Auchenlochtermuchty and buy a new set. We don't know if the village still exists, and even if it does, what if you can't buy those batteries anymore? Maybe batteries are *obsolete* in 2022. Maybe money is obsolete—maybe . . ."

"Maybe you're missing the point. Here, stop worrying and take these." Pandora passed Titus two batteries, keeping two for herself. "Stick them in your armpits, like I'm doing."

"Excuse *me*?"

"Just do it. Put them in your pits and hold them in place by clamping your arms flat against your sides like this. . . ."

Utterly mystified, Titus obeyed, shuddering as the cold metal touched his skin. "Ugh. Freezing," he moaned, puzzled at the appearance of a smile that crept across Pandora's mouth.

"Precisely. They're cold. Mrs. McLachlan taught me ages ago

that if you warm up a dead battery, you can sometimes squeeze a wee bit more power out of it before tossing it in the bin. Let's give them ten minutes and try again."

In the absence of anything better to do, they leant against the gnarled rhododendron trunks opposite the silent glass house and eavesdropped on the muttering coming from under the hood of the Aston Martin.

"What a mess," the man in overalls grumbled, standing up and gently lowering the hood. "People like that don't deserve to own such a bonnie motor. . . ." He wiped his hands on an oily rag that dangled from his overalls and then dug around in his breast pocket to produce a cell phone. After a longish pause he spoke. "Yup, Ted here . . . Aye, I've given it a full service, done ma best to repair the steering rack, but the client's really dinged it . . . Aye, aw bent out of shape. Must've been flooring it—there's wheens of metal filings in the engine ile . . . Yeah, it's a shame. . . . Aye, a real waste . . ."

"Whooo, Titus. Tsk tsk tsk. Who's been a bad boy, then?" Pandora wagged her index finger reprovingly at her brother.

"Don't, just don't. I'm so ashamed of myself. Do you have any idea what those cars cost? Thousands . . . hundreds of thousands. What a dork I'm going to be—"

"Shhh—listen. He's having a real go at you."

"More money than sense, wur Mister Borgia." The mechanic looked disgustedly in the direction of the glass house. "Oh, aye, he's rolling in it. Doesnae blink when you tell him what a whole new engine's going to cost. Sma' change to the likes of him. And *fat*? I tell you, it's a wonder the car can take his weight. Still, even wi' all that money, and yon big hoose and drop-dead-gorgeous wifie, he's not a happy bunny. Take it from me, pal, it's just like they say, money can't buy you happiness. . . ."

Pandora dug Titus sharply in the ribs and wiggled her eyebrows meaningfully. He ignored her, keeping his attention fixed on the man in overalls.

"How do I know? Because I keep ma ear to the ground, is how. I hear things, me. He hasnae spoken to his sisters for years. He chucked his parents oot the family home, demolished it, and replaced it wi' this architect-designed fish tank. . . . Why? What I heard was that it was something to do wi' having no attic that spiders could breed in or some such nonsense. . . . What does he dae a' day? He eats—a' the time. He's stuffing his face, the wifie hates him, and he's aff to see a shrink three times a week since his last suicide attempt. . . . Nahhh. I wouldnae change places wi' him for a' the money in the world. . . ."

"Titus," Pandora whispered, "give me the batteries. I think you'll overcook them—your face looks like it's on fire."

Beet-red with shame at the discovery of what a moral midget he was going to become, Titus dug the two tiny cells out of his armpits and passed them over.

Ffup leant her massive head on Pandora's shoulder and moaned. "How long *now*? I'm awash in Nestor's milk. . . ."

Snapping the batteries into place, Pandora closed the compartment, checked the display, and, praying that it would work, pressed the knob.

Titus screamed, Ffup roared, and suddenly their nostrils were assailed by a truly evil smell.

"DO YOU *MIND*?" yelled a familiar voice. "Don't jump out on me like that! Is there nowhere in Argyll that a griffin

133

can take a dump without turning it into a spectator sport?"

Squatting in the rhododendrons next to them was Sab. Pandora noticed that the griffin had a roll of toilet paper clutched in one claw and the sports section of the local paper in the other. Sab's expression veered between outrage and embarrassment as Ffup walked over to harangue him.

"The house is rather overendowed with bathrooms, you know." The dragon looked as smug as was possible, given that her chest appeared to be leaking like a colander. "You don't have to do a poo in the bushes when you could take your pick from the bogs inside."

Trying to muster any dignity while hovering above a pile of one's own steaming ordure is almost impossible, so Sab opted for full-on belligerence.

"D'you not think I *tried* that? D'you think I'm a wild animal or something? A beast that goes for a casual cack in the shrubbery? I tried the downstairs washroom; Marie Bain's got the runs and she's annexed it. I tried the guest bog; one of the guests is using the cludgie as a giant china cauldron. I went to our mistress's suite, but she's got her head down the pan, giving it big heaves; the nursery bog's got a diaper stuck in it; the family bathroom's engaged because Tock snuck in for a bubble bath; the second-floor shower room's got a mountain of tighty-whities and thongs dripping from the rail; and Latch's bathroom's being used as a frog repository—"

"STOP!" Pandora begged, covering her ears and running for the house.

"No, I won't stop. I insist on defending my griffinal right to excrete in the bushes. As I was saying—"

Branches cracked overhead and a shadow fell across them.

Looking up, Titus saw Knot's head appear over the canopy of green leaves. The yeti's furry face rumpled in an approximation of a smile when he caught sight of Ffup.

"You'd better go feed your wee babby," he said. "It's wailing its head off. . . . What's that smell?"

Breathing through her mouth, Ffup rushed off to placate Nestor. Knot sniffed several times, in a crescendo of in-snorts, each louder than the one before.

"Mmmm . . . ," he said appreciatively.

"No—*don't*. Don't say it. Bleaaargh." Titus turned pale.

"Yummm. What's for lunch? Smells delicious, whatever it is."

Titus bolted out of the bushes and ran for the house, one hand over his mouth, the other over his stomach.

"Mmmm-hmmm?" Knot stopped in mid-snort and looked puzzled. "Something I said?"

A Little Dish of Revenge

Absorbed in their studies, the group of student witches assembled in the meadow had been utterly unaware of the dramas taking place in the nearby shrubbery. In turn, they had been rehearsing the spells that they required to pass the practical part of their forthcoming end-of-term exams. Each student had chosen one standard grade enchantment from the second-year curriculum and, aided by the others, was attempting to put the magic into practice. The prospect of looming exams had focused their efforts considerably; there was no idle chitchat, no sarcastic commentary, and no amusing trick hexes to raise a laugh. The group was unusually subdued and diligent, frowning in concentration as Hecate Brinstone struggled with the visually stunning but fiendishly complex *Floreat Aetherum*.

Two witches were missing from the group: Signora Strega-Borgia, under Mrs. McLachlan's instructions, had gone back to bed; and Fiamma d'Infer was helping herself to the contents of a gin bottle that she'd hidden in the greenhouse for emergencies. Slugging down a stiff measure of neat alcohol, Fiamma peered through a mossy pane of glass at the eleven distant figures in the meadow.

"Stupid fools," she muttered, taking another large swallow from the bottle. "Idiots, with their pathetic little conjuring tricks . . ." Out of sheer spite, she snapped her fingers in front of her mouth and, in an alarming simulacrum of a flamethrower, caused fire to blaze out from deep in her throat. Seeking something to destroy, she applied herself to the ancient grapevine that grew along the back wall of the greenhouse. If plants could have given voice to their feelings, the vine would have shrieked in agony. Minutes later, satisfied that no grapes would grow at StregaSchloss for many years, she strolled out of the greenhouse and crossed the flagstones to where the formal lawn rolled down to the meadow. The air was heavy with the scent of blossom, and bees buzzed drowsily in the herbaceous borders. Fiamma noted with disgust that Hecate was managing rather well with the *Floreat Aetherum,* much to the admiration and encouragement of her classmates.

Suspended in the air above the young witch's head were thousands of tiny flower buds, their petals tightly curled as they hung magically in the still air. Hecate paused in her careful incantations and looked up, shading her eyes against the sunlight. A tentative smile hovered round her mouth and, heartened by her success thus far, she continued, *"In nomine floris—aperte!"*

Fiamma couldn't resist. Unobserved on the edge of the meadow, she muttered a counterspell under her breath, a hex designed to scramble Hecate's words and turn them into the magical equivalent of alphabet soup. Like witchcraft's version of a computer virus, its effect was catastrophic.

Before the witches in the meadow could run for cover, the hovering cloud of flower buds changed color from pale sugar-pink to a deep and angry orange. Moreover, its shape altered, appearing to vibrate as it did so. A distant buzzing grew into a loud and menacing hum. Fiamma turned her back on the resulting mayhem. Behind her, screams and oaths faded into distant squeals and grunts as the witch let herself into StregaSchloss by the door from the kitchen garden. The kitchen was empty except for Marie Bain, who was locked in mortal combat with a vast pot bubbling on top of the range. Wincing at the smell, the witch ignored the cook completely and headed downstairs through the wine cellar to the dungeons, where she hoped to find Nestor unattended, unprotected, and ripe for a spot of bloodletting.

"Ees ze sole Véronique," Marie Bain explained to Fiamma's retreating figure, continuing doggedly despite having no audience. "Ah . . . but zere was no sole, so I find some—how you say?—'keepers,' een ze smokehouse, and zen I go find some grapes for ze sauce, but *zut alors,* ze grape vin is . . . piff! Finis! Kaput! I use raisins instead. But zere ees supposed to be a glass of *vin blanc* in the sauce, and I cannot find a drop of zat, zen I see a leetle bottle of Muscat at ze back of ze fridge, so I pour eet in . . . and"—the cook paused to inhale ecstatically—*"magnifique!"*

In the dustbin under the sink, the little bottle of Muscat lay under a rancid pile of kipper heads and tails. The label on the empty bottle had an addendum scrawled across it in Signora Strega-Borgia's distinctive handwriting:

Micturia ex Multitudina c. 2000

which was not an obscure vintner's reference to the grape or indeed the vintage, but a reminder that the bottle had been recycled as a vessel in which to lay down a particularly fine example of Multitudina's urine, rat pee being a student witch's handy cupboard staple, essential for certain arcane enchantments.

"Ees ready!" Marie Bain announced. "Launch ees served!"

Lunch was also being served at the nearby Auchenlochtermuchty Arms (*Taste of Scotland*, 1989, eight bedrooms with ensuite bathrooms, four-star dining, under new management), but thankfully of a quality far superior to Marie Bain's inedible offering. The dining room was deserted save for one solitary guest, a bulky man who sat in the darkest corner, his back to the room, engrossed in reading what to even the most casual observer appeared to be an Italian newspaper. A waitress brought him the menu and inquired if he'd like a drink while he was waiting, or some wine with his meal. Squeaking his order from behind his newspaper, Don Lucifer di S'Embowelli Borgia, uncle to Titus, Pandora, and Damp and half brother to Signor Luciano Strega-Borgia, was attempting to appear as normal as possible despite his nightmarish appearance. The plastic surgery he'd undergone eight months before to reduce the size of his nose had been executed with disastrous consequences for both surgeon and patient. Immediately following the operation, the surgeon had been dropped to the bottom of the river Tiber, held fast on the riverbed by the simple device of having had his feet buried in a ton of concrete prior to immersion. The patient was on the waiting list for extensive corrective surgery to reinstate a human nose, instead of the ghastly rat-like obscenity that currently twitched and wobbled in the middle of his face. Don Lucifer di S'Embowelli Borgia had ordered the concrete overshoes in revenge for not only bungling his nose job, but also for the rat-tail that, post-surgery, he had discovered dangling from his rear, and the rattish squeakings that he now emitted every time he opened his mouth. . . .

"Eek, eek squee?"

The waitress's brow wrinkled. "I'm sorry, sir," she said. "I didn't catch what you said."

"Squee eek, 'Eek, eek squee?'" Don Lucifer jabbed his index finger at an item on the wine list.

"The house red is Rioja de Toromerde," the waitress explained. Then, lowering her voice to a whisper, confided, "I'd avoid that one like the plague—I wouldn't even use it to clean toilets. It's disgusting. How about a nice claret with your steak?"

The Don squeaked his agreement, hoping the waitress would now disappear. This was torture, trying to communicate in high-pitched noises that made him sound like he needed oil, not wine. But worse was to come.

"Now, sir. How would you like your steak?"

"Eek ike ick aww."

"Raw, sir? Not rare? You mean raw, as in cold, uncooked?"

"Eek."

"But—it's not a dish best eaten cold, sir. . . ."

Don Lucifer brought his hand thudding down on the table. "Eekeek ike eek ishh esst eek'n aww!"

The waitress retreated, clutching the menu to her chest like a shield. Charm school reject, that one. And ugly as sin. Looked like he'd lost an argument with a mincing machine. . . .

Don Lucifer was all too aware of the effect his appearance had on most members of the general public. Cloistered away from humankind after his catastrophic surgery, he'd had plenty of time to bemoan his hideously altered reflection and plan his revenge. First the surgeon, he thought, and then, that item ticked off his "To Do" list, next—next comes my half brother, Luciano Strega-Borgia. Little lily-livered Luciano, who had the audacity to escape from the death trap I laid for him. Who managed, against impossible odds, to escape from a locked and burning room in my palazzo without leaving so much as a DNA smudge from his supposedly vaporized remains. . . . Luciano, whose eldest brat, Titus, is due to inherit the millions that I, Lucifer, was promised by my dying father. Luciano, whose meddling messed up the Borgia Inheritance, an unbroken chain of money (or so my dying father had said) that had passed down the male line for centuries since—since Italians *ran* this stupid little island.

Hissing through his teeth, Don Lucifer began to write a list in the margin of his newspaper:

Item first: he scribbled, *Buy gun oil.* He'd retrieved his beloved Beretta from the ashes of the palazzo, and it badly needed to be taken apart, oiled, and reassembled to restore it to its former deadly perfection.

Item second: Reconnaissance. Had Luciano really escaped

being incinerated? He needed to find out exactly who was currently living in StregaSchloss.

Item third: Animals. He had the suspicion that Luciano kept pets, since all Christmas cards from his half brother bore the weird names of several individuals as well as those of the immediate family . . . probably guard dogs, he decided, so—

Item fourth: Buy dog food for item the third.

Item fifth: Buy flashlight—in case he did the job at night.

Item sixth: Buy waterproof trousers and jacket—to protect his clothes from blood spatter, and finally—

Item seventh: Assemble state-of-the-art incendiary device and enter detonation code into cell phone—

"Your lunch, sir." The waitress put a plate in front of him, adding, "Your *raw* steak, sir. Will that be all?"

Don Lucifer waved her away with a dismissive squeak. Pushing the gruesome plate to one side, he continued planning his lethal assault on StregaSchloss, which at this stage appeared to involve nothing more sinister than a major shopping trip to Auchenlochtermuchty.

"Your wine, sir." The waitress reappeared with a bottle and a wineglass, both of which she placed in front of Don Lucifer. "Ochhh, you're not enjoying your steak, sir. A bit too bloody, is it? Shall I take it back to the kitchen and ask the chef to do something with it?"

"Eek."

"Medium rare? Medium? Medium- to well-done? Well-done?"

To each inquiry, the surly guest shook his head. Seizing his pen, the waitress waved it in front of his face. "Write it *down*.

Tell me what you want the chef to do with it."

Snatching his pen back and stuffing his incriminating newspaper under his seat, Don Lucifer scribbled something on his napkin and held it up. The waitress peered at the pen marks bleeding into the linen.

was the terse instruction written on the napkin. For some reason this one word filled her with foreboding, and she felt her flesh creep. Without another word, she picked up the plate and fled the dining room.

O Sole Mio

Luciano Strega-Borgia scraped the untouched remains of lunch into the firebox of the range and slammed the door shut to prevent the smell escaping into the kitchen.

"If you're sure I can't be of any assistance, sir . . ." Mrs. McLachlan untied her apron and hung it on a hook by the door to the kitchen garden.

"Quite sure, Flora." Signor Strega-Borgia smiled at the nanny. "Why not take Damp out for a walk before dinner? That way she'll work up an appetite and we can get on with our work without distractions."

"Dad, where d'you want these?" Pandora edged through the garden door, her arms laden with herbs.

"On the table, and you can chop them with this." Signor Strega-Borgia passed his daughter a seriously wicked knife and turned to see how his son was faring. Titus stood over a large stainless steel pot, stirring onions and garlic as if his life depended on it.

"Not so *violently*, Titus. They're only vegetables, not mortal enemies. . . ."

"Why are you cooking dinner tonight, Dad?" Pandora looked up from chopping oregano, brushing a stray clump of hair out of her eyes.

"The rest of the household is indisposed." Signor Strega-Borgia poured a mountain of flour onto the kitchen table and, after making a small indentation in the center, dropped twelve egg yolks into it. "Your mama is feeling nauseous. Marie Bain is sulking in her bedroom because none of us touched her kippers in raisin and rat-pee sauce; your mother's colleagues are all covered in bee stings—"

"Hornets," muttered Titus, "not bees. I saw them—"

"Me too," agreed Tock, crawling out from under the table and coming over to the range to peer into Titus's pot, adding under his breath, "And that's not *all* I saw."

"Pardon?" Titus looked down to where the crocodile put his front paw to his mouth and mimed, "Keep shtoom."

"Hornets? Where on earth did they come from?" Luciano Strega-Borgia wondered aloud as he rapidly worked the eggs into the flour with his hands, causing Pandora to regard him with horror.

"Yeurrrrchhh," she groaned. "Dad, that is just utterly *gross*. It looks like sick . . ."

Secretly agreeing with his sister's assessment of the clotted mess on the kitchen table, Titus angled his body in Tock's direction and whispered, "*What* did you see?"

"That witch," Tock muttered. "Her with the ridiculous horse-drawn hearse. I'd opened the bathroom window to let the steam out after my bath and I saw her. Standing talking gibberish on the edge of the meadow, messing up that spell, turning flowers into hornets."

"Are you sure?" Titus stopped stirring and stared at Tock. "I mean, that's—that's *evil*. They're all covered in stings because of *her*."

"Yup," Tock said. "I think she's batting for the other side."

"What? What d'you mean? What other side?"

Tock's whisper was almost inaudible. "The side of Dark, not Light."

Titus paled. "You mean she's practicing Black Ma—"

"Don't *say* it," Tock hissed. "Walls have ears. I think something very nasty is going on. Haven't you humans noticed *anything*?"

Titus thought of the overall strangeness of the past few days and nodded. "I thought it was just me," he confessed. "I've been feeling . . . um, sort of . . . haunted . . . like there's something out to get me—"

Signor Strega-Borgia looked up from kneading a lump of dough that was beginning to resemble something you could put in your mouth as opposed to hurl in the trash and said, "How are your onions doing, Titus?"

"Um . . . yes . . . great. Soft and squishy and brownish," Titus guessed, adding in a whisper, "What do you think we should do? Tell Dad?"

"No. No way. When it comes to the odd behavior of student witches, your father's judgment is somewhat clouded. As far as he's concerned, Black Magic is just a darker shade of White, a tonal difference as opposed to a moral one. . . ." Tock sighed and raised his voice to a normal volume. "And speaking of clouded judgment, I'd say those onions were *black*, not brown."

"FOR HEAVEN'S SAKE, TITUS!" Luciano roared. "Can't I even trust you to do a simple thing like *brown* an onion? How the heck are you ever going to be able to feed yourself when you leave home if you can't even carry out the most elementary of culinary tasks? At this rate, you're going to starve to death before you're thirty."

The knife slipped out of Pandora's hand and fell to the stone floor with a steely *chinggg*.

The faces of both his children were ashen.

"What on earth's the *matter* with you two?" Luciano pounded the lump of pasta dough with one fist, causing a cloud of flour to erupt around his hands. In the silence that followed, Tock sidled out the door to the kitchen garden, closing it quietly behind him.

"Titus, *caro mio*." Luciano clutched his forehead, instantly full of remorse. "I am sorry for shouting. I'm an idiot. If you don't ever want to cook, well . . . that's your decision. Your poppa's money will make sure you never need worry about cooking ever again. You'll be able to hire the best chef in Europe, should you wish—your only problem will be avoiding turning into a complete butterball in the process. . . ."

Tears rolled down Titus's nose, landing with a hiss in the pot of blackened onions.

"Dad—" Pandora tried to head her father onto safer conversational topics. "The herbs are all chopped . . . um . . . what d'you want me to do now?"

Holding up a hand for silence, Luciano stepped straight into the verbal equivalent of quicksand.

"How long now? About a week, Titus? I've arranged for one of the estate lawyers to come for dinner tonight, so we can have a little chat about where best to invest your money. I mean, you can't keep it in a piggy bank, can you?"

Titus stared at his pan of spoiled onions as if it alone held the answer to all that ailed him.

"Titus. For heaven's sake, lighten up." Luciano threw his arms wide, narrowly missing Pandora's head. "Think about it: how many thirteen-year-olds do you know with so much money in the bank that they could buy a new car every year? Just off the interest alone? And not just *any* car; with that sort of money you could buy—"

"An Aston Martin," Titus said woodenly.

"*Please.* Spare me. I'm Italian, remember?" Luciano made a derisory *pffff* sound. "Not an Aston Martin, no. A Ferrari, a Maserati, something with a bit of soul—"

"Eughhh, *don't* mention sole," Pandora interrupted, seizing the opportunity to halt her father's unwittingly tactless rantings. "If that was what Marie Bain made for lunch, then I want to be in a soul-free zone for the rest of my life. . . ."

"Cars don't *have* souls," muttered Titus, scraping burnt onions into the compost bucket and dropping the ruined pan into the sink with a crash. Behind him, Pandora gritted her teeth. She'd tried to help, but both her brother and father seemed intent on conversational suicide.

"Heavens, child, do you have to be quite so literal?" Luciano abandoned his pasta dough in a mound on the table and headed for the pantry. "Titus, give me a hand here, would you?" He retrieved a stepladder from behind a flour bin and dragged it across to a wall of shelves stacked with homemade jams and chutneys, some of such venerable antiquity that they had turned black. Climbing up the steps and using the shelves to keep his balance, Luciano turned to check that he had his son's attention.

"Look, Titus." Luciano stretched up and seized a glass jam jar with its cloth cover held in place with yellow raffia. He peered at the handwritten label. *"August 1989, Strawberry and Champagne Conserve*—in your mother's illegible handwriting . . ."

"So?" Titus glared up at his father.

"So, Titus," Luciano sighed, "the contents of this jar are almost as old as you are. Your mother and I picked these strawberries in the garden with you as a baby on my shoulders. In fact, if memory serves, with you dribbling down the back of my shirt and attempting to pull my hair out in handfuls."

"Mmm . . . ," Titus mumbled, then, reasserting his adolescent need to prove that he found adult conversation deeply boring, added, "And your point is?"

"And my point *is*: this jar contains a memory of one of the happiest days of my life." Luciano patted the jar fondly. "The weather was hot and dry, there wasn't a gnat in sight, your mother was wearing a white linen dress, I still had all my hair, my firstborn child was burbling on my back, and we were about to go down to the loch and eat strawberries and drink champagne. . . ."

"So what's in the other jars?" Titus scowled up at the laden shelves in the pantry.

"Heaps of things. There's half a shelf full of quince jelly made after Pandora was born and"—Luciano indicated a large blue-and-white china jar on a low shelf—"Rumtopf that we began after Damp arrived. We were turning into experts at preserving by then. Come to think of it, we were becoming pretty expert at babies, too."

Titus winced. Some things just didn't bear thinking about. . . . "Can I go now?" he muttered, gazing down at his shoes.

"Titus"—Luciano climbed down the stepladder and sat heavily on the bottom rung—"nearly thirteen years have passed since I first held you in my arms. Nothing you do or say can change how I felt about you then, or now. You can act like you think I'm just the most terminally boring old fart it has ever been your misfortune to share a roof with, you can roll your eyes and pray that I'll just spontaneously cease to exist—but it doesn't matter. What *does* matter is that ever since you and your sisters came into our lives, we have been a family, and deny it if you must, this family is part of your soul."

"Yeah, Dad, but—"

"Hear me out. So . . . we keep all these ancient jars of jam because they are each and every one a reminder of the importance of family. When you and your sisters have grown up and gone, your mother and I are going to work our way through all these jars one by one, remembering all the joys you brought us—"

"Dad?" Titus could hardly get the words out. "Dad, there's something wrong. . . . It's . . . oh, it's just so *weird*. . . . I've got this horrible feeling—something awful's going to—"

The pantry door opened and Signora Strega-Borgia tiptoed in. "Don't mind me," she whispered. "I've just suddenly been overcome with an unaccountable desire for some of that date-and-banana pickle we made last year. . . . D'you know where Mrs. McLachlan put it, Luciano?"

"You *must* be feeling better, Baci. You certainly look better."

Luciano stood up and wrapped an arm around his wife's shoulders. "But *pickle*? Are you sure? Why not wait until dinner? We're making pasta—that is, once Titus has told me what's eating him."

Signora Strega-Borgia plucked a jar off one of the shelves and, after a cursory glance at the label, peeled off its cloth cover and sniffed the contents appreciatively. "Mmmm. Delicious . . ." She dipped a finger into the jar and withdrew a sticky lump of pickle which she promptly swallowed.

"Eughhhh. Mu-umm." Titus squinched his eyes shut in an attempt to block out the revolting sight.

Signora Strega-Borgia opened the door to leave and then paused, as if remembering something faintly unpleasant. "I'll leave you guys to it," she mumbled in between mouthfuls. "Don't forget that lawyer chap is coming at eight and he doesn't eat meat, tomatoes, garlic, or onions."

"What *does* he eat, then?" Luciano complained. "Supper *is* meat, tomatoes, garlic, and onions."

"Who cares? Let him starve," Signora Strega-Borgia said with uncharacteristic venom, closing the door behind her.

"Doesn't she like lawyers?" Titus said. "Or is it him in particular?"

"Just him. Your mother loathes anyone who has *anything* to do with your grandfather's estate."

"Why? What's wrong with it?"

"Let's just say that poppa, your grandfather, may he rest in peace, was a businessman with some rather unorthodox methods of dealing with his clients." Luciano turned back to the shelves and replaced the jar of jam.

"What d'you mean, 'unorthodox methods'? Come on, Dad, you have to tell me. After all, I am involved as well, with . . . with Grandfather's money and all that inheritance stuff."

Attempting to think of a reply, Luciano picked up a squat glass jar and tried to remember what was inside it.

"Dad? What exactly did my grandfather *do* to make all that money? What *was* his job?"

Peering into the murky depths of the jar, Luciano took a deep breath. "Only your mother and I know about this. And one other, but he may well be dead now. Titus, you must never, *ever* breathe a word of this to another living soul. Some things are best kept hidden. Your grandfather, Don Chimera di Carne Borgia, was a mafioso. A very big and powerful one. In the criminal under-world of his time he was the big cheese, *il grande parmigiano*, with big businesses, politicians, royalty, and even heads of state forming corrupt links in his chain of influence. . . ."

"The Borgias must break the chain," Titus whispered, recalling the final line of his terrifying e-mail.

"The Borgias *are* a chain. We are, Titus. You and I. The money can only pass down the male line. Thank heaven your mother and sisters are exempt."

"But all that money . . . Where did he get it?" Titus had the sneaking suspicion that his grandfather hadn't saved it up, lire by lira, in an old fruit jar.

"He killed for it—oh, not with his own hands. No. Not per-sonally, but he gave the order to kill, and one of his henchmen would do the dirty work on his behalf. He also ran casinos and dog tracks, was involved in illicit trades on the stock market, owned diamond mines, smuggled opium, and probably had a finger in every dodgy pie imaginable. . . ."

"So, it's poisoned? Tainted?"

"The money? Oh yes, but most money is. Even if you make your money by honest means, the minute you bank it you're indirectly involved in all sorts of unsavory practices—or at least your money is."

"But, *Dad*. Why me? Why did you allow him to give that money to *me*? You knew all this—stuff and you still let him go ahead."

"Titus, I *loved* him. He was my *father*. That doesn't mean I forgave what he did. I *hated* what he did. I ran away from home, left the country of my birth because of it. But when I heard he was dying . . . I—you were newborn—I took the first flight to Italy to show you to him . . . to show him that out of evil can come great goodness—"

"But you should never have allowed him to give me the MONEY!" Titus's voice rose to an anguished howl. "You *knew* it was blood money! Yet you allowed him—"

"He died two minutes after the will was signed." Luciano's face was devoid of color and expression. "It was the first time I'd seen him in over twenty years, and he died in my arms. Titus, I would have allowed him to do *anything*. It was his last wish. The man on that bed wasn't a powerful criminal mastermind, he was just my poppa, an old man that I loved . . . despite it all. . . ."

"Dad . . . ," Titus whispered. "I'm sorry. I didn't mean—"

"No, Titus. You are right," Luciano interrupted, waving a hand for silence. "On the day my father died, I did what I'm always accusing your mother of doing. I didn't *think*. And now, here we are, and I've told you something you'd rather not know, putting you in the horrible position of having to decide what on earth to do with all that money. . . . You could always give it away to charity if you just want to get rid of it."

"*Get rid of it,*" Titus mumbled. "*Destroy it, for it will destroy all who seek to possess it . . . destroy it.*"

The glass jar slipped out of Luciano's grip and plummeted to the floor, exploding on the flagstones with a crash. At once the floor was awash in blood-colored liquid and broken glass. Whatever had been preserved in the jar had long since decomposed, its tattered remains resembling some unidentifiable human organ.

Luciano and Titus looked at each other, aghast, both wondering exactly what it was they were now standing in and thinking how apt it was to be paddling in what looked like gore, given their recent conversation.

"Oh *lord,*" moaned Luciano, peering at his spattered shoes.

"Don't move," said Titus. "I'll get a brush," and leaping out of the pantry, he ran past Pandora and out into the corridor, heading for the broom cupboard.

To his surprise one of his mother's guests was already there, raking through the various brushes and mops, searching for something that, judging by the hissing and muttering coming from her hooded figure, wasn't there. She was oblivious to everything in her effort to find whatever it was that she'd lost. Titus cleared his throat to announce his presence. The witch spun round with a snarl, affording Titus a glimpse of something so feral that he nearly shrieked.

"Oh, my *heavens*! What a fright you gave me! Didn't your precious nanny ever teach you not to sneak up on people like that?" Fiamma d'Infer rearranged her face into an approximation of a smile and ran a hand through her hair. "So . . . ," she purred, taking Titus's stunned silence for normal teenage sulkiness. "Cat got your tongue?"

"We haven't got a cat," Titus muttered. "Excuse me. I need to get a broom from the cupboard."

"Be my guest." Fiamma pressed herself against the wall, allowing Titus just enough room to squeeze past her. Under her watchful eyes he felt his flesh creep. As he reached out for a long-handled brush, Fiamma murmured, "I *don't* think so. That one's Hecate's and I promise you it's got a major problem with its steering, not to mention its brakes . . . and we wouldn't want the young about-to-be inheritee to be wiped out in an avoidable broomstick accident, would we? At least not *just* yet . . ."

She paused and, pushing past Titus, grabbed a larger broom and thrust it at him. "Take this one with my compliments. Totally safe, state-of-the-art ABS, enhanced twig-ruddering, twin air bags—"

"*Air bags?* On a broomstick?" Titus couldn't help himself. He burst out laughing. "I suppose now you'll tell me it runs on unleaded and does zero to sixty in two seconds? Actually, what I'm after is a broom to sweep the floor with, not to *fly* on."

Avoiding Fiamma's offering, Titus grabbed what he fervently hoped was a bog-standard, wood-and-bristle, floor-sweeping brush and, without saying good-bye, bolted back to the kitchen.

Tarantella Spills the Beans...

The grandfather clock in the hall chimed six times as Mrs. McLachlan let herself and Damp in the front door.

"Perfect timing, pet," murmured the nanny, lifting the little girl onto the settle to remove her wellies. As she undid the zipper on Damp's jacket, the clock gave a deep and resonant *twongg* and began to chime again.

"Oh *dear*." Mrs. McLachlan hoisted the child up and made for the kitchen, pausing to peer at the clock's face as it continued to chime in what appeared to be a fit of temporal hysterics. Its filigreed hands were rotating in a counterclockwise direction that boded ill for its internal mechanism. Mrs. McLachlan checked her wristwatch and *tsk*ed.

"Heavens, the battery must be dead," she muttered, crossing to the telephone and dialing the number for the time. In her arms, Damp reached out for the porcelain jar of pens kept on the hall table—for the express purpose of jotting down

156

telephone messages but in reality used for doodling on the telephone directory during boring phone calls. Mrs. McLachlan immediately shifted Damp to her other hip, thus placing the pens out of the child's reach, and, patting her reprovingly on the nose, listened as the connection was made.

"—the time, sponsored by *cccchhtssst* will be *sshttpsscksh* precisely."

Mrs. McLachlan sighed and waited for the recording to advance to the next time.

"—the time, spons*sssht* by accu*pshhhht—ssss*—twenty-five and *pssss* seconds."

"Oh, for heaven's sake," Mrs. McLachlan groaned. "The phone's not working very well, is it?"

"—the time, sponsored by *ppppssssschhhhhh*— Please replace the handset and try again."

Mrs. McLachlan dropped the receiver in its cradle and bore Damp off to the kitchen. Opening the door, she was greeted by a mouthwatering smell and the sight of Marie Bain sitting at the far end of the kitchen table, idly picking her ears with a pencil stub as she pored over the crossword in the newspaper. The sink was clear of dishes and a stack of pasta bowls sat on the warming plate of the range. Blue-and-white china platters of salad were lined up by the window, and someone had taken the trouble to wrap blue linen napkins round each individual place setting of cutlery, tying them in place with yellow raffia.

"Very nice, dear," Mrs. McLachlan said approvingly.

Marie Bain looked up from the paper and removed a pencil from one ear, wiping it on her sleeve. She gathered her pinched features into a frown. "Ees Eetalian, zat. Anyone can do eet. Eet takes ze real culinary genius to create Frrrrench food. . . ."

"I'm sure you're right, dear," Mrs. McLachlan agreed mildly. "Do you know when dinner is to be served? My watch doesn't appear to be working."

The cook rolled up the grease-spotted sleeve of her cardigan and peered at a tiny watch on her wrist. *"Mon Dieu,"* she tutted. "My hands haff fallen oeurf. . . ."

Mrs. McLachlan blinked rapidly and then realized that Marie Bain was referring to the hands of her watch rather than the two red-knuckled appendages that poked out of the frayed sleeves of her cardigan. Mentally logging the cook's watch onto the growing list of non-functioning StregaSchloss timepieces, Mrs. McLachlan bore Damp upstairs to check the time with her Alarming Clock.

Closeted in the library in the company of his father and the estate lawyer, Titus was uncomfortably aware of loud grumblings coming from his stomach. The library windows were open onto the lawn, and in the warm evening air a distant sound of laughter could be heard coming from the meadow, where Signora Strega-Borgia and Pandora were playing against Ffup and Tock at badminton. The faint aroma of singed feathers indicated that the dragon had incinerated a shuttlecock in her enthusiasm for the game.

Titus sighed as he watched his father and the lawyer riffling through boxes of papers, all stamped with the distinctive Borgia crest. In the dusty silence of the library, the digestive process going on inside Titus's stomach was embarrassingly loud. Titus's eyes roamed around the room, desperately seeking to fix his gaze upon something that might provide more entertainment than watching adults shuffle bits of paper from one side of a desk to the other. His attention was caught by a familiar hairy leg waving from behind the half-open door of the mantel clock.

Ughhh . . . that hideous tarantula again, he thought, watching in disgust as the leg curled and uncurled like a beckoning finger. . . .

Fed up with being ignored in her efforts to gain Titus's attention, Tarantella made an exasperated *tchhh* noise and dragged herself closer to the light. This entailed moving a thimbleful of brandy (thoughtfully supplied by Multitudina for its postoperative analgesic effect), a small stack of miniature leather-bound books, and a sinister pile of bloodstained dressings. Negotiating past these was painful, and by the time Tarantella made eye contact with Titus, she was exhausted. She watched as he stood up, yawned, and walked over to the mantelpiece. Peering round the edge of the clock door, Tarantella realized that they were not alone, and she slumped back onto her sickbed, toppling the brandy thimble as she did so.

"Auuukkkk!" she wailed, as the alcohol burned a fiery trail along her recently stitched wound. "Aaaargh, ow, ouch, *OW*!" she shrieked, vaulting out of the clock in her desperation to put some distance between herself and the source of her agony.

"Aaagh, yeurrrrrch, *no*!" squeaked Titus, as the twitching tarantula landed in his hair and immediately clung on with all her might.

"Titus, for heaven's sake, we're trying to concentrate." Signor Strega-Borgia looked up from the paper mountain teetering in front of himself and the lawyer and removed his reading glasses with a sigh. "What *is* it?"

Titus was standing with his back to his father, so Luciano was unable to witness the expression on his face, which was probably just as well, since Titus looked as if he were about to expire from sheer terror. To add to his nightmare, Tarantella had scuttled down his face and was currently clamping his mouth shut in the furry grip of all seven of her remaining legs.

"Shhhh," she hissed. "*Don't* scream. Just make some excuse and get me out of here." The tarantula released Titus's lips and dropped down the inside of his T-shirt.

"Ughhh . . . ahhh . . . got to . . . got to—got to go to the bathroom," Titus squawked. He fled from the library and stumbled along the corridor to the family bathroom, where, after locking the door, he tore his shirt off, bundling Tarantella up in its folds and grabbing the showerhead for maximum protection.

"Right, spider-thing. One false move and I turn on the power shower," he said, restraining his desire to stamp on his discarded shirt. Tarantella dragged herself out onto the bathroom tiles and blinked up at Titus towering above her, showerhead trembling in his hands.

"Listen up, boy-thing, and put that ridiculous *hose* down. Believe me, being up close and personal with you was every bit as painful for me as it was for you—" The tarantula broke off, looking down at her abdomen, where a trickle of bloodstained fluid was seeping from beneath a soggy dressing. "Oh *lordy*, I've sprung a leak. . . . Pass me a bit of toilet paper, would you?"

Titus reluctantly replaced the showerhead and bent down to examine Tarantella. "You're *bleeding*," he gasped, his face turning white. "Did I do that? Heck—I'm really sorry. I never meant to *hurt* you, it's just . . ."

"It's just that you can't stand me and wish I was dead, isn't it? Nothing major, nothing I should feel too *sensitive* about. . . . Pass me something to plug the leak before I terminally exsanguinate."

Titus tore off an extravagant length of toilet paper and passed it over to the spider. "What—what happened? How did I manage to hurt you so badly? Oh *no*. You've lost a *leg*. I'm really, really sor—"

"Do shut up," Tarantella snapped, waving huffily at the hillock of toilet paper in front of her. "What am I supposed to do with all *this*? I asked for a bandage and you provide an entire Emergency Room."

"Sorry. Sorry, so sorry, I'm really—"

"Spare me. We haven't got all night, you know. Stop apologizing, tear me off a wee bit of toilet paper, and listen very carefully because this is very important."

As Titus improvised a tiny dressing from a quarter sheet of toilet paper, folded up until it was the size of Damp's smallest fingernail, Tarantella told her reluctant nurse about what she'd overheard in the guest bathroom just before being attacked and mutilated.

"You're *kidding*." Titus gasped, dropping the tiny wadded dressing, which caused it to slowly unfold once more.

"Oh, *sigh*. Do I look like I'm kidding? Do you think this is fake blood? I mean, I've heard of method acting, but ripping one's own limbs off for no better reason than thespian verisimilitude seems a tad . . . excessive."

"It's not *that*." Titus caught himself in time. "I mean,

Fiamma trying to kill you is *awful,* but . . . it's terrifying. Everything you've just told me—the mask she wears, the false teeth, the feet—her *tail.* What *is* she? And what's the Chronostone she was going on about? And who is the 'last male soul' and the 'baby magus'? What's going on, Tarantella?"

The spider sighed and examined her leaking wound. "What's going on is that I am bleeding to death while you are flapping your lips, dear boy. You'd make a lousy nurse. . . . "

"Oh lord—sorry, sorry, sorry." Titus attempted once more to fold the tiny sheet of paper.

"There you go *again.*" Tarantella covered her eyes and heaved a sigh. "Let's take your questions one at a time, shall we? 'What *is* she?' you squawk. Um, let me see, she's masked in makeup to disguise the fact that either she's thousands of years old or else has had an awfully hard life . . . wears false teeth for the same reasons . . . um, fake feet—well, if you had two cloven hooves you'd probably wear false feet, too—unless, that is, you were a pig, in which case you'd acquire two more and wear them with pride. Let's see, forked tail? Oh gosh. What animal has cloven hooves and a forked tail. Gosh and golly, that's a tough one. . . . Any ideas, team?"

"Not an animal," Titus whispered, "a *demon.*"

"And for your next question, 'What is the Chronostone?' Pass. All I know is that it's something that she and her 'Boss' want to get their hands on. Final question for many million lire: the 'last male soul' and the 'baby magus'? Come on, you know this one."

"Me?" Titus volunteered in a shaky voice. "I'm the last male soul? And Damp? Is she the baby magus?"

"Absolutely. Well done. Is that the smell of burning brain cells I detect? OUCH! Gently with that dressing, you *brute*."

"You're just lucky that I can overcome my loathing of spiders," Titus muttered, picking Tarantella up in his hands and gently securing the dressing in place with a tiny Band-Aid. "I'm going to put my shirt back on, tuck you inside it, and find Mrs. McLachlan. We have to warn her there's a monster in the house. Do me a favor and don't wriggle around. You're exceptionally hairy and you make me itch."

"And you are exceptionally dim and you make me despair—" Tarantella's words were muffled in Titus's T-shirt as, opening the bedroom door and checking that the corridor was empty, he set off to find the nanny.

...and Mrs. McLachlan Spills the Salt

As instructed by Signor Strega-Borgia, Latch sounded the gong for dinner and scratched his gnat bites absentmindedly. He'd lit a small fire in the library, for the evening had turned chilly and fingers of mist were creeping up toward StregaSchloss from the waters of Lochnagargoyle.

Chewing the remains of a toasted shuttlecock, Tock crawled out of the moat and picked a water lily to tuck behind his ear by way of ornament. He gazed at the lit windows of StregaSchloss in happy anticipation of dinner before lolloping across the rose-quartz drive toward the front door. Just as he reached the first stone step the sound of a muted squeal caused him to stop and listen. It came again, apparently from ground level—the unmistakable sound of some creature in pain. As a vegetarian, he piously hoped that it wasn't someone else's dinner putting up a protest, but nonetheless he peered anxiously around, wondering where the sound was coming from. Bats

164

flitted across the darkening sky, leaving their roost under the eaves of StregaSchloss to head for their nocturnal hunting grounds. The crocodile briefly entertained the notion that what he'd heard was the sound of the bat's high-pitched sonar squeaks; he was about to climb the remaining steps and head indoors when the sound came again, louder and clearer, repeating one word over and over in a rising scale of terror.

"*Help—help—help—help!*"

All at once Tock realized that the sound was coming from the dungeons. A ventilation shaft that allowed air to pass to and from the subterranean passages under StregaSchloss had a mesh-covered outlet next to the front door. *Something is happening down there,* Tock thought, *and by the sound of it, the something was happening to Nestor.* The baby dragon's shrieks were so shrill that they carried in the still air, out across the meadow, along the jetty, and down into the deeps of Lochnagargoyle. From a wish to offer assistance coupled with a strong desire to make Nestor shut up, Tock bounded up the steps and was dutifully cleaning his claws on the boot scraper when from the direction of the loch came a powerful roar—the awesome lung capacity of its unknown maker causing the crocodile to abandon all attempts at personal hygiene and scrabble frantically into the safety of StregaSchloss.

Chest heaving and eyes wide, he slammed the door behind him and sank back against it with a little gasp as Mrs. McLachlan came into view, sweeping down the stairs with Damp in her arms. Something about the nanny's demeanor set off alarm bells in Tock's head. Looking down at his claws, he realized that he had tracked rather a large quantity of slime from the bottom of the moat across the threshold of StregaSchloss, and by the expression on Mrs. McLachlan's face, it appeared that this lapse of protocol had not escaped her attention either.

"Wash those filthy, dirrrty claws before you come to the table," she said, turning her back and striding along the corridor to the kitchen.

"But—but—" Tock bleated, "there's something happening in the dungeons. . . . Nestor—"

"Nestor's *mother* will look after him," Mrs. McLachlan said over her shoulder, her voice chilly enough to freeze-dry the forlorn water lily drooping from Tock's ear, "and unless *you* wish to eat your dinner in the moat, you had better do as you're told."

From experience, Tock knew that resistance was futile, so he opened the door to the downstairs bathroom and meekly obeyed. Such was his fear of Mrs. McLachlan's ire that Tock didn't complain that some unknown houseguest appeared to have shaved off their chin warts with a blunt fish knife and had left all the grisly evidence of this do-it-yourself surgery dotted around the porcelain of the sink. When he emerged, squeaky clean and redolent of lily-scented soap, it was to find Titus standing in the middle of the hall, apparently engaged in conversation with his T-shirt.

"Would you *quit* that?" he demanded, unaware that he was the subject of the crocodile's puzzled scrutiny. "I think we've just missed her. She's probably taken Damp in to dinner. No— ahhh—urgggh, you're so hairy—no, *don't*."

From above came the murmur of many voices, doors opening and closing, and approaching footsteps. The houseguests had responded to Latch's summons and were gathering for their nocturnal assault on the larders of StregaSchloss.

"For *heaven's* sake," Titus hissed, peering down inside his T-shirt and, to the bewilderment of Tock, addressing one or both of his nipples. "Now I'm going to have to take you in to dinner. Keep still, or you might end up losing more than a leg—"

With a small honk, Tock bolted along the corridor to the kitchen and headed inside. The first guest had appeared at the head of the staircase and was sniffing appreciatively at the aromas wafting out from the kitchen.

"Something smells heavenly." Hecate Brinstone hastened downstairs and smiled at Titus, her face still horribly swollen from her earlier encounter with the enraged hornets. "I look an absolute *fright*," she sighed, catching sight of her reflection in the highly polished case of the grandfather clock.

"Um—no—er, I've seen far worse frights," Titus confessed with a teenager's awkward gallantry. "You look—um—fine."

A faint *tchhhh* came from inside his T-shirt as, flushing pink, Titus offered the witch his arm and accompanied her in to dinner.

There were still two empty places laid at the kitchen table as Luciano staggered to the sink with a cauldron of pasta. Tipping it with effort into a massive colander, he turned to the guests waiting at the table and wondered out loud what was keeping Pandora and Fiamma d'Infer. Just then, the missing witch appeared from the unexpected location of the wine cellar, a bottle of vintage Barolo in each hand. Luciano abandoned his pasta and leapt across the kitchen to block her path.

"I don't wish to sound churlish, but I really would prefer it if you would put those bottles back where you found them." Luciano attempted to minimize the embarrassment of ordering a guest to unhand the wine by lowering his voice to an almost inaudible whisper, but his face betrayed his anger at Fiamma's presumption that she could plunder the wine cellar at will.

"I thought these would be quite gluggable with your heroic culinary *efforts,*" the witch sneered, her body language indicating that she had little intention of obeying her host.

"Those are not 'gluggable' wines, Miss d'Infer." Luciano reached out to take the bottles from her and met with resistance. "Those are priceless vintages laid down with a special occasion in mind." Luciano began to tug at the bottles, having to redouble his efforts with every word he gasped out, as it began to dawn on him that this witch was ten times stronger than he. "This. Evening. Is. Not. Special. Enough."

The kitchen door opened to admit Pandora, who hesitated, unable to take her place at the table until Fiamma and Luciano moved out of the way. Slipping into the kitchen in Pandora's wake, Multitudina and Terminus scuttled across the stone floor and vanished beneath the dresser, not swiftly enough to avoid being spotted by Fiamma.

"Eughhh—*disgusting!*" she spat, releasing the bottles so abruptly that Luciano nearly lost his balance. "Running around the *kitchen.* Honestly, Baci darling, what with rat pee in the fish, rodent droppings in the coffee, and now free-range vermin at the dinner table, I'm beginning to wonder why on earth I ever agreed to come here. . . ."

Signora Strega-Borgia blushed deeply. As if watching Luciano playing tug-of-war with the bottles of Barolo wasn't humiliating enough, now to be confronted with her own utter lack of skills in the domestic-hygiene department was mortifying beyond belief. She looked up at where Fiamma was still standing, tapping one foot impatiently and staring at her as if to say, *Right, serf,* do *something about this.*

"*Pandora.*" Baci's voice was icy. "I've told you countless times before about letting your rats run free. For the last time, I do *not* permit free-range rodents to roam around the house. Either you keep them under control or I am going to get a cat to do the job for you." Turning to Fiamma, she continued, her voice warm and conciliatory, "I *do* apologize for my daughter's disgusting practices. Honestly . . . *children.* Do take a seat, Fiamma. Pandora, get rid of them *now.*"

Sitting round the corner of the table from his mother, Titus was aghast. Poor Pandora, he thought, she *loves* those rats. And if Mum finds out that I've got a free-range tarantula down my shirt, she'll go bananas. Why on earth is she being so *nice* to that spider-murdering woman? Doesn't she know that she's dangerous?

Next to him, Mrs. McLachlan patted his arm. "Pass the salt, please, dear," she murmured, just as Luciano brought the first tureen of pasta to the table.

Hunched on the floor in front of the dresser, Pandora was endeavoring to entice her rats out from their hiding place. Her face on fire from the humiliation of public chastisement, she peered into the darkness to where the rats cowered behind a barrier of dust balls and long-lost plastic medicine spoons.

"A *c-c-c-cat*?" Terminus stuttered. "She can't be serious, can she?"

"What's a 'cat'?" Multitudina was utterly confused. In all her lifetime she'd never encountered one, and was at a loss to understand what all the fuss was about.

Terminus, her literary skills honed by Tarantella's tutelage, was far more aware of the many dangers lurking in the world outside StregaSchloss. "Big, furry things with teeth," she explained. "Sometimes they vanish, leaving their smiles hanging in the air; occasionally they wear boots. They're renowned for riding pillion on broomsticks and hanging out with royalty, and they live on a diet of rats and cream."

"What's our trained biped doing?" Multitudina asked, distracted by the sight of Pandora.

"Trying to catch our attention, I believe." Terminus watched as Pandora squeezed her arm underneath the dresser with a small lump of Parmesan extended in her grasp.

"How thoughtful," Multitudina murmured, reaching out and snatching the cheese greedily. "And look, she's brought some more. . . ."

Pandora's hand withdrew and reappeared slightly farther away, holding a fresh piece of Parmesan. Little by little she coaxed the rats out from under the dresser until, drowsy and replete with cheese, they allowed her to pick them up and remove them from the kitchen.

"Oh my goodness!" Mrs. McLachlan blurted. "I'm *so* sorry. Heavens, that was clumsy of me," as with a dramatic gesture akin to one of Luciano's operatic armsweeps, the nanny overturned the salt dish, spilling most of its contents across the table onto Fiamma's lap. With a hiss of annoyance, the witch sprang to her feet and ran out of the kitchen before anyone noticed that, in common with all her demon kin, she was unable to tolerate prolonged contact with salt.

Mrs. McLachlan watched her hasty exit and shrugged apologetically. "Dear, dear. That seems a bit *extreme*—" she continued, absolving herself. "It's only *salt*, when all's said and done. Never mind, at least I didn't spill it in the *food*. Mmmmm, this is simply delicious—my compliments to the chefs."

Sitting farther down the table, the estate lawyer gazed at his plate in dismay. He loathed Mediterranean food, and this meal confirmed all his worst nightmares about dealing with Italian clients. Still, he comforted himself, once the boy has signed the paperwork and banked his inheritance, my days of dining with the Borgias will be over. At long last I'll be able to sever my connection with this dodgy family and return to a career that doesn't involve laundering money for the criminal underworld. Under the pretext of dabbing his mouth with his napkin, he gazed at the bent heads around the table. Eighteen of them, he counted rapidly, plus the rat-girl, the woman who'd received a lapful of salt, plus—he swallowed rapidly—plus those . . . creatures . . . slobbering and dribbling at the other end of the table. He shuddered at the sheer number of mouths avidly consuming bowlfuls of disgusting pasta and mentally consigned the entire population of StregaSchloss to perdition. Meeting Titus's eyes across the table, the lawyer attempted a smile, which faded rapidly as he realized that something large was moving beneath the child's shirt. A lump the size of a tennis ball appeared to be climbing up from his navel to his throat. The boy dropped his gaze to his lap and color flooded his cheeks.

Mumbling an excuse, Titus fled from the kitchen, the speed of his exit causing Tarantella to tumble down to his waistband moaning, "Give me a break—ow, slow *down*! That hurts, you cretin."

Ignoring her, Titus took the stairs two at a time and arrived, breathing heavily, at his sister's bedroom door. "Pan, it's me. Open up."

There was a clunk as Pandora undid the lock and let him in. Titus immediately dragged his T-shirt hem up to his throat, exposing Tarantella clinging to his navel as if her life depended on it.

"Tarantella!" Pandora gasped. "What're you doing with *him*? Oh no. What's happened to your *leg*? Oh, you poor, poor thing."

"Don't. Just *don't*." The tarantula allowed Pandora to pick her up. "Don't *leak* all over me. Oh, for heaven's sake, I may as well save my breath—"

"Poor T-Ta—" Pandora choked and could go no further, as her nose began to run in sympathy with her eyes.

"She's okay, really." Titus attempted to offer a small crumb of comfort to his sobbing sister.

"Oh, *am* I?" Tarantella glared at Titus. "And since when did *you* become an expert on arachnid well-being? Would you *stop* sprinkling me, girl? I am not fine, but I'm not about to pop my clogs either. I'm in constant pain and I'm probably going to limp for the rest of my life, but I beg you, don't add drowning to my list of woes."

"But your poor l-l—" Pandora spluttered.

"Say it, don't spray it," Tarantella snapped. "My poor leg is still jammed in the *hoof* of that monster downstairs. Forget my leg. If *I* can, so can you. Unless you wish even more terrible events to take place, you have to alert Mrs. McLachlan to the presence of a monster in our midst."

"Pardon?" Pandora blew her nose and peered at the tarantula through red-rimmed eyes. "What monster? Did I miss something?"

"Give me *strength*," Tarantella moaned. "For a supposedly superior species, *Homo sapiens* are a terrifyingly unobservant bunch. Titus, fill your sister in on the details—I'm pooped. I simply cannot summon up another ounce of energy. Before I keel over, would you please find me a safe place to sleep—one that doesn't tick or sound the hour like my last sanctuary did? I'm too ill to spin or even climb into a web and I cannot keep my . . . eyes . . . open . . . a minute . . ." The tarantula slumped in Pandora's hands, her eyes closed and her mouth relaxing into a tiny pout.

From the hall downstairs, they could hear Mrs. McLachlan calling them.

"Titus, Pandora. Hurry *up*. Your dinner's growing cold."

"I'll put her in the old doll's house," Pandora decided, crossing her bedroom to the shelves where her favorite possessions from earlier childhood were displayed. The old doll's house was an antique, passed down from Signora Strega-Borgia to Pandora, and ultimately destined for Damp. Every item of furniture within had been made by hand, down to the tiny carpets that had been embroidered in silk by one of Signora Strega-Borgia's great-aunts—who, over the course of a decade, lovingly stitched tiny tapestries designed specifically for the interior of the doll's house. Pandora unhooked the front and carefully placed the slumbering Tarantella in the master bedroom, lifting the minute goosedown comforter from the four-poster bed and tucking the spider in before drawing the bed's curtains closed around her.

"Come *on*," Titus urged. "I'm starving."

"You have to tell me about the monster first." Pandora turned out the light and opened the door to the hall just as Fiamma d'Infer strode past, giving the children not so much as a passing glance on her way back downstairs.

"Right. I think I'll just *lock* my door," Pandora muttered, closing it gently behind them. Titus nodded his approval and began to explain in whispers about Tarantella's brush with death.

"That's her. She's the monster. The one who had the fight with Dad over the wine. The one who moaned about the rats. She tried to kill Tarantella and—"

"*What?* And no one has told her to pack her bags and go? I'll soon see to that—"

"NO! Pan, no *way*. Don't go near her. *Promise* me you won't. She's not what she seems. . . ."

They had reached the kitchen door and hesitated in the corridor outside.

"Pandora," Titus pleaded, "I know you love your spider and anyone who harms so much as a hair on her body ought, in your opinion, to be torn limb from limb but—we're not dealing with just anyone here. That woman . . . she's a demon in human form. She's after far bigger prey than a wee spider. She wants Damp—and—and, um, me, actually."

"Damp? And *you*? What, like a kidnapping?"

"No—uh, I'm not exactly clear about what bits of Damp and me she's interested in, but Tarantella seemed to think that Mrs. McLachlan would understand what is going on and would know what to do. So, we have to pretend nothing is wrong, go back and finish dinner, and then try to talk to Mrs. McLachlan without anyone overhearing, and tell her *everything*."

Pandora's eyes filled with tears again.

"What? What's the matter?" Titus's stomach growled impatiently as he waited for his sister to reply. "Come *on*. We'll have to go back in there in a minute."

"It's Mrs. McLachlan," Pandora sniffed. "She practically tore my head off before dinner. I've never seen her so angry . . . she went absolutely ballistic, and her *eyes*— Oh, Titus, it was *awful*."

"What about her eyes? Why was she angry? What—oh *no*— she found out about us borrowing her clock?"

Pandora nodded slowly as fresh tears tracked down her cheeks.

"Oh *heck*," Titus groaned. "That means I'm in deep poo as well. Oh lord, I can hardly wait—"

"No," Pandora whispered. "I took the blame. I told her it was just me 'borrowing' it. I didn't mention you . . . or the trip to 2022 or . . . any of that. I decided I'd better leave you out of it, since you'd been so freaked out by what we saw in the future, and—oh, those terrifying e-mails, and—well, I figured you'd had enough."

Titus gazed at his sister in amazement, stunned at her magnanimity.

"Think of it as an early birthday present," Pandora sniffed.

"After all, there's no point in my buying you anything if you're about to inherit all that money, is there?"

Titus's jaw dropped. For the last hour his thoughts hadn't once strayed in the direction of his inheritance. Suddenly the whole tangled mess of the tainted money and his unappetizing future as a bloated plutocrat came crashing back in. "Pandora . . . you're a—" he blurted incoherently. "I'm, um, not so—"

"Come on, Titus. I can hardly hear the call to dinner over the racket coming from your stomach." Fixing a brave smile on her face, Pandora turned the handle to open the kitchen door, propelling her brother ahead of her and adding in an undertone, "Mmmm-hmmm, don't those onions smell . . . *burnt*?"

Written in the Stars

Dinner had been a huge success, Luciano decided, peering myopically at the dusty bottles in the wine cellar. He carefully replaced the two Barolos in their rack and, kneeling down, removed two half-bottles of Tokai for after-dinner consumption. From the dungeons downstairs he could hear Nestor wailing his protests at the earliness of bedtime, and, over that, the sound of Ffup racing through a bedtime story in order to return upstairs and join the company.

"And-then-the-handsome-dragon-opened-his-mouth-and-ate-the-ugly-princess-and-some-of-them-lived-happily-ever-after-the-end-good-night-kiss-kiss-lights-out-not-another-squeak-good-bye. . . ."

Luciano found himself holding his breath in sympathy with Ffup, remembering how he himself had gone through similar bedtime rituals when the children were babies. Night after night, he'd turn out the light and get halfway down the corridor from the nursery before a wail would summon him back crib-side.

"Wahhhhhhh," came Nestor's response.

Luciano exhaled noisily. Poor Ffup, he thought.

"Oh, for heaven's sake, would you close your big yellow eyes and GO TO SLEEP?" the dragon hissed.

"Wahhhhhhh."

Luciano could almost hear Ffup's resolve crumble, and moments later, he heard her sigh deeply and relent.

"If I read you *one* more story, will you promise me you'll go to sleep then?"

Smiling, Luciano stood up and carried the dessert wines into the kitchen. All family and guests had removed themselves to the comforts of the drawing room, leaving Marie Bain muttering balefully to herself as she washed the dishes. Choosing to ignore the fact that the cook appeared to be intent on smashing the china rather than cleaning it, Luciano piled a silver tray with tiny almond cantuccini biscuits, unwrapped a panforte and cut it into bite-sized morsels, and uncorked both bottles of Tokai.

Behind him, Marie Bain hurled empty tureens into the sink, pausing only to sneeze productively into the dishwater. Ffup appeared with Nestor clinging to her hip.

"Won't he settle down?" Luciano picked up the laden tray and smiled at the dragons.

"Eughhhh. *Babies*. What a complete *pain*." In contrast to her words, Ffup planted a kiss on Nestor's head and shifted his weight in her arms. "He's worked himself up into a complete froth: utter hysterics every time I try to sneak back upstairs. He refuses to let me out of his sight for some reason. . . ."

"Come and join us in the drawing room." Luciano opened

the door onto the corridor. "Who knows, we might be able to *bore* him to sleep."

A resounding crash from the sink indicated that Marie Bain had abandoned her attempts to clean the clay casserole in which the pasta sauce had simmered. Wincing as Ffup picked her way through pot shards, Luciano held the door open to allow her to carry Nestor safely out, then closed the door firmly on Marie Bain's dishwashing tantrums.

To Titus's frustration, an opportunity hadn't yet occurred for him to speak privately with Mrs. McLachlan about Fiamma, although he was beginning to suspect that the nanny was more aware of lurking dangers than he had given her credit for: the salt-spilling at dinner had looked, to Titus, to be an act of magical terrorism, and the rapid disappearance of the demon from the dinner table seemed to confirm this. Fiamma had reappeared later, and even now was perched on a footstool by the fireplace, determinedly avoiding some of her colleagues' entreaties to join them in a game of charades.

She hooded her eyes and affected total ignorance of the fact that Nestor was trying to flame-grill her feet. Much to Ffup's embarrassment, her baby son now appeared to be unable to share a room with Fiamma d'Infer without trying to cremate her. Eventually the witch stood up, and on the pretext of having to make a few phone calls, headed upstairs to her room. To the relief of the assembled company, Nestor immediately fell fast asleep.

Before Titus could seize the opportunity to draw Mrs. McLachlan into a quiet corner, the estate lawyer came over to sit beside him, perching awkwardly on the edge of the sofa as if poised for flight.

Cramming a handful of cantuccini into his mouth, Titus attempted to look at least awake, if not very interested.

"Your father and I have laid out the relevant documents ready for your signature." The lawyer drummed his long fingers on his knees and raised his eyebrows pointedly. "So, if you'd just take a minute to work through them, then I can be on my way."

Across the room, Black Douglas muttered in Signora Strega-Borgia's ear, "What d'you call a lawyer who's been chained, gagged, and dropped in cement shoes into the sea?"

"A good start," she replied. "More coffee, anyone?"

"Mmmfffle." Titus hadn't quite realized how badly cantuccini need to be accompanied by liquid, preferably wine. His mouth felt as if it were crammed with dusty boulders, and crunch and swallow as he might, he couldn't manage to reduce the volume of masticated biscuit-rubble enough to allow him to speak. In despair, he heard his father excuse himself from the guests and invite the lawyer and Titus to join him.

Swallowing jagged lumps of biscuit, Titus followed the adults upstairs to the library, where someone had thoughtfully lit a fire and turned on the lamps, but had neglected to close the windows. Drawn by the light, a significant proportion of the insect population of Argyll was flitting across the ceiling, occasionally dispatching its more challenged members to their deaths by toasting on lightbulbs. Giant shadows of moths and daddy longlegs danced across the spines of the Borgias' collection of thousands of books, and Titus inwardly gave thanks that

Tarantella was no longer residing in his T-shirt. The prospect of having tarantula drool dribbling down his chest distracted him from the more immediate problem of how to avoid ingesting a lungful of gnats with each indrawn breath.

"Should we adjourn to another room?" the lawyer asked, praying that the answer would be affirmative.

"It's only a few *gnats*." Being Italian, Luciano regarded the scourge of Argyll to be a watered-down version of the more macho mosquito; only a real lightweight would consider altering his plans to accommodate such a pathetic infestation. "Anyway, this shouldn't take too long, should it, Titus?"

Titus was miles away, struck by a particularly vivid memory from earlier childhood, happily replaying it in his head and thus deaf to his father's question.

. . . it had been a night just like this, same time of year, probably even the same number of insects. He'd been—oh, six, seven—yes, seven years old. His birthday, in fact, because he remembered helping Mum carry his birthday cake and a cooler full of bottles of lemonade and champagne. Pandora was on Dad's shoulders, giggling as he ran down the bramble-lined path to the lochside, bouncing her with each step, till her unself-conscious five-year-old's laughter rang out across the still water.

There had been an old rowboat moored at the end of the jetty, its peeling sides knocking gently against the steps in time with the waves that lapped the tide line of the pebble beach. They'd all clambered into the boat—Dad had rowed out into the middle of the loch, and Mum had lit the candles on the cake. He had a vague memory of feeling sad when the candles had been blown out and he'd consumed far more of his fair share of cake, and thus was lying back on the floor of the boat, bloated and anticlimactic, watching the stars pass by slowly overhead and feeling faintly depressed that he had a whole 364 days to wait until his next birthday.

Then had come the miracle.

A cry from his mother made Titus sit up and look to where her pointing finger indicated a patch of what resembled stars reflected on the water of the loch. A closer inspection revealed this to be a cluster of millions of points of light: tiny, luminous pinpricks just below the surface of Lochnagargoyle.

"What are they?" he asked, leaning over the edge of the boat, all the better to see.

"It's a form of phosphorescence," Luciano said. "I've never seen it like this before."

Something in his father's voice made Titus fall silent. He leant into Luciano's embrace and watched in awe as the entire loch came alive with flashes of light.

"Mummeeee!" Pandora exclaimed, jumping up and down and causing the boat to quiver in the sparkling loch. "Look, Mummy, the stars have fallen in the water!"

Titus plunged his hand into a dark patch of water to see if it felt different. It didn't—but to his delight, when he withdrew his hand from the chilly loch, it had been magically transformed. Each finger glittered and sparkled, and as the water ran down his wrist, it etched a blazing comet trail in its wake.

"Oh WOW!" Pandora had just made the separate discovery that by slapping her hand on the surface of the water, she could, in effect, hurl stars across the loch into the distant darkness. Fingers trailed in the water left a slowly fading line of stars in their wake. . . . Titus wrote his name in the loch and watched as the last starry "s" slowly faded to black.

"It's gone," he sighed. "Why does it disappear like that?" He wrote his name again, as if by repetition it would remain engraved indelibly on the loch.

"Nothing lasts forever." Signora Strega-Borgia smiled. "Titus, even if you wrote your name on stone, it would still vanish eventually." Seeing her son's face fall at the discovery of his human frailty in the face of Time, the Ultimate Eraser, she sought to comfort him. "But think of this, Titus. Lochnagargoyle will remember your name: on some atomic level it was there, it *is* there, invisibly written on the water."

"It's like sand," Titus said, remembering an afternoon spent drawing dinosaurs at the beach. "All those drawings we did in the wet sand, and then the tide came in and took them away out to sea. . . ."

"Exactly." Luciano fitted the oars in the oarlocks and began to head back to the jetty, each dip of the blade causing a brief phosphorescent flare. Behind him, the silhouette of StregaSchloss grew out of the darkness, its lit windows golden against the night.

A white wraith flew across the meadow, its silence absolute; its identity unguessable until, with an inquiring hoot, it landed on an oak and waited there till an answering toowit released it to soar once again above the tree line. StregaSchloss beckoned and now, to Titus's delight, he saw a tiny figure outlined in each of its windows in turn as Latch pulled the curtains shut against the night, moving from room to room as if tucking the house in for the evening. For Titus, the sight of home, in all its solidity and permanence, was hugely comforting.

Unseen by the family, over a turret on the far western corner, a star blazed across the sky, winking out as it appeared to fall into the black mass of trees skirting the foot of Mhoire Ochone. The bottom of the little boat scraped along a submerged rock as Luciano shipped the oars, then reached out for the mooring rope to pull them gently alongside the jetty.

"But Dad," Titus persisted, sensing bedtime drawing near and wishing to delay this by whatever means possible, "where did my name go? Where did the dinosaurs on the beach go when the water took them away?"

Suddenly longing to put the children to bed and curl up by the fireside with his wife, Luciano sighed. "They . . . ah . . . they went . . . they became part of a bigger pattern. . . . Oh lord, help me out here, Baci."

Signora Strega-Borgia closed her eyes and concentrated, trying to frame an explanation that Titus could understand. "Titus . . . ," she said at last, "we're all part of everything—we in our boat, the loch, the meadow, the stars—everything we can see and everything we can't. It's all kind of joined up like the biggest puzzle you could imagine. Just because we can't see something doesn't mean it's gone. . . . It's still there, but it has changed into something different. Sweetheart, it's awfully hard to explain, and I'm not sure that I even understand it properly myself, but think of it like this: I said 'Nothing lasts forever,' but that's not the whole story. What I should have said was, 'Nothing lasts forever unchanged.' Things change, Titus—they move on from one state to another."

"Like Mortadella," Pandora supplied helpfully.

"Um, yes . . . just like Mortadella," her mother agreed, privately unsure if recalling Pandora's dead rat was such a good idea.

"She swole up and died," Pandora said matter-of-factly. "Then she went moldy, so we buried her in the garden and she turned into flowers."

"Bravo!" exclaimed Signor Strega-Borgia, standing up very carefully to avoid capsizing the boat, and grabbing hold of the ladder on the jetty. "I thought we'd all forgotten about her—"

"I hadn't," Pandora said.

"Of course you hadn't, darling, but do you remember how, a year afterward, a little patch of forget-me-nots sprang up in the exact spot we'd buried her?"

"Rats don't change into flowers," Titus said with seven-year-old certainty.

"Yes they do, Titus," Luciano insisted. "Think—a tree starts with a seed from another tree, blown by the wind, dropped by a bird—"

"In its poo."

"Thank you, Pandora. Yes, sometimes seeds are dropped by a bird 'in its poo,' as you so quaintly put it. Then the seed grows into a sapling, then a tree, then it makes its own seeds for growing into other trees, and in time it grows old, withers, blows down in a storm—"

"Or we cut it down. For firewood," Titus insisted, ever a stickler for detail.

"And yes—we burn it on our fires, but that isn't the end of the tree. It doesn't vanish—it turns first into flames and heat, then ash for the garden, and part of it turns into smoke and flies up out of the chimney. . . ."

"But it's gone," Titus wailed. "It's not a tree anymore."

"No," Luciano conceded. "It has changed into smoke and ash, and in time, the clouds and the wind will carry it away and it will rain down on other trees in other places, and those other trees will drink it up through their roots—and in this way it will become a tree again."

"Oh! That's just so perfect. Well done, Luciano." Baci sprang to her feet and flung her arms round her husband's neck—and before they could blink, the boat overturned, plunging them all into Lochnagargoyle. . . .

"Titus—hello? Hello?"

He blinked, recalled to the present by his father's voice. To Titus's relief he wasn't struggling in the chilly loch, but slouched across a chesterfield in the library. Luciano stood before him, backlit by the logs burning in the fireplace, scratching irritatedly at a gnat bite behind one ear.

"Sorry, Dad. *Phwoof,* I was miles away," he mumbled, aware from his father's expression that something more was expected from him. "Um—what? Why're you staring at me like that?"

"You look different, somehow." Luciano tilted his head to one side and narrowed his eyes, peering at his son doubtfully. "I hesitate to say this because you'll probably regard it as an insult, but you look . . . oh . . . *young* and happy. Happi*er*. Much, much happier than you were earlier this evening."

Titus smiled, somewhat baffled by his father's comments. Of course he looked *young,* he reasoned—compared to the two wrinklies in his present company, he was almost a newborn. And happy? Oh *yes,* he confirmed, feeling something vast and full of light streak across his thoughts. Yes, I'm so happy I could *burst,* actually. In a week's time I'm going to be pure dead grown-up. Thirteen! A teenager at long last. And . . . at long last, I know exactly what I want for my birthday . . . and, more to the point, exactly what I *don't.*

"Dad," Titus said, turning his back on the estate lawyer, "can I have a wee word—just you and me, for a moment?"

Spilt Blood

In a fit of rash generosity that she later regretted, Signora Strega-Borgia had given Fiamma a bedroom on the second floor, the walls of which were covered in panels of raw Chinese silk dating back to the P'Ing Imperial Dynasty. Sitting on the bed, her charred high heels digging holes in the coordinated silk quilt, Fiamma lit a tiny black cigar and sank back against the pillows with her cell phone tucked under her chin.

"I need you to look something up for me," she said, tapping ash onto the floor. "It's not available on the Internet, otherwise I'd have done it myself—so don't give me grief about your not being my personal search engine. You have to get up off your scaly haunches and go find the relevant file."

There was a stunned silence from the other end. Then Fiamma was put on hold while the lesser demon applied itself to the task. Minutes ticked by until the bedroom was filled with evil black smoke and Fiamma had ground her cigar out on the bedside kilim.

"So soon?" she hissed, her eyes briefly flashing vermilion. "Took long enough, didn't you? Right. The chapter on *Sang di Draco*, if you would, with particular reference to the subsection dealing with fluorescence . . ."

There was a shuffling of parchment as, on the other end, the minor demon did as it was bid.

"Right, minion. Tell me if the Pericola d'Illuminem does indeed make dragon's blood glow." Fiamma's voice had dropped to a whisper as she peered at a tiny vial held between her thumb and forefinger. "Perfect," she purred, transferring the vial to the palm of her hand and closing her fingers around it. "I thought it did, but I just wanted to be absolutely sure before I start hurling blood around the place. . . ." A smile played around her mouth, and a small trail of drool crept down her chin. "Catch you later, serf," she added, switching her phone off.

Fiamma stood up, her breathing shaky, her inner agitation making it impossible for her to remain still. I'm almost *there*, she gloated silently. First the stone, then the souls . . . and then I'm out of here, back home to Hell. Even if I do say so myself, that was a stroke of utter *genius*, drawing blood out of that malformed baby dragon. . . .

Before she'd left the Hadean Executive on this particular mission, they had been installing tanning beds for the exclusive use of high-level members who needed regular exposure to ultraviolet light to counteract the effect of spending their entire lives in the sunless depths of Hell. A colleague of Fiamma's had made the useless discovery that UV light caused dragon's blood to fluoresce—under the ultraviolet rays of a tanning bed the blood glowed deep neon-pink. This information was duly filed and forgotten, and would have been entirely lost to demon-kind were it not for the fact that here, now, Fiamma was about to make demonic history. For the Chronostone emitted a particular wavelength of light that corresponded to ultraviolet on the electromagnetic spectrum.

"All *I* have to do . . . ," Fiamma whispered to her reflection in the dark glass of her uncurtained window. "All I have to do to find the Chronostone is sprinkle little drops of dragon's blood around this Scottish mausoleum and wait to see if they *glow*."

The small matter of dispatching the boy and the baby? A mere bagatelle. Fiamma unstoppered the vial and dipped a tiny glass rod into the red liquid within. With a flick of her wrist she sent a single drop of Nestor's blood spinning up in the air, and then straight down onto the floor. On contact with the floorboards, the drop exploded into tens of droplets, which arranged themselves in the classic spatter pattern beloved of detective fiction. In the gloomy light of the Chinese bedroom, the blood failed to do anything other than soak indelibly into the floorboards. Not in the least discouraged, Fiamma restoppered the vial and tiptoed out into the corridor, pausing at the head of the stairs to repeat the experiment.

It wasn't until she reached the great hall that she struck gold. But by then, it was far too late.

Titus Grown

"As your lawyer, I must advise you that what you are doing is . . . foolhardy beyond belief."

Titus wrote steadily, ignoring the splutterings coming from behind him.

"Once done, this cannot be undone." The estate lawyer was pale with the effort of making sure that his young client was aware of what he was doing.

"Look," Titus said, waving his father's fountain pen for emphasis, "I don't *want* any more advice, thank you. Please, could you keep quiet—or I'm going to sign my name wrong. . . ." He bent his head and laboriously scrawled

Titus Andronicus Chimera di Carne Strega Borgia

for the fourth time in ten minutes. Silently, Titus passed the pen to Luciano, who signed his name under that of his son. In a silence broken only by scratching from the pen nib and loud hissing from a particularly resinous log on the fire, they all became aware of the sound of footsteps approaching from downstairs. An urgent knock was immediately followed by Latch's head appearing round the library door, his words tumbling one over the other in his haste to be understood.

"Sir, you've got a prob— There's a— You've got to come downstairs now, right now, or he's going to—"

"Latch?" Luciano slowly unfolded himself from the woodworm-scarred embrace of his chair. "Latch—you're shaking like a leaf—what's the matter?"

The butler's eyes were wild and his hands trembled as he pointed behind him to the open library door. "Please," he begged, "now. He said if I don't bring you both downstairs immediately he'd—he'd—"

"Who? What? He'll what?" Signor Strega-Borgia was by Latch's side, infected by the butler's state of panic and half-aware of Titus getting up from the desk and moving toward the door in slow motion. A shot rang out from downstairs, and Titus heard the unmistakable sound of Pandora screaming.

The front door stood wide open, and consequently the great hall, like the library, was full of opportunistic insects whose attraction toward warmth and light made them unaware of the present dangers inside StregaSchloss. Fiamma d'Infer lay sprawled across the floor at the foot of the grandfather clock, her hand outstretched toward the shadows beneath it, a large bloodstain evidence of the bullet that had torn through her buttock and embedded itself in the wall behind the banister. Regrettably, her chest's slow rise and fall indicated that she was not slain, merely unconscious. Spilling from under the demon's body was a mysterious puddle of neon-pink liquid, which was slowly leaching away into gaps between the flagstones.

Titus took in these details in little memory snapshots—*door/insects/body/clock/luminous pink puddle*—automatically recording each image with scant emotion and even less interest. Since hearing the gunshot, he'd entered a nightmarish zone akin to the still center at the eye of a hurricane. He'd run downstairs behind his father, but he'd felt like an automaton, robotic in his utter lack of thought or feeling. All he could hear was his sister's scream. All he could think of was Pandora.

The door to the drawing room stood ajar and now, coming from behind it, they could hear a weird, high-pitched squeaking sound followed by another gunshot.

Left behind in the library with instructions to phone the police, the lawyer discovered that the telephone line into StregaSchloss had been cut. Replacing the dead receiver, he turned to rake through his briefcase, then remembered that he'd left his cell phone in his car.

Perhaps he'd seen too many movies or had failed to realize that, at fifty-eight, deciding to rappel down the south face of StregaSchloss on the end of a moth-eaten damask curtain was a bad idea. Or maybe the sight of the Borgia money going to such an undeserving home had simply robbed the estate lawyer of the will to live. But miraculously, his rappelling suicide attempt didn't kill him. He was just crawling, bleeding, out of the shrubbery—and checking how many bones he'd fractured in his fall from the library window on the second floor—when a bullet turned him into the subject of a fulsome obituary in the following week's *Daily Telegraph*. Unaware of his posthumous fame, the lawyer spun round once, sank to his knees, and collapsed facedown in a thistle patch.

On the threshold of the drawing room Titus stopped dead, a howl of protest dying in his throat. The smell of explosives assailed his nostrils as he caught sight of his mother in the grip of a man with a face straight out of a nightmare. Aghast, Titus realized that the object the man was pressing against Baci's throat was a snub-nosed gun. Around her, frozen in place, the faces of her family and guests mirrored the terror Baci felt at being held hostage by this hideously maimed assailant. Under hissed instructions from Latch, Titus and Luciano restrained themselves from running to Baci's aid. On a sofa in front of a vase full of blood-red roses, Pandora sat trembling next to Mrs. McLachlan, who held Damp in her arms. A muted growling came from all five beasts, miserably aware that they had failed utterly to guard their family from harm.

"L-L-Lucifer?" Signor Strega-Borgia stammered, barely able to recognize his half brother's ruined face. "Is that really you?"

"Eek," came the terse reply, as Lucifer waved his free hand in Latch's direction. With a whispered apology, the butler approached as instructed, producing a notebook and pen which he handed over.

"What happened to your face . . . your voice?" Luciano quavered.

Ignoring this, Lucifer transferred the gun to his left hand and wedged the notebook open between Baci's shoulder blades, holding it in place with his forearm. Not taking his eyes off the others, he scribbled something in the notebook and passed it back to Latch.

"He says, *Shut up*," Latch read, an impatient movement from Lucifer making the butler return the notebook. Lucifer's yellow eyes didn't once drop to the page but maintained their watch on the room as he scrawled out several lines of instructions. Wearily, Latch received the notebook and, holding it at arm's length, read out Lucifer's demands.

"'*Nobody try anything or the Signora gets it. Luciano, get your brat to transfer the money over to me. I'm taking your wife with me as security until the money reaches my bank account. Any tricks and you'll never see her alive again.*'" The butler's face was strained with the effort of allowing such words to pass his lips. From the other side of the room, Titus spoke, his voice ringing out in the silence.

"You're too late, 'Uncle' Lucifer. You've wasted your time coming here tonight. Earlier this evening we wired the money from Grandfather's estate account into yours. We were just completing the paperwork when you . . . interrupted."

Pandora's head jerked upright. Titus had voluntarily *given* his inheritance to this creep? Uncomprehending, she watched as Lucifer relaxed his grip on Signora Strega-Borgia.

"Phone your bank if you don't believe me," Titus said, adding, "That is, if you haven't already cut the telephone cable into the house."

Still without taking his eyes off anyone, Lucifer produced a cell phone from his breast pocket and pressed a button on its keypad. His eyes darted from Luciano to Titus, back and forth, recognizing in Titus shades of the little half brother he'd spent his childhood torturing. He squeaked something incomprehensible into his phone, but evidently the voice on the other end was used to dealing with a client who not only acted like a rat but spoke like one, too—for Lucifer fell silent, his face reflecting the discovery that half an hour before his nephew had made him one of the wealthiest men on the planet. His lips curled upward in a hideous rictus as he confirmed that Titus had not lied.

However, if he wasn't mistaken, there was a corpse in the shrubbery outside—and a roomful of witnesses to the fact that he'd murdered an innocent stranger, shot a woman in the hall, and threatened the life of his half brother's wife. With a vicious shove, Lucifer pushed Baci to one side, grabbed the notebook from Latch, and began to write with such force that his pen gouged holes in the paper. He flung the notebook on the floor at the butler's feet, and backed away toward the French windows leading onto the lawn. Latch briefly closed his eyes and took a deep breath before reading Lucifer's message.

"He says the money changes nothing. Apparently we're all still dead meat." Latch's voice was utterly flat and devoid of emotion as he read out this death sentence in the silent room, but everyone watching noticed the telltale quivering of the notebook he clutched in his hands. "Apparently," he continued, "while we were dining downstairs, this murderer was crawling around in the attic, wiring up a massive incendiary device—"

Ariadne Ventete gave a small squeal and collapsed into a log basket.

Unperturbed, Latch carried on calmly, "—a device that he intends to detonate by keying in three numbers on his cell phone—"

All adult eyes in the room swiveled to where, with gun in one hand and cell phone in the other, Lucifer had almost reached the open windows.

It was at precisely this moment that Damp, impatiently wriggling in Mrs. McLachlan's arms, reached out to grab one of the roses in the vase behind her nanny. Instinctively, Baci made a lunge for her baby daughter and fell on top of Mrs. McLachlan. Damp lost her balance, clutched a particularly thorn-studded rose stem and, shrieking like a banshee, cast the first major spell of her lifetime.

Sleeping Boaty

or a split second, Pandora thought she'd been blinded. Being plunged from the fading light of the drawing room into pitch darkness left her completely disoriented, but the voices of her mother and Mrs. McLachlan complaining about the lack of light made her realize that whatever had happened and wherever she was, she wasn't alone.

"Oh lord, what *now*?" Baci struggled to disentangle herself from Mrs. McLachlan, her hands touching the reassuring soggy diaper of her youngest daughter. "Damp, is that you, darling?"

"Hold on just a wee moment, madam." The nanny's voice was followed by a faint click. Immediately there was light—admittedly only a mere glimmer—but enough for Pandora to see the faces of her mother, Damp, and Mrs. McLachlan, who appeared to be holding her Alarming Clock in both hands. The nanny's eyes twinkled in the glow from the clock face.

"Such a *useful* clock, this one," she said, stretching out to illuminate the bodies littering the floor around them.

"Oh no!" gasped Signora Strega-Borgia, staring in horror at the still forms of her husband and son, who lay crumpled on the floor.

"They're not dead, madam. They're asleep," Mrs. McLachlan said hastily, patting Baci's arm. "It would appear that your younger daughter has inadvertently cast a spell."

"Sleeping Boaty," Damp agreed, sucking her sore finger as she glared at the vase of blood-red roses. "Nasty yuck flower. Burrrny."

"My *younger*—? Damp? Are you telling me that *Damp* did this?" Baci waved a trembling hand at the sleeping bodies littering the drawing room. "How? She's just a baby. Infants aren't supposed to be able to work magic. It takes a real witch like m-m-m—" Baci's voice trailed off as she grasped the significance of Damp's newfound abilities.

"She's a magus," Mrs. McLachlan said sadly, adding, "The poor wee soul."

Baci gasped, but Pandora disregarded this information.

"Yes, but—where are we? What is this? What time . . . ?"

Mrs. McLachlan looked at her wristwatch, sighed, and then peered hopefully at the mantelpiece clock. "It's round about half-past eight," she said, frowning at Pandora.

"But it's *dark*," complained Signora Strega-Borgia.

"That's part of the spell." Mrs. McLachlan stood up with Damp in her arms and pointed to the door. "Come this way, we have work to do."

Pandora and Mrs. McLachlan left Signora Strega-Borgia and Damp in the candlelit nursery, promising to return soon. Damp sat surrounded by picture books, apparently content to be left reading till summoned. Closing the door behind her, the nanny led the way downstairs. Still sprawled across the hall floor, Fiamma d'Infer snored quietly, a trail of drool puddling on the floor near her mouth, like the antithesis of Sleeping Beauty.

"First things first," Mrs. McLachlan said, returning to the drawing room and picking her way across to the window with the aid of a lit candelabra. The window, like every window and door at StregaSchloss, was now crisscrossed with an impenetrable thicket of briar roses, their wicked thorns forming a barrier to both the passage of daylight and human traffic. They were effectively trapped inside the house by Damp's invocation of the *Sleeping Beauty* spell.

"What time did you say it was?" Pandora said, peering at the girth of one of the briar stems, which was as thick as her wrist.

"If you mean what *year* did I say it was, I didn't. However, since you ask, the *time* is now ten to nine, but the year is still 2002," Mrs. McLachlan snapped, her unfriendly tone of voice causing Pandora's self-control to dissolve in a flood of tears.

"You're still a-a-angry at m-m-meeee," she wailed, collapsing abruptly on the sleeping mound of Knot, and noting distractedly that while the yeti was sleeping due to Damp's enchantment, his fur certainly wasn't. It seethed with lice, the infestation apparently immune to the workings of magic. Pandora was too miserable to care.

"Everyone else in this family gets away with murder except *me*," she howled. "Because of Titus, we've got a psychotic gunman in our midst, Damp gets away with casting spells that plunge us all into some insane version of *Sleeping Beauty*, but when I allow my rats to go loose and accidentally touch your precious alarm clock . . ." She paused to blow her nose on the slumbering Knot, allowing the yeti's unhygienic arm to flop back onto the floor, as with a deep sniff she continued, "The only one in this whole household who understands me is Tarantella, and she's—she's—" Reminded of the little injured body she'd tucked up in her doll's house, Pandora's face crumpled. This time, however, she found herself wrapped in Mrs. McLachlan's warm arms—held in an embrace within which Pandora realized that she was not only loved, but forgiven.

"Och, pet," the nanny murmured, "I'm far angrier with myself than with you. . . . I should have kept that alarm clock locked up, out of sight. You were just being naturally curious, but I was being utterly stupid." Mrs. McLachlan produced a clean handkerchief from her pocket and passed it over.

"But . . . could we use it?" Pandora brightened, suddenly struck with the possibility of helping Tarantella. "Your clock— could we go backward in time? To just before when Tarantella lost her leg? We could stop it from happening—"

Mrs. McLachlan took both of Pandora's hands in hers and drew a deep breath. "Child—you've just demonstrated the colossal danger of using the Alarming Clock. The answer to your question is no. No. Never. We cannot *ever* change the past, no matter how much we may wish to. We mustn't even allow our thoughts to stray in that direction, especially when we have the means to revisit the past in our possession. Can you understand what a perilous thing this clock is?" Pandora's puzzled expression drove Mrs. McLachlan to continue, "Try and think of it like this: if by using the clock, you could go back in time and undo one of the biggest evils of the past, then where would you start?"

With hardly any hesitation, Pandora plucked an atrocity from her sketchy memory of history lessons. "Um . . . Hiroshima. The atomic bomb. I'd try and undo that one."

"And how would you do that?" Mrs. McLachlan prompted. "Stop the inventor of the atomic bomb from being born? But how would you propose to do that? Cause his mother to have a fatal accident before his birth? Smother him in his crib?"

"NO!" Pandora was outraged. "That would be *murder*."

"Some would say an *insignificant* act of murder compared with the destruction wreaked by his invention. Let's try another scenario: perhaps you could sabotage the bomb, cause it to fall harmlessly into the sea instead of in the middle of a Japanese city?"

"Yes, that's a much better idea, but—" Pandora hesitated.

"Exactly. But. *But*, in a few years' time, the people who rely on that sea for their survival would be dying by the thousands, their livelihood contaminated, their unborn children damaged beyond medical repair. And maybe—who knows?—one of those children, but for the bomb that fell in the sea, might have grown up to become the greatest peacemaker in the history of the planet. What appears to be a simple black-and-white puzzle is, in reality, a minefield etched in varying shades of gray. What we would call a moral labyrinth."

"Um . . . ahhh . . ." To Pandora's annoyance, language was deserting her.

"Listen to me, child. The Alarming Clock is not a plaything. It is a powerful and dangerous tool. It was designed to be used for seeing into the future, and thus to return to the present forewarned. That's exactly what you and your brother did—" The nanny held up her hands to forestall Pandora's attempt to deny Titus's involvement. "I *know* you both used it, and I'm beginning to wonder if it was something that Titus witnessed with the Alarming Clock that caused him to pass on his inheritance to that thug. A brave attempt to avoid the fate you both foresaw outlined for him. However . . . certain rules of conduct apply to those who use the Alarming Clock, and one of them is always to carry spare batteries."

Pandora looked down at her hands and blushed.

"Another rule," the nanny continued, "is no messing. No tweaking of the past or the future. No minor adjustments. No leaving of litter and no taking of souvenirs. You children have no idea how narrowly you missed destroying everything you love."

"But then why have *you*—?" Pandora's voice was very small and frightened.

"Why have I got the Alarming Clock?" Mrs. McLachlan stood up and extended a hand to help Pandora to her feet. "I needed something to protect you children from that—fiend." She nodded toward the hallway, where Fiamma d'Infer's slumped body was just visible from the drawing room. "I wanted to borrow a shield, but all I could get was an Alarming Clock."

Pandora's mouth opened, and she managed half a question before a frown from Mrs. McLachlan made her halt in midsentence.

"Dear child"—the nanny smiled, shaking her head slowly—"you have the most inquiring mind it has ever been my pleasure to encounter. Most people sleepwalk through their entire lives, their minds deliberately closed to the millions of possibilities open to them. Your parents and your brother are hardly aware of anything that goes on outside the limits of their own heads. But you and Damp are both explorers, your compasses permanently fixed on some distant star—your bags packed, and your little boats gently rocking at anchor—ready at any time to set sail for uncharted territories. For now, think of the Alarming Clock and where it came from as places that aren't on a map. You've heard rumors that they exist, but either they're too far away for your little boat to reach, or the seas are too unpredictable. And thus, for now, you have to wait and dream of a day when you find the map, or build a bigger boat—or even come on board with a more experienced navigator."

Gazing into Mrs. McLachlan's shining eyes, Pandora was reminded of the old chart downstairs in the map room, the one hanging over the mantelpiece with illegible writing and "here beye monsteres" written in the fading script of a long-dead ancestor. Titus hadn't given it a second glance, his attention as ever focused on his computer screen in preference to the larger world beyond his eyes. Mrs. McLachlan picked her way around the sleeping witches to the window where Lucifer lay snoring on the polished floorboards. She bent down and removed the cell phone from his unresisting hand. Pandora watched as Mrs. McLachlan stood up, took aim, and hurled the offending object through a gap in the bramble thicket. The phone flew through the air and plunged with a splash into the mud at the bottom of the moat, giving out a small eruption of bubbles that meant its circuitry had been fatally flooded with moat-water.

"There," the nanny said, dusting her hands and turning back

to face Pandora. "That should do the trick." She reached under Lucifer and retrieved his handgun, engaging the safety switch before tucking the weapon into the waistband of her skirt.

"Why not just get rid of it?" Pandora asked, then lowered her head into her hands in embarrassment. "There I go *again*— another question."

"Because it might come in handy when we wake everybody up," Mrs. McLachlan explained, nudging Lucifer with her foot. "*This* one doesn't understand anything unless it's accompanied by a gun. He's a nuisance, but he's nothing like as dangerous as the demon in the hall. Come on, let's get it over with, shall we?"

Twenty minutes later they emerged, soaked to the skin, from the waters of the moat. Lacking the tools to hack their way through the thorn-studded branches enveloping StregaSchloss, Pandora and Mrs. McLachlan had crawled through the partially flooded tunnels that ran beneath the house like a granite honeycomb, forming a link between the dungeons and the moat. Shivering, they ran across the meadow and halted at the foot of a rowan tree.

"Are you sure this will work?" Pandora peered up at the leafy branches, in some doubt as to whether such a fragile-looking tree could withstand the ferocity of a thwarted demon.

"It's the best I can think of right now." Mrs. McLachlan began to tear rowan branches off the main trunk with an energy that belied her age. "And with a hefty sprinkling of salt, it might afford us some protection."

Carrying Damp, who clutched a dog-eared picture book, Signora Strega-Borgia walked past Fiamma d'Infer with an astounding lack of curiosity as to why the demon resembled nothing so much as an oven-ready turkey. Trussed in a colorful selection of Pandora's tights and scarves, liberally sprinkled with salt, and surrounded by sprigs of greenery, Fiamma looked as if she were lacking only an accompaniment of roast potatoes in order to become the main course of Sunday lunch. Pandora and Mrs. McLachlan followed Baci and Damp into the drawing room, and all four resumed their positions on the sofa in front of the vase of roses.

"Ready?" Mrs. McLachlan paused, smiling broadly at Damp.

"*Now* what?" Signora Strega-Borgia inquired peevishly, wishing her own magic powers were less ineffectual.

"Now we undo the spell," Mrs. McLachlan replied.

"I'm not exactly like the handsome prince in your picture books," Pandora said apologetically, kneeling down beside Titus and smiling up at Damp. The little girl watched her big sister bend down over her big brother and clapped her hands in delight as Pandora planted a smacking kiss right on Titus's lips. To Mrs. McLachlan's amusement, Pandora grimaced, then swiftly wiped her mouth with the back of her hand.

Titus's eyes flickered as he woke up, peering blearily at his sister. "Eughhh," he remarked pleasantly, rolling over and sitting up. Around him, the waking witches were doing the same, sleepy and bewildered, but immediately snapping back to full consciousness as Lucifer roared in outrage at the thwarting of his plan.

"EEEK SQUEE URK," he bawled, raking through his pockets in disbelief.

"Your phone has gone, Mr. Borgia," Mrs. McLachlan informed him, crossing the room with Lucifer's Beretta held firmly in one hand. "And unless you wish to join it at the bottom of the moat, I suggest you make your farewells and depart."

"Eek?" Lucifer peered at the nanny in some confusion.

"I have your gun here, so don't waste your time looking for it. You've got what you came for, so kindly don't be so ill-mannered as to outstay your welcome—" Mrs. McLachlan's tone was breezy, brushing off the astonished gangster as if he posed no more threat than a housefly.

Lucifer gaped, his little pink eyes narrowing as he processed this information. For the first time in his life, he realized he'd met his equal. Snatching his notebook and pen, he rapidly scribbled something, tore the page out, and passed it to Mrs. McLachlan. Without a squeak of good-bye, Don Lucifer di S'Embowelli Borgia turned and walked out through the open windows.

In the stunned silence that followed, they could all hear his measured tread fading away down the drive. Pandora bit her lip and tried to restrain herself from asking what he'd written in his note to Mrs. McLachlan. Titus closed his eyes and hoped he hadn't just condemned his uncle to death by passing on the inheritance, and Signor Luciano Strega-Borgia gave silent thanks for his family's continued survival.

From the hall came an enraged shriek, as Fiamma found herself trussed like a turkey.

"What on earth?" Luciano's head jerked upward as ear-splitting screams echoed round the hall, accompanied by roars so powerful that the floorboards vibrated. Tendrils of yellow fog began to curl round the door to the hall, and the temperature plummeted within the drawing room. The twilit sky outside the windows turned to night, then day, causing the hands on the mantelpiece clock to describe such a rapid orbit that they glowed red-hot, as Fiamma demonstrated the ease with which she could manipulate time itself. As if to underscore this, the grandfather clock, which had stood ticking erratically in the hall for centuries, exploded in a hail of glass and wood, its whirling pendulum spinning into the drawing room and missing Damp by a hair. Ffup snatched Nestor up in her arms as howls of demonic laughter echoed around the hall.

Titus paled. He knew that Fiamma was coming for him and Damp. He turned to Mrs. McLachlan and realized with a sickening jolt that she was every bit as petrified as he was.

"Oh *dear,*" the nanny whispered, aware that rowan branches and salt were about as effective against this demon as bows and arrows against an armored tank. The noise from the hall swelled and grew, causing floorboards in the drawing room to break free of the nails that held them and bang up and down underfoot.

"Stand clear," Black Douglas commanded, pushing his way past till he stood first in line at the doorway. "Let me deal with this," and before anyone could stop him, he slipped round the door and vanished into the hall.

Kraken Kin

The first living thing the Sleeper encountered after leaving the loch to answer the distress call of his kin was a strange squeaking thing fleeing along the track. Unable to outrun the vast Sleeper, the squeaking thing had collapsed to its knees, tears rolling down its ruined face as it attempted, he assumed, to beg for mercy. Bending down to give it a good sniff, the Sleeper decided to let it go. For one thing, it appeared to have done something rather unpleasant in its pants, and for another he'd always hated snacking on human flesh—its fatty consistency disagreeing mightily with his digestion.

Turning his back on the gibbering Lucifer di S'Embowelli Borgia, the Sleeper resumed his undulating progress toward StregaSchloss. The meadow presented him with few problems, its grassy sward parting beneath his body like water, but by the time he'd crossed the drive, his tender underbelly was studded with painful little chips of rose quartz, and he was in no mood to be trifled with. The Sleeper barreled through the front door of StregaSchloss, slithered across the hall, and, hearing noises coming from the drawing room, barged right in.

Holding Damp in her arms, Mrs. McLachlan realized that her only remaining option was to save herself and the little girl. Titus lay on the floor, his eyes open, his chest barely moving. Fiamma d'Infer stood astride him, hunched and waiting for the boy's soul to emerge on its final journey. A ring of green flame surrounded them, forming a barrier that nothing human could cross. First Luciano, then Baci, had tried to rescue their son, and both had been flung aside as they attempted to break through the circle of fire. Fiamma had assumed her true shape, casting off her human disguise like a snakeskin, and causing some of the witches to faint in terror at what was revealed beneath. Discarded socks, scarves, and rowan branches were embedded in the ceiling, witness to the force with which the demon had shed the ties that bound it.

And Pandora? Mrs. McLachlan's mind reeled. Pandora had disappeared completely. One minute she'd been there, trying to shield Titus with her own body, and then. . . . Crushed by her failure to protect all those she had loved, Mrs. McLachlan found her face wet with tears.

"Och no, wee lassie," she whispered. "I won't let the same thing happen to you. . . ." She hugged Damp tight, giving one last silent plea for some form of divine intercession. She was on the point of pressing the button on her Alarming Clock when help came from a most unlikely source.

"YOU!" roared a voice. "You're the one who knifed ma wee

son. Dinnae deny it, you vicious wee dod of pond-life—I can smell ma wee son's blood all over you!"

Mrs. McLachlan's hand paused on the button, her heart hammering in her chest.

"Dadda-Dadda-Dadda," Nestor squeaked, the unaccustomed words falling from his mouth and causing Ffup to peer at her infant son in some puzzlement.

"Hang oan, son," the voice commanded as an immense darkness extinguished the ring of flames and arrowed straight for Fiamma d'Infer.

There was a ghastly clotted gargling sound as the demon found itself engulfed in coils of oily black.

"Och, dinnae put up a fight, you," the voice continued, effortlessly squeezing the life from its prey. A high-pitched scream emerged from the demon's crushed throat as it shape-shifted from demon to witch, then back again, in an attempt to avoid its fate. To Mrs. McLachlan's relief, the black coils merely tightened their grip, squeezing and suffocating until—with a last bellow of rage—the demon expired, with a puff of vile-smelling smoke erupting from its mouth. Titus closed his eyes, curled into a ball, and began to weep, oblivious to the legendary beast that stood over him, the corpse of Fiamma d'Infer clutched in its fatal embrace. Signor and Signora Strega-Borgia knelt by his side, their arms wrapped round their son, giving and drawing scant comfort from the embrace. In between howls, Mrs. McLachlan heard Titus call his lost sister's name, as if by doing so he could turn back the clock. Damp wriggled out of her nanny's arms and wobbled across to fling herself on top of her brother.

"Panda," she said, her childish abbreviation of Pandora's name redoubling Titus's anguish. "Pandalina," Damp added, repeating this made-up word with increasing determination until she was yelling, "PandaLINA, PANDALINA," in an effort to make Titus sit up and take notice. In frustration at her brother's apparent lack of understanding, Damp thumped him over the head with her picture book.

"PAN-DA-LINA IN THE FLOWER!" she shrieked, stamping her feet in a fury.

Mrs. McLachlan's mouth fell open. Damp dropped her picture book on the floor and crawled quickly toward her.

"Damp?" Mrs. McLachlan whispered. "Did you put Pandora in the flower?"

The little girl nodded. At last, her expression seemed to say, *someone* with a brain round here.

"Like Thumbelina?"

"*Panda*-lina," Damp corrected, adding, "Nasty yuck flower."

"The roses?" Mrs. McLachlan dove across the room and, hardly daring to breathe, searched through the vase of blood-red flowers till she found what she was looking for. So astounded was she that she didn't notice the vast shape of the Sleeper towering behind her, his expression distinctly unfriendly. Tossing Fiamma's corpse aside, he glared down at Mrs. McLachlan.

"You again?" he said with little evidence of delight. "You're the one that woke me up yon time."

Mrs. McLachlan admitted that yes, regrettably, this was indeed the case.

"And fir whit?" the Sleeper demanded. "To defrost that

squitty wee loch? So you and yer pals could carry oan fishing? Seems like a pretty dodgy excuse for dragging me back frae the land of nod."

Mrs. McLachlan agreed, trying to look as apologetic as possible while shielding the flower vase from the Sleeper's gaze.

Across the room, Ffup could be heard muttering to herself. "What *nerve*. Turns up four months late, no warning, not even a phone call, and does he apologize? I don't *think* so. Doesn't even so much as give me five minutes' grace to brush my wings, slap some moisturizer on my scales. . . . Just turns up, pulps a guest, and demands his parental rights—"

The Sleeper shook his head and swung round to glower at Ffup. "What're you oan about now, wumman?"

Dwarfed by the gigantic beast, Ffup blinked, shifting Nestor's weight to her other hip. "See this wee beastie I've got attached to my side?" she demanded. "This here's your son. And where were you when I was going through the traumas of dragonbirth? Absent, that's where. Where were you when he wouldn't sleep at night? Ditto. Elsewhere. What happened to all those promises you made me last December?"

"Aww, come *oan*, hen . . ." The Sleeper looked around in some embarrassment, aware that certain people in the room were paying close attention to Ffup's tirade.

"Don't you 'come oan, hen' me, you faithless toad," Ffup shrilled inaccurately. "This poor wee baby needs *two* parents, not one. He needs a *father*, not an absent monster whose only claim to fame is for boosting Scotland's tourist trade with rare appearances in Loch Ness. I mean, it's not even as if you've got a *proper* job. Itinerant monster with special responsibilities for entertaining visiting Americans? And—" She paused, waiting till she had everyone's attention before delivering her parting shot. "—If you think your son's going to be proud to call his daddy 'Nessie,' you can think again." With a snort, Ffup turned on her heel and stalked out of the drawing room, with Nestor clinging to her hip. Moments later they could all hear the dungeon door clanging shut.

Sab clambered down from his perch on the pelmet and patted one of the Sleeper's black coils. "Don't worry," he said, in a blokeish, beast-to-beast kind of way. "She'll get over it. Bit highly strung right now—"

The Sleeper groaned. He exhaled and rolled his eyes, clearly not used to being lambasted by outraged females. "It's jist—" He groped for words. "Ochhh . . . I'm no' very guid at aw that soppy stuff. I'm weel oot of practice. I mean—it's been centuries since I last—"

"Yes, yes. Fine. We quite understand." Sab shuddered. "Spare us the details. My advice is: let her get a good night's sleep, then—" The griffin leant close and began to whisper in the giant beast's ear.

Collapsed on sofas, chairs, and carpets, the family and guests paid little attention. Their more pressing concerns lay with the missing Pandora, the sobbing Titus, and the fate of Black Douglas. Carefully avoiding Fiamma's remains, Mrs. McLachlan crouched down beside Titus, still being comforted by his parents and Damp.

"My dears," she began. Their tragic faces turned toward her, aware that, for some reason, the nanny was beaming from ear to ear. Mrs. McLachlan held a dark red rose in her hands, its velvet petals curled around a tiny creature. . . .

Signora Strega-Borgia blinked.

. . . a tiny creature that waved and squeaked, its voice too wee to be heard . . .

Titus's eyes grew large.

. . . a tiny creature that slapped its forehead in apparent frustration at being unable to make itself heard . . .

Signor Strega-Borgia burst into tears of relief, and at last they could all hear Pandora's voice, admittedly on the far side of audibility, despite the fact that she was yelling at the top of her tiny lungs,

"GET ME OUT OF HERE—THIS ROSE IS *FULL* OF BUGS!"

"D'you promise not to eat me?"

"How many times do I have to go through this? Oh, *sigh*. Read my lips, girl. I don't do humans. Flies, yes—gnats, always—daddy longlegs, occasionally—and wasps, well—only when they're sun-dried. Now move over, you're hogging my quilt."

"*Your* quilt? Whose doll's house d'you think this is?"

"The *doll's*, stupid," Tarantella replied, grabbing the tiny eiderdown with one leg and hauling it over herself. Pandora lay beside her, gazing in amazement at her beloved tarantula. This is decidedly weird, she thought. Being turned into a fairy-tale character to do battle with gigantic aphids in a rose the size of a circus tent was bizarre, but being tucked up in bed in your own doll's house—only to discover that you're half the size of your favorite spider was, to be honest, more than a little upsetting.

Titus's gigantic head came into view. "I'm GOING to CLOSE

the DOOR NOWW," he bawled. "BUT MRS. McLACHLAN will be back in an HOUR. SHE says to TRY and GET SOME SLEEP. . . ."

"Does he *have* to roar?" Pandora moaned, deafened by her brother's onslaught on her eardrums.

Tarantella removed a hairy leg from each ear. "You sound like that, too," she said. "Normally. All humans roar. They breathe gales and typhoons as well. And while we're on the subject of human excess, when you lot walk around—it's like an earthquake. I can hear you crashing around in the kitchen even when I'm several floors upstairs in my attic. Get used to it, kid. This is life as we know it in the arachnid-zone."

"Don't you feel scared?" Pandora asked, wincing as Titus whistled tunelessly, his thunderous footsteps receding as he headed downstairs.

"I'm used to being scared," Tarantella muttered. "It's the price I pay for cohabiting with humans, not to mention their illiterate rodents and homicidal guest-demons."

"I'm so sorry about your poor leg."

"Not half as sorry as I am." The tarantula gazed into the middle distance. "I only wish *I'd* been able to get my revenge. Now the demon is dead, there's little chance of that happening. . . ."

Had she but known it, Tarantella's vengeful musings were identical to those of Black Douglas. One minute he'd been spectacularly heroic, rushing out into the hall to confront Fiamma, armed with nothing more than his fiddle; only to find himself demonically transmogrified into the principal source of cat-gut violin strings and booted out of the way by the outraged fiend. Now he sat warming himself by the range, keeping a watchful eye on his colleagues as they attempted to return him to a human form. To pass the time, Black Douglas washed himself from paws to tail, pausing to spit as he tasted the sulfurous traces Fiamma had left in his fur. Signora Strega-Borgia peered at him in revolted fascination as Black Douglas expertly tucked one leg behind his head and applied himself to the task of laundering his bottom.

"Douglasssss," she demurred, closing her eyes in embarrassment, "could you please hold off from doing that until we change you back?"

"Oh yeah? And when's that going to be?" he inquired between licks, his peevish voice emerging as unintelligible yowls that prompted Signora Strega-Borgia to crouch down and try to pick him up. Hissing, he sprang backward and bolted through her legs, heading for the quiet of the pantry, where a saucer of milk awaited him. At the kitchen table Hecate Brinstone sighed, rubbing her eyes and closing the vast grimoire in front of her.

"No luck?" Signora Strega-Borgia leafed through one of her spelling notebooks.

"The trouble is, I don't know what kind of spell Fiamma used on him," Heck admitted. "If I knew *that*, then it would be a fairly simple matter to look it up and undo it. But, as things stand, it might be safer to leave him as a cat—"

From the safety of the china cupboard, Terminus was not inclined to agree. Black Douglas might have been a cat for only a short while, but already he'd demonstrated just how quickly he'd adapted to his altered status. In the space of ten minutes the enraged pussy had shredded the silk cover of a chaise in the drawing room, peed in a corner of Signora Strega-Borgia's bedroom, clawed Knot to ribbons when the yeti had ill-advisedly sniffed Black Douglas's intriguingly perfumed backside, and even now was spraying the pantry in an attempt to mark out his territory. To Terminus's relief, Signora Strega-Borgia stood up and produced a wand from the drawer of the kitchen table.

"I think I might have just the enchantment for our poor colleague," she said, crossing the kitchen to the pantry, where she crouched down, feeling faintly foolish. "Here, puss puss puss. . . . Here, kitty kitty kitty . . ."

Prowling along the topmost shelf in between fossilized jars of jam, Black Douglas hissed. "What are you on about *now*? What's this *puss* nonsense? Give me a break—" And then, his yellow eyes widening in alarm, he realized that Baci was waving a wand in his direction. He stiffened, his fur sticking straight out from his body. Baci? The most incompetent witch in the history of the institute? Casting a spell? With a terrified *meow*, Black Douglas launched both himself and several jars of jam into midair, in the faint hope he might thus be able to avoid being the target of one of Baci's dire misspellings.

"Vexing hex be thus undone—cat to mate to man become."

Baci gasped, ducking to avoid the lethal hail of jam jars crashing down from the top shelf. This spell would, for once, have been perfect had it not been for a brief lapse of attention due to falling preserves. Baci's second stanza became a garbled *"c-a-tomato man become"* as, to her horror, Black Douglas turned into the main ingredient of pasta sauce and hit the floor with a loud *splattt*, scattering tomato seeds and pulp everywhere. Mercifully for Baci, consciousness left her at this point, and she slid to the floor in a faint.

Scissors, Paper, Stone

atch swept the splintered remains of the grandfather clock into a tidy pile and tried not to eavesdrop on Signor Strega-Borgia's one-sided telephone conversation with the local police.

"He's in the border. . . . No, the *herbaceous* border, not the Scottish Borders . . . Good heavens, Constable, is this so hard to understand? There is a corpse lying in my flower bed."

There was a pause while Signor Strega-Borgia rolled his eyes and drummed his fingers on the hall table. Latch worked on, the pile of broken glass and wood growing by the minute. Then the butler paused, his eye caught by something glinting in the dust.

"Yes. Good evening, Inspector." Signor Strega-Borgia drew a deep breath and began again. "*As* I explained to your colleague, I'm phoning to report a murder. . . . No. NO! Not my *mother,* a murr-derr, as in 'death by unlawful killing.'"

Latch bent down, his attention focused on the shiny crystal

in front of him. Wonderingly, he reached out to pick it up, just as Mrs. McLachlan emerged from the kitchen, the freshly restored cat-edition of Black Douglas yowling under one arm.

"Behave, you rogue," she cautioned, adding, "And just count your blessings we didn't simmer you into a sauce for tomorrow's lunch."

Subdued by this reference to his brief incarnation as a tomato, Black Douglas fell into a silent sulk, even allowing the butler to stroke his glossy fur.

"I've found something odd," Latch said, pointing to the crystal at his feet. "I wonder if it was part of the grandfather clock? Or maybe one of the crystals from the chandelier that shattered last New Year? I seem to recall sweeping up endless bits of broken glass afterward—I must have missed this one."

Mrs. McLachlan peered at the egg-sized stone. A faint alarm bell sounded in her memory. Hadn't Pandora mentioned something about seeing a big diamond during one of her illegal forays with the Alarming Clock? And once Titus had realized that Fiamma was indeed as dead as one could wish for, he'd told her that the demon had been hunting for a thing called a Chronostone. . . .

"I wonder," the nanny said, bending down to pick it up. "Latch, I'm just going to look this up in the library. If it's what I think it is, we're in great danger—"

"Again?" The butler paled. "How much worse can it get? We've had the Mafia dropping in for coffee, we've been unknowingly extending full-on hospitality to a colleague of Satan's and, to cap it all, the Loch Ness Monster just gatecrashed our wee gathering. . . ." He heaved a sigh and picked up the broom to resume sweeping. "All that's missing now is an alien takeover bid," he observed to Signor Strega-Borgia, who'd tucked the phone under his chin and was doodling on the back of the telephone directory.

Mrs. McLachlan frowned in exasperation. Latch simply had no idea what he was talking about. She suppressed a desire to inform him that the forces she suspected would now be coming for the Chronostone made Fiamma look about as dangerous as a snail. Tucking the crystal in her pocket, Mrs. McLachlan carried Black Douglas upstairs to Pandora's bedroom.

Signora Strega-Borgia's eyelids fluttered open—she focused blearily on the heads bending over her, their eyes full of concern, their combined breath hot and faintly fishy.

"Welcome back," Tock whispered, his claws embedded in Signora Strega-Borgia's pillow.

"We've been told to guard you and Damp," Sab explained, aware that his mistress might be somewhat peeved at the presence of all five beasts in her bedroom. Wishing to assure her that they were there on a legitimate errand, he added, "Your husband said to tell you to stay here while he deals with the police."

Beyond the windows, dawn was breaking over Lochnagargoyle, and Baci checked her alarm clock, dimly aware that she must have been unconscious for hours.

"What?" she croaked. "Where's Black Douglas?" recalling with shame her part in turning her guest into a squashed mess on the pantry floor. This thought made her stomach roll in protest; with a desolate moan, she fell out of bed, ran for the bathroom, and made it to the sink just in time.

Outside the door the beasts discussed her abrupt departure.

"I *had* a bath last week," Knot said defensively. "I'm sure it's not my smell that's done it—"

"I think she's eaten something disagreeable," Sab decided. "She did this yesterday as well."

"What, a Technicolor yawn?" Ffup said, seeking greater clarity. "She *hueyed*? Gave it big rrrralfs? Up-chukkies?"

Tock clamped his front paws over his ears with a small moan. "Enough," he whispered. "We get the point. Yes. She threw up on the front step yesterday."

Behind the door, Signora Strega-Borgia gave an all-too audible demonstration of this newfound skill.

"In the morning?" Ffup persisted, a wistful smile playing across her mouth.

"I fail to see where this is leading," Sab protested, leaping back from the bathroom door as Signora Strega-Borgia emerged, pale and wobbly, tottering across the floor to collapse facedown on the bed.

Ffup folded her wings carefully behind her back with a smirk. "Well, well, well—," she said, grinning widely. "Who'd've thought it?"

Signor Strega-Borgia's head appeared round the door, his anxious expression giving way to one of relief when he saw his wife was awake.

"Luciano . . . ," she groaned. "How is Pandora? And what's happened with Black Douglas? And the police? Oh heck, it's all such a *mess,* and I feel so dreadful—"

"It'll pass," Ffup muttered, adding darkly, "But you can kiss good-bye to nights of unbroken sleep."

Ignoring the dragon, Luciano hurried to his wife's side. "Don't worry—Pandora is fine. So is Black Douglas. The police have taken that poor lawyer off to the morgue. And they've put out a search warrant for Lucifer, alerted airports and all points of exit from the country, and . . . You know, Baci, you don't *look* too dreadful. In fact, you look—um . . ."

"Radiant," whispered Ffup in Sab's ear. "Bet you he says 'radiant.'"

"Radiant," Signor Strega-Borgia decided.

Baci burst into tears and fled to the bathroom, leaving Luciano to turn to the beasts in some confusion. Embarrassed, they turned away, except for Ffup, who drew Signor Strega-Borgia to one side and whispered something that caused him to sit down abruptly on the floor, a stunned expression on his face, his mouth opening and shutting, but with no words coming out.

"What are you up to?" Sab demanded, tapping Ffup on the shoulder. "What *is* going on?"

"It's a girl thing, pet," the dragon murmured, so condescendingly that Sab had to grit his teeth to stop himself from shaking her as she added, "Trust me, you wouldn't underst— Ow, ow, don't *do* that, you big brute." Ffup bolted from the bedroom and fled down the corridor, pursued by Sab. Their raised voices faded into the distance . . . and the air filled with birdsong, greeting the birth of a new day.

Mrs. McLachlan hadn't actually *lied* to Latch when she said she was going to the library; but, on reflection, she decided that she had perhaps been a mite economical with the truth. With

Pandora's tiny body safely stowed away in a pocket and the cat under one arm, she set off at once. Regretfully, the journey to the library didn't agree with Black Douglas, who dug all his claws into Mrs. McLachlan's flying rug and yowled his protest at such a brutal form of transportation. On arrival at their destination he shot through the library door and sprayed everything within range, including the librarian, until he calmed down enough to realize he wasn't under attack. Now he sat on guard beside the library fire, alert and suspicious, eavesdropping on Mrs. McLachlan and the centaur, Alpha.

"Where's the clock?" the librarian demanded. "I can't possibly allow you to withdraw *anything* else until you return it to the library."

Mrs. McLachlan closed her eyes in despair. In her haste to remove the Chronostone from StregaSchloss, she'd completely forgotten about the Alarming Clock.

"Look . . . ," she began, removing the crystal from her pocket and placing it on the countertop between Alpha and herself. "Never mind about the clock. I've brought you this thing, which, I think you'll agree, is a wee bit more important." She watched with satisfaction as the little centaur bent over the stone and gave an admiring whistle.

"Oh my . . . ," he breathed, coming round the counter to stand beside the nanny. "Is this what I think it is?"

"I think so," Mrs. McLachlan said softly. "The Pericola d'Illuminem—the Perilous Light—" She drew a deep breath. "On the other hand, it might just be a fabulously valuable diamond, in which case I'd better put it back where I found it."

"Do you know *how long* this has been missing?" The librarian shook his head in amazement. "I can't believe it's actually here, in front of me . . . after all this time."

"Can you verify that it's the real thing?" Mrs. McLachlan tried not to betray her sense that time was running out. She was positive that Fiamma had been only the first emissary from Hades—her successor or successors might not prove so easy to subdue.

"May I?" The librarian picked up the crystal and gazed into its luminous depths. "I just want to be able to tell my grandchildren that I held it in my hands, just once . . . improve their opinion of librarians no end—"

"Actually, I'm in a bit of a hurry." Mrs. McLachlan placed Pandora on the countertop. "This wee thing needs to go home, preferably normal size, and that blasted cat glaring at us from the other side of the room needs to be turned back into a human."

"Let me get you a Quikunpik, then I'll run a test on the stone." Reverently placing the crystal on the counter, the librarian headed to the display cases to find what he needed.

"HE'S STARK NAKED!" Pandora yelled, trying to make her tiny voice heard. "What is he? And where are we? How did we get here?"

Mrs. McLachlan smiled wearily. Pandora had shrunk, but her appetite for questions certainly hadn't. The centaur returned with a small tool, which he passed to the nanny. Holding its coiled rubber handle firmly in one hand, she ran the other end of the device across the ball of her thumb.

"For a Quikunpik, it's extremely sharp," she murmured, examining the tiny pair of silvery scissors at the other end of what looked like an insulated wand.

"All the better to sever enchantments." The librarian removed his wristwatch and placed it on the counter next to the Chronostone. Removing a set of cloth-wrapped watchmaker's tools from a drawer, he selected a tiny screwdriver and used this to undo the back of his watch. "Better get the child out of harm's way," he advised, indicating where Pandora stood, watching him in apparent fascination.

"Hold verrrry still, dear," Mrs. McLachlan advised, bringing the business end of the Quikunpik uncomfortably close to Pandora's head and making several swift cutting motions in the air.

"WHAT IS THAT THING? WHAT ARE YOU DOING? IS IT AS DANGEROUS AS IT LOOKS?" she squeaked, trying not to flinch as the nanny painstakingly snipped at something invisible near Pandora's stomach.

"Nearly there," Mrs. McLachlan muttered, her eyes narrowed in concentration. *Snip, snip, sneck* went the Quikunpik, its silvery scissor-head flashing dangerously close to Pandora's eyes.

"NO!" the librarian yelled. "Watch *out!*"

There was a final glittery *snick* from the Quikunpik, and Pandora found herself falling off the countertop, her flailing arms causing the Chronostone to roll onto the librarian's wristwatch. Mrs. McLachlan threw herself full-length on top of Pandora as, with a tremendous cacophony of clanging bells, ringing alarms, and chiming clocks, the Chronostone proved beyond a doubt that it was indeed the genuine article. The countertop imploded in a deafening crash of shattered glass and the Chronostone fell to the floor, bounced across the flagstones, and rolled across to where—ears flattened against his skull—Black Douglas was doing a passable imitation of an enraged lavatory brush. Of the wristwatch, nothing remained save a lump of fused metal and glass.

"Wow . . . ," Pandora breathed, struggling out from under Mrs. McLachlan. "What on earth—?"

"Um . . . yes," the librarian bleated, picking himself up from where he'd been flung across the room. "I guess it's the real thing then," he added reproachfully, gazing around at the wreckage.

"But it *ate* your watch," Pandora said.

"Not exactly." The librarian trotted across to the fireplace and, ignoring the malevolent hissing coming from Black Douglas, picked up the Chronostone. "What you saw was it reabsorbing the time-chip in my watch. All the library chronometers have a tiny bit of the original crystal embedded in their Moebius drive."

"What, like the Alarming Clock?" Pandora turned to Mrs. McLachlan for confirmation.

"Oh *lord*," the nanny muttered. "Drop me right in it, why don't you?"

The centaur frowned. "This child has *seen* the Alarming Clock?"

"Actually, I've used it," Pandora admitted.

"I can explain . . . ," Mrs. McLachlan began, but to her astonishment, rather than imposing a massive fine for unauthorized use of library materials—or even banishing her from the library for all time—the librarian was trotting across to his computer and beginning to type.

"Name?" he barked.

"Flo-Flora Mc—"

"Not *you*. The child." The librarian rolled his eyes.

"Pandora Strega-Borgia," Pandora whispered.

"Age?"

"Ten and three-quarters."

"Address?"

Pandora was about to reply when Mrs. McLachlan interrupted.

"You're *enrolling* her?"

The librarian turned round from the screen. "Look," he said kindly, "you've returned the most precious thing the library has ever had in its possession. D'you have any idea how long the Pericola d'Illuminem has been 'missing'? We'd completely given up hope of it being returned. Then you turn up, late as usual, with the stone lying casually at the bottom of your pocket. As far as I'm concerned, from today onward you can borrow anything you like, keep it for as long as you want, and I'll enroll anyone you suggest as a member. Er, d'you want me to start with the cat?"

Mrs. McLachlan burst out laughing. "I think *not* the cat. I'd better sort him out and return home before we're missed. But—does this mean the Chronostone is safe? No more psychotic demons coming out of the woodwork? No more dragons claiming it was their missing earring?"

"Absolutely." The librarian turned back to gaze at his screen. "Not only is it safe, it's *never* going out on loan ever again. Now"—he patted Pandora's arm—"if you'll excuse us? Your address, please?"

Water Babies

Sitting on the jetty, Titus watched dawn break over Lochnagargoyle. The surface of the loch was pitted with ripples as the Sleeper performed his morning ablutions under Titus's watchful gaze.

"Is that better?" the beast roared, peering dubiously at a small sapling he'd been using to brush his teeth.

"Show me. Say *ahhhhhh*," Titus said, suppressing a scream as the beast revealed a vast acreage of greenish fangs for his inspection. "Pretty good. I think that despite herself, Ffup'll be impressed. Now you have to practice what you're going to say to her."

The Sleeper groaned. "Dae I have to? It's aw soppy stuff. . . ." A faint blush crept across his scales, turning his vast head an alarming shade of purple. Realizing there was to be no escape, he cleared his throat, hawked spectacularly into the loch, and then mumbled, "I . . . I missed you, hen—"

"*Not* hen. She's a *dragon*," Titus hissed.

"I missed you, dragon . . . I dreamt aboot you . . . um . . . I couldn't think aboot onything else. . . . I l— Ah *l*—*l*— Och *no*. I cannae dae it withoot feeling like a right numpty," and coiling himself up into something that resembled a house-sized pretzel, the Sleeper sank below the surface of the loch, the waters hissing as they closed over the beast's flushed cheeks.

Titus waited till the loch was silent and still, then took the Alarming Clock out of his pocket. I'm only borrowing it for a moment, he reminded himself—in an attempt to justify the fact that he'd sneaked into Mrs. McLachlan's bedroom and snatched the device, fully aware that the nanny would go ballistic if she found out. Titus had been feeling positively saintly since giving his inheritance away. Saintly and utterly, dismally, irrevocably skint. No Aston Martins for this chap, he reminded himself. However, the loss of all those tainted millions seemed like a small price to pay if it meant that he wasn't going to die—fat, ugly, and unloved—at the relatively tender age of forty-two. He needed to check, to be absolutely sure that this was indeed the case. And so, taking a deep breath, he closed his eyes and pushed the button.

Hardly daring to inhale, he opened his eyes to find a small boy staring down at him.

"Where did you appear from?" the child gasped, backing away in alarm.

"Um . . . ah . . . I've just arrived. Don't panic—" Titus reached out to reassure the little boy, but his gesture had the opposite effect. With a wail, the child fled along the jetty, his voice raised in a howl of terror, screaming, "Flora! FLORA! THERE'S A BIG BOY ON OUR BEACH!"

I'm going to have to be quick, Titus resolved, giving chase.

He hurtled through the brambles, skirted the edge of the meadow, and plunged into the shade beneath the rhododendrons, their thick foliage shielding him from the house. StregaSchloss glowed pink in the early-morning light, its continued existence the source of considerable relief to Titus. No glass monstrosity, he noted, and no flash cars lined up on the drive, either. An elderly woman appeared at the front door, the wailing child in her arms. Titus frowned, unable to see clearly at this distance who she might be, but nevertheless sure that it couldn't be Flora McLachlan. Titus crept silently through the rhododendrons until he reached a vantage point from which he shamelessly eavesdropped. In the still air, the voices from the front door carried perfectly.

"Show me where you saw the man."

"Not a man. A big boy," the child insisted.

"A big boy, is it now? Och . . . you're talking nonsense. There's no big boys awake yet. They're all asleep upstairs."

At this, the child's wails redoubled and the elderly lady set him down firmly on the steps. "That's enough, pet," she said, hands on hips. "Hush now—you'll wake the house with your racket. . . ."

Another figure appeared at the front door, dressed in a sensible tweed skirt. The child wriggled out of the elderly lady's grasp and flung himself on this new arrival, who commented mildly, "Och, you poor wee chook."

Hearing the unexpectedly familiar voice, Titus leaned forward to peer through the bushes. His mind reeled in denial. Mrs. McLachlan? Still there? She must be *ancient*.

"Don't you worry, pet," the nanny soothed. "I've made some

pancakes for your breakfast and there are some of Grandpa's favorite raspberry muffins ready to come out of the oven—"

Grandpa? Raspberry muffins? Titus clutched a rhododendron trunk for support. This was all too bizarre, he decided—but his traitorous stomach growled in happy recognition at the mention of its favorite food.

"Away you go back down to the loch, and let Grandpa know his breakfast's getting cold," Mrs. McLachlan continued, turning round and disappearing into the shadows inside the house. Obediently, the little boy ran back across the meadow, all fear forgotten in his haste to call his grandfather inside for muffins. Titus's stomach growled again. The elderly lady on the doorstep remained standing, apparently having a senior moment as she talked to herself.

"He's as obsessed about fishing as he used to be with those computer things," she observed, apparently addressing the stone griffin that still graced the entrance to StregaSchloss. "And *muffins* . . . I would have thought he would be sick of them by now." She bent down, stretching out a hand to something too small for Titus to see.

Just then it all fell into place in his head. The ancient granny on the doorstep was Pandora, a fact he confirmed when a familiarly grumpy voice muttered, "Just because *you're* a geriatric doesn't mean you have to treat *me* as one."

Titus saw a small black fur-ball scuttle up Pandora's arm and cling to her collar as it said helpfully, "D'you know . . . that lipstick . . . does *nothing* for you."

That could only be Tarantella, Titus thought gloomily, still obnoxious as ever. On the doorstep his wrinkly sister turned to go inside, leaving Titus to debate whether to follow her or not. On reflection *not*, he decided. If discovered, his presence at StregaSchloss would require explanations of such complexity that he doubted his ability to sound anything other than completely insane. However, he *had* to see himself just once in the future flesh before returning. Retracing his steps down to the lochside, he found he was growing more nervous at the prospect. He halted, rubbing his face with clammy hands and breathing heavily as if he'd been running. Through the brambles and scrub oaks that partially blocked his view of the loch, he could hear the child's voice calling for his grandfather.

Apparently the grandfather hadn't heard, for there came the sound of footsteps running along the jetty. Again, the child called, and this time came a distant, deeper voice, raised in warning. The silence was again broken by a harsh overhead squawk from a seagull, and Titus peered through the brambles just in time to see the little boy lose his balance and fall with terrifying slowness into the deep water off the end of the jetty. For a split second that felt like a lifetime, Titus froze, caught in an agony of indecision. He couldn't swim and had never learned. As he plunged through the brambles, ran across the beach, and hurtled along the jetty, he knew that all he was about to accomplish was two drownings, not one. Such reasoning, sensible as it was, gave him no comfort. Just out of reach—seventy years in the future—his grandchild was drowning and he could do nothing whatsoever to prevent it. Casting around desperately for a branch or a bit of driftwood to hold out for the child to cling to, he realized that he'd forgotten someone.

Ahead of him, out on the loch, came a yell accompanied by a massive splash. Seconds later, Titus saw a bobbing bald head swimming frantically across the gap between a distant rowboat and the ripples marking where the child had fallen in. What the bald swimmer lacked in aquatic finesse he more than made up for in the speed with which he plowed to the rescue. Reaching the ominously calm water by the end of the jetty, the swimmer trod water—ducking his head down in an attempt to see where the child lay beneath the waters of the loch.

"THERE!" Titus yelled, able to see exactly where the child hung suspended, feet tangled in weed and little body horribly still. The swimmer dived downward in such a flurry of bubbles and foam that for one moment, nothing could be seen from above. Then, with a great gush of water, the swimmer broke surface, the child's body in his arms. He made for the jetty, where Titus knelt with arms outstretched to receive the little boy.

In that instant, as their eyes met, there came a gleam of recognition in those of the swimmer. For Titus, it was the strangest sensation to meet his older self, face to face. As he later explained to Pandora, the feeling was like a hammer blow to the chest, driving all breath from his lungs in an involuntary gasp, breath that was replaced by heat and accompanied by a dazzling shimmer at the corners of his vision.

"Wow," Pandora breathed respectfully. "Sounds weird . . . but what about the wee boy?"

"You mean my *grandson*?" Titus said, rolling the words experimentally round his mouth. "He was fine. He threw up spectacular amounts of loch-water, burst into tears, but otherwise he was okay. I must say, though, for an old wrinkly I was the most amazing swimmer . . . and brave? Phwoarrrr. All in all, a real hero of a grandfather."

"And so modest, too," Pandora sighed. "Tell me, though . . . what did he say to you? I mean, what did the heroic wrinkly Titus say to you? He must have wondered who on earth you were, and where you'd sprung from."

"Ah, yes . . . " Titus looked embarrassed. "I had thought he'd say something profound, something about the amazing fact that here I was, a living, breathing version of himself, only several decades younger . . . but instead he said, 'Time you learned to swim, laddie. Ignorance is no excuse,' and then he just turned his back on me and ran back to the house with his— my—oh heck, *our* grandson in his arms. Which brings me to my birthday present."

"Eh?" Pandora frowned. "I fail to see what your birthday has to do with—"

"Swimming lessons," Titus interrupted. "Don't you see? I have to learn how to swim so that . . . well, um, so that I can be a hero like . . . um . . . well, like I'm going to be, so I'd like you to teach me how to swim as a birthday present."

"Fine by me." Pandora put her head to one side and stared at Titus. "But—you know, I'm dead impressed that you gave away all that money. Still, I have wondered if, when it comes to your birthday, aren't you going to wake up and think, What did I do *that* for? All that money?"

"No," Titus said firmly. "Who needs it? Besides—that old guy, me as a grandfather, in a funny sort of way he was seriously cool. Wrinkly and old, but . . . the kind of grandfather I wish we'd had. A grandfather who would have taken us out on his boat, who knew about fishing, and who would probably have arm-wrestled me for the last muffin in the pan. He looked . . . happy, Pandora. He looked as if his life had been pretty good to date and he was looking forward to more of the same. Nothing like that fat, lonely millionaire who lived in the glass house, and probably nothing like the grandfather who left me all his tainted millions. So," he concluded, staring out the window at Lochnagargoyle, "I know which one I'd rather become."

Pandora stood up and reached out a hand to Titus. "Come on, then," she said, hauling him upright. "No time like the present for your present."

"What?" Titus frowned. "Now? Right now? The loch'll be *freezing*. Can't we wait till my proper birthday?"

"No," said Pandora in a manner that made Titus's heart sink. "Get your swimsuit. I'll meet you down by the jetty. Think of these lessons as a bonus, Titus. I've actually already found you the most brilliant birthday present, but you can't have *that* till the day itself."

Pandora headed downstairs, leaving Titus rummaging through his wardrobe, bleakly aware that unless he appeared at the jetty fully dressed, his sister was going to be treated to the sight of him sporting legs hairier than Tarantella's. Praying that Pandora wouldn't tease him about his recent pubertal sproutings, he pulled on a pair of decently baggy shorts, dragged a T-shirt over his head to conceal the dozen or so chest hairs that were his secret pride and joy, and ran downstairs before he could change his mind.

Father of Lies

Arriving back in Hades after his abrupt demise at StregaSchloss, the demon Astoroth was peremptorily debriefed, dumped in the limbo-tank for what felt like eons, and then rudely ejected to face the wrath of the Boss. Following meekly behind a lesser demon, the disgraced Second Minister from the Hadean Executive had plenty of time to consider exactly what form his punishment might take, and to hope fervently that his next incarnation wouldn't be a female one. Their labyrinthine passage through the corridors of Hades had taken even longer than usual, checkpoints and barriers appearing at every turn—each requiring him to fill out endless forms and questionnaires before he could proceed onward toward the upper levels where the Boss had his domain.

With each stop the paperwork grew more finicky and time-consuming; Astoroth was obliged to answer the same series of questions he'd just completed moments before. Moreover, all too keenly aware that he was in deep poo, he couldn't allow his temper to erupt and thus had to endure the leaky ballpoints and poor-quality paper that each set of forms required him to deal with. As soon as he laboriously filled in each of these, they were promptly shredded—unread—as an exercise in complete futility. Finally, after completing a particularly pointless forty-two-page questionnaire printed on what appeared to be gray blotting paper—with a blunt turkey feather dipped in raw sewage—a distant door flew open at the end of the corridor ahead.

A blood-red figure emerged, crooked its finger at Astoroth, and said, "He's in a meeting, but if you'll just come in here and wait, I'll let him know you've arrived."

Astoroth took a deep breath and stepped forward, inhaling the homely smell of hot iron and sulfur that coiled invitingly from behind the open door. The red demon stepped aside to allow access to the Boss's antechambers, then returned to his position behind a large obsidian desk. Ignoring Astoroth, he lowered his eyes to concentrate on a laptop—which, together with a black telephone and a watercooler, constituted the only items of a nonorganic nature in the room. The walls and carpet were made of woven human hair; this, in all its rich tonal and structural variety, gave the bizarre illusion of being trapped inside a giant fur-ball. The transparent watercooler was filled with virulent green liquid and little signs everywhere read

NO ABSTAINING

In obedience to this, the red demon extended a tray on which lay tobacco in all its various forms. Astoroth accepted a small cigar and bent his head to light it at one of the flames that burned continuously in little alcoves round the room.

Coughing gratefully, he squatted on his haunches and waited to be summoned.

After what felt like several weeks, the black telephone rang and Astoroth found himself being ushered into the Presence. On trembling legs he walked through a door into a darkness so thick he could almost chew it.

"KNEEL," came a command, and Astoroth fell to the floor at once.

"GROVEL," the voice continued, adding, "MORE . . . LOWER . . . UP THE SELF-ABASEMENT FACTOR, *WRETCH*."

Taking this last for an instruction, Astoroth obediently retched, gagged, and threw up on the floor. Immediately the lights came on, and he found himself kneeling on a glass floor, beneath which were rumored to burn the eternal fires of the Pit. At a glass table in front of him the Boss pushed his lunch aside with a groan. Snapping his fingers, the First Minister summoned an underling to deal with Astoroth's ejected stomach contents.

"TELL ME, SCUM, WHAT POSSIBLE EXCUSE DO YOU HAVE FOR LOSING MY PRECIOUS CHRONOSTONE?"

"Um." Astoroth swallowed. "Most Awesome Foulness, if you would just give me one more chance, I'll get it back for you. . . . Please, Master of the Pits, Earl of Earwax, allow me, your devoted slave, to perform this one last service for you—" Aware that he was groveling inexcusably, Astoroth grew silent.

"ONE MORE CHANCE?" The Boss considered this as he glared down to where Astoroth knelt, hands clasped in supplication. "ONE MORE CHANCE? YOU'RE FIRED, REMEMBER? THIS IS *NOT* NEGOTIABLE. YOU'RE NO LONGER SECOND MINISTER FOR THE

HADEAN EXECUTIVE. YOU'RE NOT EVEN A MINOR DEMON WITH-OUT PORTFOLIO ANYMORE. YOU'RE LOWER THAN A SUCCUBUS."

"I know," Astoroth whimpered. "I've got the firepower of a soggy match and the bite of a gummy grandmother, but—give me another chance and I'll prove I'm not finished yet. . . . Please? Pleassssse? Pretty please?" He crawled across the floor and prostrated himself.

"OH, VERY WELL . . ." The Boss sighed. "ALTHOUGH, I WARN YOU, YOU'RE GOING TO FIND YOUR NEXT INCARNATION RATHER LESS LUXURIOUS THAN WHAT YOU'VE BECOME ACCUSTOMED TO OF LATE—"

"M-M-Minister?" Astoroth quavered. "D'you mean I'm to be reincarnated as a *servant*? Or as a *woman*, again? Or"—an awful possibility occurred to him—"or as a *child*? Oh please, no, not that—anything but that."

The Boss stood up, wrapping a fur-lined cloak around him-self, apparently unconcerned that the ambient temperature was hot enough to roast meat. He bent over Astoroth, purring in his ear, "DON'T WORRY, SCUM. I WON'T SEND YOU BACK AS A CHILD. YOU WON'T BE A SERVANT, EITHER. NO"—he gave a little mirth-less snicker—"NO, NO. YOU'RE GOING BACK TO POOLS OF COOL WATER, A LIMITLESS FOOD SUPPLY, AND ENOUGH WILLING MEM-BERS OF THE OPPOSITE SEX TO KEEP A RED-BLOODED CREATURE LIKE YOU HAPPY FOR A LIFETIME. . . ."

"Th-thank you, Minister," Astoroth stammered, unable to believe his luck. Shaded swimming pools, endless banquets, and bags of nubile attendants? Suddenly the future looked so bright he was almost dazzled. He struggled to his feet, eagerly anticipating this promised incarnation—unfortunately forget-ting that the prime requisite for becoming First Minister of Hades was the ability to lie through one's teeth.

4,748 Days Old

Latch had removed Strega-Nonna from her freezer the night before Titus's birthday, and consequently the old lady sat defrosting by the warmth of the range, hopeful of being sufficiently thawed in time to wish her great-great-great-great-great-great-grandson many happy returns. Pandora stepped carefully around her, laying a birthday breakfast tray for Titus, the centerpiece of which was a large raspberry muffin steaming tantalizingly in the middle of a blue china plate. The muffin had remained deliciously warm ever since Pandora had borrowed it from the library a fortnight before, its name of Multiplimuffin giving some clue to its magical properties. Across the table, Signora Strega-Borgia nibbled at a piece of dry toast and willed her stomach to desist from its attempts to repel all boarders.

Mrs. McLachlan swept into the kitchen bearing an armful of dirty linen, mildewed black velvet corsets, gray bloomers, and dark stockings so full of holes they were unlikely to survive the laundering process. Damp followed solemnly behind, holding one decomposing sock at arm's length. The little girl halted in the middle of the floor, a wide smile appearing on her face as she caught sight of Multitudina, who was cleaning her whiskers at the open door to the wine cellar. The nanny dropped her bundle of grubby clothes on the floor next to the washing machine and began to sort through what was in need of immediate laundering. Producing a small collection of coins and tissues from various pockets and folds, Mrs. McLachlan stopped to unfold a crumpled piece of paper. After a cursory glance, she gave a disbelieving snort and threw it into the coal scuttle beside Pandora, who stood waiting for the kettle to boil.

"So what did it say?" Titus mumbled, spraying crumbs across his bed and watching in amazement as the Multiplimuffin spontaneously regenerated itself for the eleventh time, the gap where he'd taken a mouthful filling back in with warm and fragrant cake.

"It said something like, *Marry me, Signora. Let's make beautiful bambinos together. I may have the face of a rodent, but I have the bank account of an emperor. I await your reply c/o Hotel Baglione, Bologna, Italy.*"

"Eughhh." Titus gagged. "Disgusting . . ."

"Not the Multiplimuffin, surely?" Pandora frowned. "I was assured that it would taste heavenly no matter how long we kept it for—"

"No. Heck no, it's perfect," Titus hastily reassured her, taking another bite for emphasis and watching the muffin miraculously regenerate. "No. It's that note to Mrs. McLachlan from our dirty old beast of an uncle. How dare he proposition *our* nanny? Anyway, she's far too old for that sort of thing—" He paused, then pleaded, "Isn't she?"

"I don't have a clue how old she is." The continuing mystery of Mrs. McLachlan's exact age remained a closed book, one that Pandora suspected would remain so for years to come. "But even if she wasn't old, I'm sure she would never marry someone like Uncle Lucifer, no matter *how* rich he might be." Pandora stood up and took the breakfast tray from Titus. "Come on, you. Enough muffin for now. Time for your swimming lesson."

"Do I *have* to?" Titus collapsed backward onto his pillows. "Can't I have a day off? I mean, it is my birthday after all—"

Rolling her eyes, Pandora ignored him. Every morning was the same: a list of excuses, protests, and pleas for leniency, followed by Titus's reluctant arrival on the jetty. Then she would turn a deaf ear to his endless complaints about the earliness of the hour, the freezingness of the loch, and the hideousness of his swimsuit—until, exasperated by this daily litany, she would push him off the end of the jetty. After that, Titus was fine. Quite a willing pupil, in fact, she reminded herself, taking several thoughtful mouthfuls of the Multiplimuffin before tucking it into a napkin and hiding it behind a stack of computer manuals. She listened to the diminishing sound of her brother's footsteps and waited till she heard his voice drifting up from the garden below. Titus was ululating in a bad imitation of Tarzan as he ran across the meadow toward the loch, causing clouds of gnats to boil up into the still air, disturbed by his passage through the long grasses. Scratching reflexively, Pandora grabbed her towel and headed downstairs.

Dusk had drained the color from the surrounding mountains as the Strega-Borgias pronounced themselves replete. For a day in Argyll at the beginning of May, the weather had been positively Mediterranean, and thus the family and guests had lazed on the lawn and lochside after breakfast, nibbling until lunch, hung around for afternoon tea, and now, digesting dinner, were all too full to move. Even Signora Strega-Borgia had joined in, apparently overcoming whatever it was that had ailed her and devouring course after course of Titus's birthday banquet— badly prepared by Marie Bain and surreptitiously adjusted by Mrs. McLachlan.

There had been a few near-misses, the nanny thought, helping herself to a nectarine and remembering the tripe that she'd turned into trifle, not to mention the bacteria-laden sushi she'd been forced to transform into Sacher torte. . . . In addition to the cook's efforts, there had been bowls of tiny wild strawberries and dewy figs imported from the village of Luciano's birth, along with fat grapes to replace those destroyed by Fiamma d'Infer's wickedness in the greenhouse. A vast chocolate meringue cake had been reduced from its billowy heights to a tiny leftover sliver on a glass plate, and Knot was unashamedly licking the syllabub bowl clean, covering himself in primrose-yellow cream in the process. Hecate Brinstone had revealed a talent for baking bread, and her braided challah, marzipan-filled stollen, and crusty ciabatta had emerged from the depths of the range—causing Marie Bain to mutter bitterly into her soiled handkerchief as she ostentatiously buttered herself a stale slice of store-bought white.

Tock had caught a wild salmon, and under Sab's instructions had employed Ffup's fiery exhalations to smoke it whole, serving it up on a water-lily platter. Even Black Douglas had provided a black bombe, firing this ball of frozen chocolate ice cream out of one of the cannons protruding from the flank of his beautiful boat. He aimed the edible missile at the meadow, where it floated down on a tiny parachute to be retrieved, regrettably decorated with a powdering of flailing gnats, by Knot, who had assumed the insects to be animated vanilla seeds.

"Coffee?" groaned Signor Strega-Borgia, loosening his belt to its final notch, and praying that the walk to the kitchen wouldn't cause his stomach to explode. "Coffee, and then your birthday present, Titus?"

"We'll leave you to it," Black Douglas said, climbing slowly to his feet and yawning widely. "We have to pack up and get ready to sail tomorrow," and taking this as their cue, the student witches began to gather their belongings, bidding each other sleepy good-nights as they trailed effortfully toward the house in Signor Strega-Borgia's wake.

In the silence of the wine cellar, Luciano retrieved one of his precious bottles of Barolo and one each of elderflower champagne and peach nectar. He placed these in a waiting picnic hamper along with some crystal glasses and Titus's birthday cake. Heading into the kitchen, he was rummaging in the cutlery drawer for a corkscrew when he became aware that he was being watched. Looking up, he noticed a strangely dressed woman peering at him through tottering piles of dirty dishes.

Signor Strega-Borgia blinked. Had he missed one? Was this one of Baci's colleagues he'd somehow managed to overlook during the previous week?

The stranger smiled and removed her tricorned hat by way of greeting. "At *last*," she said, in evident relief. "Perhaps you can help—"

Luciano stared. The stranger was dressed like a coachman straight out of a fairy tale, with white wig and knee breeches adding to the overall effect.

"Um . . . I don't think we're interviewing for staff at the moment," he murmured, wondering where on earth this vision had appeared from.

"I don't want a *job*," the stranger sighed. "I want to go back to being a rat again." Seeing Luciano's expression instantly change from one of slight confusion to total bewilderment, she explained, "I'm *Multitudina*. You know? Your house-rat? Mother of multitudes, including Terminus? Pandora's trainer? The Illiterat? Oh, come *on*—"

"Lovely . . . ," Luciano mumbled, backing out of the kitchen, convinced that he was conversing with a madwoman. "Sorry, must dash—"

Eavesdropping halfway along the corridor, Astoroth was almost as confused as Signor Strega-Borgia. Upon arrival back at StregaSchloss, newly reincarnated as an insect, he'd been dismayed to find that the Chronostone was nowhere to be seen. He could have sworn it had been under the grandfather clock in the great hall; this sighting was backed up by the fact that he'd seen the dragon's blood fluoresce just before taking a bullet in his rear end. But now, to his dismay, not only was there no clock, but the stone appeared to have vanished, too. To add to his difficulties, the Boss hadn't lied about the presence of thousands of willing members of the opposite sex. . . . Everywhere Astoroth went there appeared to be millions of leering males, baring their teeth and waggling their proboscises in a truly loathsome fashion. The promised pools of cool water turned out to be stagnant puddles—and thus far, the guaranteed food supply that had been part of the job description had failed to materialize, and Astoroth was *ravenous*. Caught in the draft caused by Luciano's hasty passage along the corridor, the reincarnated demon found himself being swept out the front door and straight into the company of all the Strega-Borgias, beasts, and staff, who had assembled on the lawn to witness Titus opening his birthday present.

"Most extraordinary . . . ," Luciano muttered, laying his hamper down on the grass. "Do you know I just found a complete stranger in our kitchen claiming that she's our house-rat, Multitudina? Not only that, but she appears to be dressed like a coachman out of *Cinderella*. . . . Baci, is she one of yours?"

Signora Strega-Borgia was staring at Damp. So, too, were Pandora and Mrs. McLachlan. Looking up from the pages of her picture book, Damp realized that she was the focus of their attention, and her bottom lip popped out in protest. Wishing to avoid tears before bedtime, Mrs. McLachlan scooped her up and turned to Titus.

"Right, laddie," she said. "Time for your blindfold."

"What?" groaned Titus. "What's going on?"

The nanny produced a clean tea towel from the picnic hamper and bid Titus tie it round his eyes. Once blindfolded, Titus was carefully led by Signor and Signora Strega-Borgia across the meadow, down the bramble-clad path, and out onto the jetty, by which time he was growing understandably nervous.

"Please, not *more* swimming?" he begged. "Really. I've done my bit for today, haven't I, Pan?" He stood swaying at the end of the jetty until Mrs. McLachlan stepped forward to put him out of his misery.

"You can remove the blindfold now, pet," she whispered.

Fumbling with the knotted tea towel, Titus wondered what his family was up to. Nearby he could hear the tide lapping at the pebbly beach and, from the sound underfoot, he knew he was standing on the jetty, but why was he here? He blinked in the light of the twilit sky, its lilac reflections scattered across Lochnagargoyle, the blindfold falling unnoticed at his feet.

"Oh yes . . . ," he breathed, catching sight of what waited for him, bobbing gently in the water. "Oh yes—oh YES—OH YESSSSSS!"

Forthcoming Attractions

Astoroth leapt aside as two colossal bottles rolled toward her, halted, and then—for no obvious reason—reversed their direction and rumbled back in the direction they'd come. The deafening crashes as the contents of Luciano's picnic hamper rolled around were causing the demon to feel all too mortal. Squeezing through a gap in the wicker, she found herself once again in the open air—and, if she wasn't mistaken, within range of something edible. . . .

I can't *believe* I'm doing this, Astoroth said to herself, alighting on a vast chunk of pale raw meat. Inhaling deeply, all the better to savor its aroma, she plunged her proboscis straight into Damp's leg. Since gnat bites are rarely painful, Astoroth's young victim hardly registered the intrusion. Giving a quick squirt of histamine to make Damp's blood run freely, the demon-gnat settled down to the feast. So engrossed was the demon that she failed to register the presence of a spider bearing down on her.

248

A spider with a distinctly murderous gleam in her eyes. A spider lurching in her direction with a less than full complement of limbs, which was more than made up for by her overabundance of spleen.

Tarantella paused, listening to the repulsive slurping noises coming from her enemy. She laid down a minuscule homemade crutch, with a finality that boded ill for Astoroth. It had been the stench of sulfur that had alerted the spider to the gnat's true identity. Astoroth looked like a gnat, flew like a gnat, and certainly had the appetite of a gnat, but the brimstone reek of Hades marked her out as a demon, albeit a very tiny one. Tarantella sighed with pleasure, produced a tiny lipstick from somewhere under her abdomen, and liberally applied this to her mouthparts, the absence of a mirror proving no hindrance to her skills at applying what was, in essence, war paint. Grooming her remaining legs with a bone comb, she assessed how best to dispatch the demon. Tear its legs off? No, no, no—*way* too simplistic. Tit-for-tat was *such* a mug's game. No, what was needed was a creative way to best exact her revenge on the monster that had amputated her eighth leg. . . .

Waving from the shore, Mrs. McLachlan was unaware that the Strega-Borgias were in such close proximity to the newly reincarnated demon Astoroth. Had she known, she wouldn't have hesitated to fling herself fully clothed into the loch and swim out to where the family floated in blissful ignorance of the demon in their midst. They rocked gently as Titus plied the oars on the little rowboat that was the best birthday present he'd ever had in his thirteen years on the planet.

"Look," Pandora said, "your boat's so new that there's still sap oozing out of its planks. . . ."

Under one of these planks that formed a seat in the bow, Tarantella reached out a hairy limb and plucked Astoroth off Damp's leg. Before the demon could open her gnat's mouth in protest, she found herself overwhelmed by something sticky and suffocatingly redolent of pines. Whatever the something was, it crushed her antennae, flooded her staring eyes, seeped past her mandibles, and trickled into her gizzard—thus coating her, inside and out, in viscous glop. Tarantella regarded her handiwork with satisfaction before flicking the resinous droplet into Lochnagargoyle to jump-start its chemical transformation from pine sap to amber, the ultimate preservative. Amber—the substance in which insects dating back to the Stone Age have been found conserved, their tiny bodies imprisoned for eternity.

"I love that smell," Signor Strega-Borgia said, sniffing appreciatively. "Reminds me of the forests near my father's house when I was small. . . ." He reached into the picnic basket and withdrew a bottle and three glasses. "Elderflower champagne, or peach nectar?"

The diminutive figures of Latch and Mrs. McLachlan waving from the shore receded as Titus sculled out farther into the loch. The sky had faded to a deep purple and the evening's first stars were beginning to appear. Overhead, Ffup and Sab circled, their wings hardly moving as they worked the thermals rising from Lochnagargoyle's surrounding hills. With a discreet *pop*, Luciano withdrew the cork from his hoarded Barolo, and poured a tiny mouthful for his wife and a glassful for himself.

"I'd, um—ah," he began, looking across to where Baci smiled encouragingly at him. "Yes . . . er, children. Raise your glasses to—er . . ."

Titus and Pandora peered at their father in confusion. Damp, not understanding the importance of glasses full of peach nectar, hurled hers over the side of the boat. Recognizing the bottle of Barolo to be one of the pair her father had rescued from Fiamma d'Infer, Pandora's curiosity grew exponentially. She was at the point of asking what exactly they were celebrating when the answer arrived fully formed in her mind.

"No—NO, *DON'T!*" Titus shrieked, as a gigantic head broke the surface of the water ahead, followed by several serpentine coils that reared alarmingly above their tiny boat.

"Dinnae get your knickers in a twist, son," the Sleeper hissed. "I've no capsized a boat yet, and I'm no about to start now." Then, clearing his throat with a sound like an industrial espresso-maker, the Sleeper began to serenade his distant girlfriend,

Ae fond kiss . . . and then we sever.
I love youse and . . . och, whatever.

"That's not the version that I'm familiar with . . . ," Baci murmured, her eyes sparkling.

Bonnie little dragon-mither
Ae fond kiss . . . I'm yours forever.
So marry me, and dinnae dither.

Overcome with embarrassment, the gigantic beast sank back beneath the surface of Lochnagargoyle and, to the family's delight, initiated the most stunning display of phosphorescence they'd ever seen.

"Okay, okay—I'm *impressed*!" Ffup shouted, arrowing down to the loch to retrieve her embarrassed swain. She splash-landed with wings outspread and her jaws in a wide grin. The Sleeper's head reappeared, beet-red with mortification, and he immediately closed his eyes as Ffup launched herself across the loch to wrap her wings round his neck.

"I will!" she squeaked. "I do . . . I mean *yes*!" She flapped a paw in the direction of the watching Strega-Borgias. "And they'll be *delighted* to do all the catering, the flowers, the invitations, and all that stuff. Oh, I can't *wait* to tell Nestor. . . . I'm going to be a teenage bride—"

Overhead, Sab flew back to the shore to inform his fellow-beasts about Ffup's forthcoming nuptials. "What an *air*head," he muttered, dreading the girly excesses to come, but pleased that someone, at last, was going to make an honest dragon of his colleague.

"Is that what we're raising our glasses to?" Titus said, peering at the bubbles rising to the surface of his elderflower champagne.

"I *don't* think so," Pandora whispered, wondering when her father was going to stop staring off into space and Get On With It. From the faraway shore came a round of applause and wild whoops as Sab delivered the glad tidings of Ffup's wedding to the waiting beasts. Damp crawled over Titus's legs and into Signora Strega-Borgia's arms, gazing up at her father, who appeared to be about to say something, since he kept opening his mouth and then closing it again.

"So . . . ," he managed at last, his voice strangely hoarse. "I'm, ah . . . we're, um . . . that is to say . . . er—your mother . . ."

Baci rolled her eyes. At this rate it would be dawn before Luciano managed to get the words out and, if she wasn't mistaken, Pandora knew already, judging by the huge smile on her face.

"Children"—Signor Strega-Borgia took a deep breath—"your mother and I are delighted—" He stopped, raised his glass to his lips, paused, brought it up to eye level, and looked into it, as if it alone understood what he was going through, then continued, "We've just found out . . . well, no, actually it was this morning when—the most amazing thing. . . . Next New Year there'll be a . . ."

Taking pity on her father, Pandora patted him on the arm and raised her glass, nudging Titus with her foot. "A toast—to all of us, especially our new baby."

Titus's jaw dropped, then, catching Pandora's eye, he immediately closed his mouth.

"Congratulations, Mum and Dad," Pandora continued. "Well *done,* both of you."

Titus blushed. Stop . . . stop, please, he silently begged his sister. Too much information. He knew where babies came from, but he'd tried to forget exactly how they got there in the first place. Eughhhh. Grown-ups? Dis*gus*ting. However, he reminded himself, he had concrete evidence that one day he would be one, too. But not, thankfully, for *ages* yet. Cheered enormously by this thought, he raised his glass and toasted the new little stranger in their midst.

"What shall I *wear*?" Ffup muttered to herself, unable to settle to sleep in the dungeon. Beside her, Nestor snored faintly, his long tail coiled round himself, an old teddy of Titus's tucked in one paw.

"Purple velvet? Red? Ugh, no, it would *clash* with my scales—um . . . blue? Oh, divine . . . perfect—blue velvet, with silvery details . . ."

"Shut *up*, would you?" groaned Sab, rolling over and stuffing his ears with straw in an attempt to block out Ffup's ravings.

"And my flowers . . . ," the dragon continued, oblivious to her fellow dungeon-mates. "Blue, I think . . . and white, um—"

"Forget-me-nots," suggested Tarantella.

"No I *won't*," declared Knot, outraged at the suggestion. "I'll never forget you."

"I *wish*," growled Sab, sitting up and glaring at Ffup. "How long are you going to drag out this wedding? How many more nights of broken sleep am I going to have to endure before you finally get married to your giant *eel*?"

"He's *not* an eel," Ffup squeaked. "He's a beast, just like we are."

"Speak for yourself," Tarantella muttered. "*I'm* an arachnid, myself. Although—" She dropped her voice to a whisper and added, "I'm not going to be by myself for much longer. . . ."

Down at the jetty, Titus's birthday present rocked gently at anchor. Inside it, under one of the seats, hundreds of baby spiders hung suspended in an egg-sac waiting till the time was ripe for hatching. A little sign written in lipstick beside them read:

DO NOT DISTURB
new Web site under construction

Gliossary

ALLOPATHICA FOR ARACHNIDAE: This is a surgeon's manual of correct procedure when operating on eight-legged hairinesses. Nope, I don't know how to pronounce it, either.

AND FIR WHIT?: Meaning, and for what? Pronounced exactly as it is written.

ASTON MARTIN: The car of this author's dreams. Made in England, by hand as opposed to machine, this car is so fast and so ridiculously expensive that only the seriously wealthy can afford one. When the engine is turned over, the ground around the car vibrates. The seats are covered in hand-stitched leather hide, the dashboard is carved from a single piece of wood and burnished to a deep gloss by a wee man wielding a tin of beeswax and a cloth. It's the kind of car that makes heads turn, grown men weep, and petrol-heads the world over salivate uncontrollably. As driven by Mr. James Bond. Pronounced ass-tin mart-in.

AVE: As in "*Ave*, Caledon." Not a reversal and contraction of Caledon Avenue, but a form of greeting employed by Ancient Romans. Meaning roughly, "Hi, Caledon." Pronounced ah-vey.

AWFY SAD, YON: Translates as "that's deeply tragic, that is," said with deep sincerity and accompanied if possible by eyes that are on the verge of "gaunny chuck it doon." Pronounced aw-fay sad, yawn.

Aww, come oan, hen: Placatory Glaswegian phrase, always used by a male to a female. Hen is the female form of jimmy, which is a blanket term for a Glaswegian man. "Aww, come oan, hen," thus loosely translates as "don't give me a hard time, woman." Pronounced aw, come oh-ahn, hen (in a faintly whiny voice).

The bogs: Scottish slang for bathroom. Pronounced bawg-z.

Bonnie little dragon-mither: Compliments in Glasgow rarely come higher than this, with occasional use of **pure dead brilliant** as a long-winded addition to **bonnie**. Straight translation is "beautiful little mother to dragons." Awww, the Sleeper *does* love his wee Ffup. Pronounced baw-nay little dragon mih-theh-rr.

Cara mia: Italian for "my darling." Aww, isn't that nice, Luciano does love Baci. Pronounced car-ah mee-ah.

A casual cack: Slang for a recreational dump/poo. Derived from the Italian *caca*. Pronounced to rhyme with snack. On second thought, perhaps not. Let's try to rhyme with sack.

Cludgie: Affectionate name for toilet. Although why one would want to refer affectionately to what is, in essence, a poo depository, is quite beyond the limitations of this glossary. Pronounced cluh-jee, to rhyme with budgie.

Dinnae dither: Literally, don't dawdle, get a move on. Pronounced dih-nay dih-theh-rr.

DOLL MADS: The correct spelling, according to locals on the Greek island of Crete, is "dolmades." Totally delicious (no, really) little parcels of minced lamb and mint wrapped in vine-leaves and oven-baked till ready. Pronounced doll-mad-ez.

ENGINE ILE: Dialect for engine oil. Pronounced igh-ill (who'd've thought such a wee word could have two syllables?)

FIREBOX OF THE RANGE: Not a reference to firearms, or shooting ranges, but merely a nod to the Strega-Borgia's oven. Dear reader, imagine a vast range-type cooker/oven, in this case a cream enamel color, powered by a mixture of coal and wood that burns within the firebox, thus heating the following: four ovens behind four doors at the front of the range, a plate-warming oven, a simmering oven, a baking oven, and a roasting oven. On top of the range are two vast, round, hinged lids, which when opened reveal a simmering plate and a boiling plate. To one side of these is a flat metal sheet known as the warming plate. Always on, always warm, the range is an essential part of Scottish country houses on the same scale as Strega-Schloss. Without it the Strega-Borgias would freeze to death.

FLOREAT AETHERUM: Arcane enchantment dating back to Roman times. A rough translation is "the continued health, happiness, and flowering of the etheric medium." Nope, I'm not going to tell you how to do it. What d'you take me for? A witch? Pronounced flaw-ray-at eeth-er-um.

GAUNNY CHUCK IT DOON: Translates roughly as "it's going to pour with rain." Said with unusual relish (especially to visiting tourists) in Scotland, which is unused to precipitation on such a grand scale. Pronounced gaw-nay chuck it doon.

IL GRANDE PARMIGIANO: Slang for the Boss, the C.E.O., he-who-must-be-obeyed. Pronounced eel gran-day par-meedj-eeh-ah-no.

IN NOMINE FLORIS—APERTE: Without giving too much away, this means "in the name of the goddess Flora [not Mrs. McLachlan, incidentally]—open." Frequently muttered by amateur Celtic gardeners during a wet summer, when one's flowers remain squeezed shut. Pronounced een naw-meen-ay floh-ris—ah-per-tay.

LEGLESS: In this case not a reference to a state of being without lower limbs, but to a state of being intoxicated by alcohol. Also known as puh-shhed, shlaughtered, shquiffy, and—boringly, tediously—drunk. Pronounced leg-lesh.

MAH: Not a blood relation, but merely Glaswegian for the possessive pronoun "my."

PANFORTE AND CANTUCCINI: Gosh, it must be getting close to lunchtime. **PANFORTE** (literal translation—strong bread) is a kind of Italian cake made from almonds, honey, candied citrus peel, and a tiny amount of flour to keep it all hanging together. Pronounced pan-for-tay. **CANTUCCINI** are little dry, dry, dryyyy biscuits studded with whole-shell almonds. Pronounced can-too-chee-knee.

POOR WEE BAIRNS: Translates as "the poor little children," said with maudlin sentimentality. Pronounced poor wee bay-rin-z.

PURE DEAD BRILLIANT: In common with this book's predecessors (**Pure Dead Magic** and **Pure Dead Wicked**), this Glaswegian phrase means "very fine indeed, verging on the excellent." A word of warning, however. If pronouncing this title in Glasgow, to avoid being slandered as a complete *numpty*, you might want to say it: pew-rr dehhd brull-yant.

A RIGHT NUMPTY: Presumably the opposite of a left numpty. This quaint insult translates approximately as "a complete idiot" and is much bandied around in barrooms to the detriment of all and sundry, bar fittings and fixtures, and, in due course, the police cells into which the numpties are dragged. Pronounced numb-tay, but if you could squeeze the "p" in the middle without adding another syllable, it would sound more authentic.

ROBERT THE BRUCE, BOB THE BRUTE: More formally known as King Robert I of Scotland (A.D. 1274–1329). Legend has it that at a particularly low point in his military career, Bob spent several freezing months hiding in a cave in the wilds of Scotland, and was hugely encouraged by the sight of a tiny spider struggling to build a web. Twice the fragile structure was blown away by the kinds of winds common in Scottish caves, but on the spider's third attempt, the web held. From this, Robert the Bruce was to draw the conclusion that "if at first you don't succeed, try, try again." But, hey, we know better, don't we? The true moral of this tale is "two legs bad, eight legs good, but never travel without a spare Band-Aid."

RUMTOPF: Rumtopf is a Northern European delicacy, usually eaten at Christmas as a rather superior form of dessert. It consists of layers of strawberries, gooseberries, black currants, figs, and peaches, but since each successive layer is preserved by submersion in brandy, it's the kind of food that should have a health warning writ large upon it. Pronounced rum-taw-pfff.

SANG DI DRACO: Not a vampire's lament, but literally translated as "blood of dragon." Pronounced sang dee drack-oh.

SETTLE: Wooden bench seat with back. Spectacularly uncomfortable, thus ensuring that guests do not linger in one's Great Hall. Pronounced seh-till.

SOLE VÉRONIQUE: Heaven on a plate. Take a skinned sole, poach gently in mixture of one glass of white wine, juice of half a lemon, large spoonful of chopped parsley, about six black peppercorns, one chopped shallot, smear of butter, pinch of salt, and cook until the flesh is just growing opaque in color. Reserve liquor from fish (discarding soggy shallot and parsley into compost bucket) and keep fish covered and warm. Still with me? Good. Now comes the tricky bit. Peel and de-seed twelve green grapes (aaaargh), and fold them into velouté. Pour sauce over fish and devour immediately. Pronounced (with enormous pride, especially if you've just cooked it) sohl vay-row-neek.

SOUL MIRROR: A mind-reading device employed by Mrs. McLachlan in *Pure Dead Wicked*. Also known by the name of I'Mat.

VALE: Ancient Roman valediction/way of saying good-bye. As in "*Vale*, Caledon," meaning, in context, "Good-bye, Caledon, fnurk, fnurk." Prounouced vah-lay and not to be confused with **valet**.

WHEENS OF METAL FILINGS: Translates as "loads of metal filings" in engine oil. This indicates that the driver of the car has thrashed it beyond its capabilities, thus stripping particles of metal off the pistons. Pronounced just the way it reads.

WOAD: A dye made from plant of same name and used by ancient Celts to adorn their bodies and frighten Roman invaders. Pronounced woe-d.

YIN: Not to be confused with yin and yang, but referring to the number one. Pronounced yih-n.

YOUSE: Plural of you. One wonders if medieval Glaswegians also said "thou" and "thouse"? Pronounced yoo-z.

Don't miss the Strega-Borgias
in their next adventure,

PURE DEAD TROUBLE!

Nothing to Declare

The Strega-Borgias stood out from the crowd clustered around the silent baggage carousel at Glasgow Airport mainly because of the pallor of their skin and the somber black of their clothing. Surrounded by sunburnt holidaymakers scantily clad in shades of lagoon turquoise, screaming orange, and eye-watering pink, the Strega-Borgias looked as if they had recently returned from a funeral; indeed, as if all five of them had narrowly escaped being buried themselves.

Signora Baci Strega-Borgia propped herself against the handle of a baggage trolley and yawned. Her husband, Signor Luciano Strega-Borgia, shifted the sleeping weight of their youngest daughter, Damp, onto his other shoulder and closed

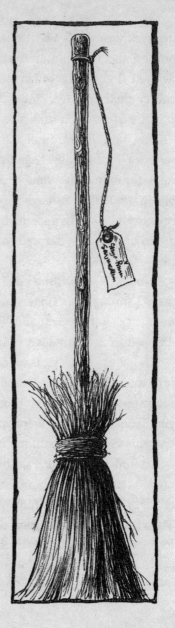

his eyes wearily. It was three hours past midnight and every one of the two hundred and fifty passengers just off the delayed flight from Milan had several desires in common: to collect their luggage, find a bathroom, and head for a horizontal surface upon which to fall into a much-needed sleep.

The baggage carousel lurched to life with a juddering series of hiccups and began to turn, each orbit bringing suitcases tumbling into view, some of which had suffered horribly in transit. A teenage boy lurking on the fringes of the carousel buried his face in his hands and uttered a heartfelt groan of denial at the sight of his backpack wobbling toward him.

"No . . . ," he whispered. "Please, let it not be mine." He peered through his fingers at the eviscerated luggage bearing the Strega-Borgia crest and his name scrawled on a label that drooped from a shredded strap.

"If I were you, Titus, and thank heavens I'm *not*, I'd just turn and walk away." Pandora Strega-Borgia raised her eyebrows and regarded her brother through slitted eyes. "Mind you," she added, "if I were you, I'd never have tried to import five ripe Gorgonzolas in my backpack either. . . ."

Around Titus and Pandora the crowd thinned abruptly, noses wrinkling in disgust, muttering about the catastrophic effect of nasty foreign food on innocent Scottish stomachs. As Titus dragged his backpack off the carousel, the smell of rotting cheeses intensified, causing Pandora to cough and turn swiftly around in search of less-polluted air.

Across the concourse, Baci Strega-Borgia caught sight of

2

her familiar black hatboxes and flight cases that held her essential travel kit of broomsticks, collapsa-cauldrons, and ceremonial hats, not to mention the little ventilated crate in which her portable frog collection had traveled the long hours between Italy and Scotland. It's hard to imagine a white face turning even paler, but somehow Baci managed it.

"The frogs . . . ," she whimpered. "Oh heck. . . ." She reached out with black-gloved hands and plucked the battered remains of the ventilated crate from the carousel.

"If that's what I think it is," Luciano muttered, "we'd better grab the rest of our stuff and get out of here, pront—"

Climbing past the rubber flaps through which suitcases trundled from the hold of the plane into the airport was a naked young man, loudly complaining about the flight, the weather, the lamentable lack of footmen, and his current state of undress. Behind him came another vociferous complainant, also regrettably unclad. Around them the crowd parted, some covering their eyes in embarrassment, others round-eyed and open-mouthed in amazement, their attention focused on the growing number of naked young men clambering off the carousel to join their kin, who stood shivering in a huddle on the concourse floor.

In the confusion, the Strega-Borgias hurled their luggage onto a trolley and stole away, hissing instructions to each other as they headed for Customs and Excise and, hopefully, their waiting car.

"Don't turn back." Luciano propelled his wife ahead of him, her long black cloak billowing behind her.

3

"But they're my *frogs*," Baci wailed, torn between delight that her amateur dabblings in magic had worked and horror at her part in turning her crated amphibians into escapee royals-in-the-buff.

Luciano quickened his pace, causing Damp to wake up and gaze over her father's shoulder to where Titus and Pandora were following behind, faces no longer pale but brick-red with shame.

"I don't think I've ever been quite so embarrassed in my entire life," Pandora complained as the family drew to a halt at the customs booth. Behind them, Titus saw several armed police officers moving purposefully toward the baggage carousel.

"Keep moving," Luciano said, attempting to look as innocent as possible for the benefit of the customs official, who regarded the family with complete indifference. Holding their breath, the Strega-Borgias rolled past, along the Nothing to Declare channel and out, at last, into the waiting throng of chauffeurs, taxi drivers, and other people's relatives, all waiting for travelers off the delayed flight from Milan.

In vain the Strega-Borgias scanned the faces in front of them, looking for their butler, Latch, who had been instructed to meet them on their return. After three fruitless circuits of the crowd, during which he'd been run into with laden trolleys, had his toes stepped on by women in high heels, and been mistakenly embraced by a drunken Glaswegian, Luciano lost what remained of his temper.

"Oh, for heaven's *sake*!" he exploded, causing Damp to

cover her ears and emit a startled squeak. "Remind me *never* to go on holiday ever again. It's been a *complete* catalog of disasters from start to finish. Not only have we just endured a journey from Hell in an overcrowded sardine can accompanied by decomposing cheeses and rampaging frogs, but now we can't even return to the comforts of home because our feckless employee hasn't bothered to sh—"

"Darling, calm down." Baci tugged at her husband's arm, uncomfortably aware that heads were beginning to turn in their direction. "Look, if Latch has forgotten, we can always take a taxi, or rent a car, or—"

"Perhaps we could just unpack one of your precious broomsticks and *fly* home," Luciano hissed, shaking off Baci's arm and glaring at his family.

Titus wearily removed a cell phone from his pocket, keyed in the number for home, and passed the phone across to his father. Baci slumped over the handle of their luggage trolley while Pandora tried to give the impression that she was in no way whatsoever related to this family of deranged travelers. In her father's arms, Damp listened to the unanswered ringing as Luciano waited for someone at StregaSchloss to pick up the phone.

A long way north, the moonlit silence in the great hall was broken by the insistent shrilling of a telephone. The sound echoed off walls, suits of armor, mirrors, and windows, penetrated through wooden doors, chimed along rows of crystal glasses and china, and at length reached the pantry, where

Multitudina, the free-range Illiterat, lay snoring beside a half-gnawed KitKat. Her whiskers twitched and her pink nose wrinkled peevishly as she surfaced from sleep, blearily aware that something was demanding her attention. Multitudina stretched all four legs, flexed her claws, and sniffed the air for clues. She dragged herself upright and scuttled out of the pantry, across the flagstones of the kitchen floor, and along the corridor leading to the great hall.

"Somebody get that, would you?" she squeaked, outraged that her beauty sleep was being disturbed by thoughtless callers. "I don't do telephones," she explained to the empty hall, adding, "Come on. Pick—up—the—phone."

Just as suddenly as it began, the ringing stopped, but by then Multitudina had stumbled upon the body of Latch, lying like a human draft stop across the front doorstep.

The rat was all too aware that humans didn't voluntarily lie in crumpled heaps unless something was seriously amiss. She also dimly understood that it was up to her to do something about it. That something probably involved calling for medical assistance, so she hauled herself onto the hall table and regarded the telephone with little idea of how to make it work. In some confusion, she peered at the instructions written below the receiver.

"Fire, please, amblans . . ." she translated, her illiteracy normally a source of rodent pride, but on this occasion proving to be a major handicap in her efforts to summon help. "Fire, please, amblans . . . ," she muttered, and then, in a flash of understanding, "Fire, police, ambulance!" Delighted with herself, she peered at the number and began to press the requisite buttons, but no matter how many times or how determinedly she thumped the numbers written next to FIRE POLICE AMBULANCE, all she could hear was a computerized voice demanding that she replace the handset and redial.

The Broken Latch

Asullen gray dawn was beginning to break over Lochnagargoyle as a taxi pulled up at the gate on the northern boundary to the StregaSchloss estate. Barely awake, Titus fumbled with the taxi's door and dragged himself out into the damp air. Ahead of him, faint shapes reared out of the mist: ancient oaks in full leaf, the distant silhouette of the jetty, and the dew-soaked meadow looking like a sheet of beaten silver. Stiff and sandy-eyeballed, Titus drew in a deep lungful of Argyll air and, lifting the latch, pushed the heavy metal gates open and waved the taxi on. With a yawn that made his jaw creak, Titus slumped back into the vehicle's interior, wondering as he did so why it was that at five a.m. he felt so utterly ravenous. He was barely conscious, but his stomach was loudly signaling that it was wide awake and impatient to begin the day's work. Titus laid his head against the glass of the window and groaned. Since Latch had forgotten to pick the family up at the airport, he'd probably also omitted to replenish the contents of the fridge, pantry, and bread box.

In the front passenger seat, Signor Strega-Borgia stared straight ahead, his thoughts running parallel to those of his son. Even the sight of StregaSchloss and the knowledge that cool linen sheets, feather pillows, and deep, dreamless slumber were within reach failed to give Luciano any comfort whatsoever. He closed his eyes, attempting to divert his thoughts onto matters more conducive to sleep than his current desire to slam doors, hurl suitcases, and vent his rage at Latch for letting them all down. Luciano had just managed to talk himself into staying calm, saying nothing, and dealing with his feckless employee after catching up on some much-needed rest when the taxi driver drew to a halt on the rose-quartz drive and demanded a sum of money so outrageous it made Luciano's eyes water.

"You *can't* be serious," he squeaked; then, adopting a more macho tone and forcing his voice to drop two octaves, he added, "That's daylight robbery. Our *flights* cost less than that."

The taxi driver regarded him with utter indifference, his fish eyes betraying no sign that the sum in question was open to negotiation.

"Come on," Luciano attempted. "Be reasonable. I'm not a millionaire. I'll give you half of what you're asking, but that's as far as I'm prepared to go."

Titus caught sight of the taxi driver's expression in the rearview mirror and immediately averted his eyes toward the front door of StregaSchloss, wishing he was on the other side of it instead of being forced to witness his father doing this full-on tightwad number.

"Listen, pal," the taxi driver growled, "this here's anti-social hours, you live in the back of beyond, I've ripped the bum aff my motor driving up yon track. I'm never gonnae get a return fare back to Glescae, your wain needs a diaper change, and there's something that's *stinkin'* in your luggage. . . ." He paused, narrowed his eyes, and poked Luciano in the chest with an extended finger. "And youse're telling porkies about no being millionaires. Lookit yon"—he indicated the honeysuckle-draped walls of StregaSchloss—"only someone wi' wads of dosh would own a hoose like yon. So get a move on, pal. Ma meter's still running."

"Dad. . . ." Titus leant forward and grabbed Luciano's arm.

"Don't interfere, Titus," Luciano hissed. "Highwaymen are, as a rule, exceedingly dangerous and don't take kindly to being interrupted while robbing innocent travelers." He removed his wallet from an inside pocket and peered at the lamentable lack of cash within.

"Dad, it's *urgent,* look—"

"Titus, will you quit trying to interrupt?" Luciano snapped, turning back to the taxi driver. "Um. I'm frightfully sorry, but I don't appear to have any cash. D'you take credit cards? A check?"

"DAD!" Titus yelled. "There's a *body* on the doorstep. . . ."

In the confusion that followed, all thoughts of taxi fares and running meters evaporated. Running across the drive and up the stone steps, Luciano discovered why Latch hadn't arrived at the airport. Lying sprawled across the brass doorstep, Latch showed no flicker of consciousness whatsoever in his open eyes. Only the slow rise and fall of his chest beneath his shirt indicated that he was still alive.

"Dinnae try to move him," the taxi driver advised as he bent over the butler, his face gray with concern. "You find something warm to cover him with, and I'll phone for an ambulance."

From her hiding place in the hall cupboard, Multitudina silently wished him good luck. God knows, she'd tried her best, but the telephone had refused to cooperate. . . . She decided to offer assistance and scuttled across the hall, skidding to a halt beside the taxi driver's sneaker-clad feet, where she paused for a few moments to catch her breath. Overhead, the taxi driver was issuing directions to StregaSchloss for the benefit of the ambulance crew; silhouetted against the pale light of dawn coming through the front door, the Strega-Borgias were gathered around their fallen butler, their faces hollow with fright as they tried to comprehend what had happened. Luciano gently laid a picnic blanket over Latch, bending low to whisper in his ear, "Don't worry, help is on its way. Just hang on and we'll get you sorted out. . . ."

Scaling the taxi driver's leg in two seconds flat, Multitudina emerged on the telephone table, where her arrival produced dramatic results. With a scream, the man dropped the receiver and backed away. Multitudina, sensing that yet again she'd failed in her attempt to assist, tried to make amends. Leaping back down onto the hall floor, she hurtled toward the open door, clambered onto Latch's blanketed form, and, to everyone's horror, began to administer the kiss of life to the inert butler.

At this, all Hell broke loose, but throughout the screams, sobs, and general hysteria, Latch lay unmoving, his brown eyes as empty of intelligence as if they were made of glass. Baci knelt beside him, gently stroking his outflung hand, ignoring the histrionics of the taxi driver who, after consigning all inhabitants of StregaSchloss to perdition, fled out of the front door as if pursued by demons. As Luciano pointed out afterward, the one bright spot in what had proved to be one of the worst days of his life was the fact that he'd escaped having to pay two hundred and fifty pounds to a highway robber. But this saving brought scant comfort when set against the sight of Latch being wheeled into a waiting ambulance and taken away in the pouring rain.

Signora Strega-Borgia headed upstairs carrying Damp. After discovering that the fridge was indeed empty, Titus had also gone to bed, but with little hope of sleep due to the noises coming from his stomach as it demanded, in turn, breakfast, elevenses, and now lunch. Titus lay in darkness, curtains drawn, the familiarity of his surroundings failing to soothe him into sleep; for no matter what configuration of pillows, duvet, and limbs he adopted, he was unable to shake the image of rain falling into Latch's open eyes. Watching the ambulance driving slowly away from StregaSchloss, Titus had been horrified to find his own eyes growing damp, a situation he couldn't blame on the dismal weather since he'd been inside the shelter of the front door at the time. Beside him, Pandora looked every bit as stricken as Titus felt, and as the ambulance disappeared into the rain, she turned and fled upstairs.

Shortly afterward the police had arrived and the door to the kitchen had been firmly closed, remaining thus for the hours measured out by Titus's bedside clock as it ticked past morning coffee, then lunchtime, and began its approach to the hour when its owner might expect afternoon tea. Showing no respect whatsoever for Latch, Titus's stomach launched into a loud and peevish complaint.

SOMETHING WICKED IS HEADED FOR STREGASCHLOSS!

After a vacation in Italy, the Strega-Borgia clan arrives home to a shocking discovery: Their faithful butler Latch is lying comatose on the front doorstep, reeking faintly of sulfur. Horrified and troubled, the clan eventually becomes distracted by their own problems. Only Nanny McLachlan realizes the truth. Will she alone be strong enough to protect the family?